Decadent: Kent's Desire

Club Wicked Cove

Book 6

Linzi Basset

Decadent: Kent's Desire

A Dark Suspense BDSM Novel

By

Linzi Basset

Linzi Basset

Decadent: Kent's Desire

Copyright © 2020 Linzi Basset
Editor: Anumeha Gokhale
Published & Cover Design: Linzi Basset
ISBN: 978-1975976774

This book is a work of fiction. The names, characters, places, and incidents are products of the writer's imagination or have been used fictitiously and are not to be construed as real. Any resemblance to persons, living or dead, actual events, locales, business establishments, or organizations is entirely coincidental.

Warning: This book contains sexually explicit scenes and adult language and may be considered offensive to some readers. This book is for sale to adults only, as defined by the laws of the country in which you made your purchase.

Disclaimer: Neither the publisher nor the author will be responsible for any loss, harm, injury, or death resulting from use of the information contained in this book.

Contents

WARNING: BDSM & THRILLER

This series contains scenes including, but not limited to, explicit graphic sex, voyeurism, exhibitionism, humiliation, ropes, cuffs, spanking, whipping, flogging, anal sex, ménage, strong language, bondage, and some S&M. Furthermore, expect controversial subjects such as unplanned pregnancy and BDSM activities.

This is a thriller/suspense combination genre and contains scenes of violence and death.

Liberties have been taken with places and notions that may resemble those of real life, such as insta-love and geographic locations.

Please, only proceed if you are comfortable with the above!

AUTHOR'S NOTE

Dear Reader,

Please note: Punishments in these books ... well, they aren't meant to be pleasurable and are, as their name indicates, punishing.

These stories develop over a very short time span. In real life, care should always be taken with your emotions, lifestyle, and sex. Remember: always safe, sane, and consensual.

Thank you for visiting Club Wicked Cove, my second BDSM suspense thriller series.

In book 6 in the series, Decadent: Kent's Desire, Kent Gibson took on the biggest challenge of a lifetime ... a woman whose scars he couldn't fix with surgery.

Kent Gibson knows the anatomy of scars.

As a celebrated plastic surgeon, he knows that some scars are skin deep, while some are embedded in our souls. Since losing his wife ten years ago, Kent has filled the void in his life by playing a Dominant Master at Club Wicked Cove. Life is good; he's got the looks and money's aplenty, good friends and subs galore. What more could he ask for?

Sharon Watts has lived through sheer hell and survived to tell the tale. She carries her scars like a roadmap of her torturous past. Try as she might, she can't jerk off the baggage of her nightmarish experience. Until an impromptu scene with Kent brings her back to life.

As soon as he touches Sharon, Kent knows he's in for it. When, through a twist of fate, Kent wins Sharon as his slave in an auction, it's time to throw caution to the winds and take a leap of faith. As a healer, Kent knows he has the most exquisitely fragile woman in his hands who needs careful mending, inside and out. She is gorgeous to him and makes his blood boil with a mere look. Kent and Sharon are falling hard and fast for each other.

But the evil is reaching its crescendo. The Occhipinti family is poised on a precarious juncture. What looks like an impenetrable castle, may very well turn out to be a house of cards. One way or another, Colt and his friends have had enough.

It's time to hunt. It's time to kill.

It has come full circle. It ends now.

And that, as they say in the movies folks, is the end to this saga of the Occhipinti family. Thank you for everyone who supported this tale and waited patiently for the end.

Wishing you all well and trusting you will enjoy this story.

Warm regards,

Linzi Basset

PREFACE

Welcome to the elite, underground, BDSM escape named Club Wicked Cove.

Club Wicked Cove is a very exclusive, underground BDSM club on a farm located thirty miles outside of Jacksonville, Texas, on the banks of Lake Jacksonville. It's a place where people go to escape and lose themselves in their own kinks and pleasure. In such a small, close-knit community, people treasure their privacy, therefore they wear masks, wigs and even colored contacts to ensure their identities remain intact.

Colt Fargo is the owner of Fargo Produce, one of the most successful farms in Texas. He is also the owner of the club, which stands on the outskirts of his farm on a separate plot of land. No one associates him with the club, which suites his need for plausible deniability.

Club Wicked Cove is a series woven around Colt, his best friend and co-owner of the club, Nolan Shaffer, along with four of their friends, Parnell, Seth, Kent, and Raul.

Colt's dark past and the Occhipinti family wove an evil web around the club and its Masters. Each to be challenged in a different way as violence, sex and death scattered their paths to happiness.

DICTIONARY

Basta di questo	-	That's enough
Brucia all'inferno	-	Burn in hell
Cazzate	-	Bullshit

Cazzo ho scelto quello sbagliato - I fucking chose the wrong one.

Cazzo fuoco	-	Fucking Tired
Che non va	-	What's wrong?
Dannazione	-	Goddamnit
Divertirsi un po	-	Have some fun
È giunto il momento	-	The time has come
Fanculo	-	Fuck
Finalmente	-	Finally
Gesù	-	Jesus
Ho finite	-	I am done
Il cazzo di bastardo	-	The fucking bastard
Lui nuota con i pesci	-	He'll swim with the fishes
Mi senti	-	Do you hear me
Mio cazzo primogenitura	-	My fucking birthright
Mio figlio	-	My child
Nessuno	-	No one

Non andrai da nessuna parte - You're not going anywhere

Non cazzo con	-	Do not fuck with me
Non cazzo niente	-	Fucking nothing
Non lo fa	-	No, it doesn't

Non provare la mia pazienza - Don't try my patience
Non sono un idiota -   I'm not an idiot
Perché cazzo hai sparato - Why the fuck did you shoot
Quella   -   That
Quello che cazzo vuoi - What   the   fuck   do   you want?
Responsabilità   -   Accountability
Sei pazzo   -   Are you crazy?
Se non è meglio -   If not better
Silenzioso   -   Silence
Tenere la cazzo bocca chiusa – Keep your fucking mouth shut
Ti sto avvertendo -   I'm warning you
Tutti questi cazzo anni - All these fucking years
Vaffanculo   -   Fuck off
Vergognatevi   -   Shame on you

Linzi Basset

CHAPTER ONE

NOTE: Although this is a suspense thriller with an erotic BDSM twist, it is <u>first and foremost</u> a thriller. It is a <u>DARK</u> series involving mafia crimes, hate, revenge, violent acts, and deaths.

PLEASE NOTE: This book involves the dark traits of the American Mafia and there are details to the murder of a small child throughout the story. Please do not read this book if such content will trigger or upset you in any way.

Club Tiberius—Anacapri, Capri Island, Italy.

"Ah, there's nothing like the smooth taste of good single malt, Zak. I'm glad to see you've stocked up on the good stuff."

Kent Gibson took another sip and rolled the decadent amber liquid on his tongue, savoring its woodiness before he swallowed.

"Moira and I appreciate you attending the reopening of the club, Kent. Hopefully, Nolan isn't too upset that you've missed his wedding?" Zak Powell, co-owner of the Club Tiberius, asked. He was leaning with his elbows on the bar, glancing around with a glint of satisfaction in his gaze.

"You know Nolan. He can't help but grumble and complain. Besides, the opening of Club Tiberius had been scheduled before his wedding date was set. He should count his lucky stars that the rest of the guys stayed behind for the wedding."

"Nevertheless, with Mason's kidnapping, I'm sure you'd rather have gotten on the plane the moment Seth phoned you with the news. Hell! I wanted to, myself. I love that little guy and Ceejay and I, we've always been very close, although since … well, that's water under the bridge," Zak said. He was Ceejay's cousin and was still battling to overcome his own emotional scars from his own abduction at the hands of Jay Vick a year-and-half ago.

"I wanted to, but Seth assured me they have everything under control. But I'm cutting my trip short and will be leaving tomorrow afternoon instead of next week. I'll come back for an extended visit later."

Kent looked around the stylish, open plan, entertainment room. It was a large room with a restaurant in the one section and a large dance floor in the center of the room. Plush, gray, and red leather sofas were arranged at the other end of the room to give it an intimate ambience, where members could relax.

"I never saw the interior of the club before, but I like what you've done with the place," he said. "Have you kept the dynamics of the previous club?"

"You mean hardcore? Hell, no. I'm still a newbie to BDSM myself and the day I walked in here for the first time, I was flabbergasted at some of the things I witnessed. Moira and I agreed that it wasn't the kind of club we wanted to run. We immediately shut it down and informed all the members about the new rules."

"Did you lose many members?"

"Some, but less than we'd anticipated, and we made up by gaining others who preferred a less hardcore environment. Why don't you take a look? Dungeon and private rooms are through that arch. You're welcome to play, my friend. I noticed how the subs have been eyeing you since you walked in."

Kent shrugged before he swallowed the last of his drink.

"I'll see if there's anyone who catches my eye. I wouldn't mind a good whipping scene for a change."

"Be my guest. The equipment is top class. It's the one thing Roberto Vitale did well in this club."

Kent sauntered into the dungeon, his mind on the conversation he'd had with Parnell an hour ago.

"Jesus! How did he manage to steal Mason away with all the people around?" Kent asked, his mind swirling with concern for Ceejay and Colt.

"The kids were in the playroom during the marriage ceremony. According to Molly—the nanny, he came through the backdoor and was dressed like one of the wedding guests. Until he pulled out a gun and threatened to shoot one of the kids if they screamed," Parnell explained.

"They?"

"Molly and Carol, Ceejay's mother. He took her as well."

"Ceejay's mother?"

"Yes. It's the only consolation they have. That Mason isn't alone with that fucking bastard."

"Jesus! I still can't believe he's the same Jay Vick I knew and cared for as my business partner at the clinic." Kent felt the anger boil inside him at the thought of such deceit at the hands of the man he'd regarded as his best friend for years.

"Has he made any demands yet?"

"No, but Colt knows what he wants. This whole business is fucked up. It has destroyed so many lives over the years. And for what? To gain power over a fucking mob? How sick could the world get?" Parnell

didn't bother to hide the distaste in his voice.

"I'll be back on Monday. Do you have any idea what Colt plans to do?"

"No, but we need to discuss this with him. It's time to change the game plan. We've all been pawns in the game they've been playing. Enough is enough. It's time they become the hunted. I'm sick and tired of living in fear for the ones we love. It has to stop."

"I'm with you, Parnell."

Kent joined a group of people watching a whipping scene. His gaze sharpened on the blonde sub tied to the St. Andrew's cross. She seemed completely relaxed even though the double whipping left red welts covering her back, legs and part of her buttocks bared by high-cut leather shorts.

No, she isn't just relaxed; she's bored. Ken disliked it when a sub wasn't fully committed to a scene.

Although she made all the right moves and sounds one would expect from a sub during an erotic whipping, she was unaffected by their efforts. He couldn't see her face from where he stood, but he noticed her looking around the dungeon. Her body language spoke volumes.

I wonder if she even feels the sting of the whips?

No Dom appreciated being played for a fool. Kent had an aversion to deceitful subs. From the noticeable tension in the Doms' shoulders, it was clear they were onto her but nothing they tried, offered the satisfaction they were striving for with the scene.

A scene between a Dom and a sub wasn't purely for the benefit of the sub. *It takes two to tango.* A Dom experienced the emotions too, same as the sub did. When a couple agreed to a scene, it wasn't for pure pleasure or pain; it was about connecting on an emotional level, to levitate in the sensations both parties experienced during the scene. Being deceived like this was deflating, to say the least. The two Doms were young and it was evident that they had no idea how to deal with a sub who had completely disassociated from the scene.

Kent shouldered his way through the

audience to the front. He looked around and found what he was looking for. Neat shelves along one wall featured a selection of impact tools, ball gags and blindfolds.

"Come now, sirs, is that the best you can do?" the sub scoffed. Her voice was husky and dripped with sarcasm.

It hit Kent smack in the center of his chest. He knew that voice. His gaze travelled over the confident tilt of her chin, the invitingly arched back, narrow waist and surprisingly rounded buttocks that tapered into long, shapely legs. Her skin was silky, even with the red stripes from the whip lashes adorning her body.

Well, well, I'll be damned. This, I'm gonna enjoy.

He selected a long-tail whip and a black blindfold before approaching the two Doms. They appeared relieved to hand over the scene to him and joined the crowd to watch instead.

Kent waited until the sub began to squirm against the cross. Her annoyance at the interruption was clear. He pressed his chest against her glowing skin.

Her breath hissed at the contact and she drew a breath to snap at him. The blindfold was over her eyes and tied behind her head before she could utter a word. He ran his hands expertly over her arms to test the tightness of the cuffs holding her in place.

"What the fuck—"

"Quiet, sub," he snapped. His voice had deepened and the submissive in her reacted immediately to the power he exerted.

"Who are you," she asked in a subdued voice. Her stomach tightened when she felt his hands brush over her hips and up, to cup her generous breasts and pinch her nipples. She squirmed against him subconsciously arching her neck. A low cry escaped her lips when his seeking fingers found her clitoris under the shorts and rubbed over it in a figure eight pattern.

Kent chose not to respond to her question.

"Explain the scene you agreed to, sub," he ordered.

"A double, erotic whipping," she responded readily and gasped when he slapped her ass with his bare hands. *Hard.* It stung. The pain surprised her when it registered in her brain. Usually, she barely felt the sting of the whips, but *this,* his bare hand connecting with her skin, zinged painfully through her core to set her clit throbbing.

"No sex?" Kent asked. He'd be surprised if she said yes. If she had no interest in being aroused during the scene, it was highly unlikely that she'd be interested in finishing it with such intimacy.

She shook her head and another hard slap cracked against her butt cheeks in warning. "No!" she gasped quickly.

He continued slapping her ass, alternating it with massaging her skin. He pressed his body against her back again and ran his hands over her breasts, pinching her nipples and teasing her clit until she writhed against the wooden cross, panting in arousal.

"Strange. Somehow, I got the impression you weren't interested in such a scene. Explain to me the purpose of an erotic whipping, sub."

"I want to be aroused over and above the pain; where the agony culminates into the ultimate pleasure. Oohaah," she cried out in surprise as he snapped his wrist; the whip striking across the curve of her buttocks with a soft snap.

"I hate when a sub plays the Dom for a fool during a scene and humiliates him in the process. Making him believe he's incompetent, when you're the one being deceitful and not committing to the scene you agreed to. Now, I intend to correct that oversight," Kent promised darkly. "You will not come, sub. Is that understood?"

Her snicker was instinctive, which he punished with a particularly harsh snap of the whip on the inside of her thigh. Her scream of pain echoed through the room.

"Don't think about playing the same game with me, sub. I promise you; you will lose. Now, I ask again, do you understand my instruction?"

"Yes, Sir," she whispered. "But I intended no disrespect. It's just that no one has been able to make me come. Not for a long time," she admitted softly.

"Maybe if you didn't top all of them from the bottom, you would. Now, I don't want to hear another word, sub, or should I gag you?" Kent asked sharply.

"That won't be necessary, Sir," she intoned and relaxed her muscles in preparation for the sting of the next lash.

The crack sounded loud in her ears but it left her with a thrilling zing that shot directly to her clit. The lash flickered; a dance of passion over her skin, confusing her. He settled into a soothing rhythm. It was the most sensuous thing she had ever experienced. Every lash felt like a caress—an extension of his hands—rather than a sting.

Kent threw the whip over his shoulder and stepped against her to rub the skin he'd just lashed. He fondled her breasts and pressed his hard body against her back.

"You have lovely tits, sub; very firm and responsive. One day, I'd like to whip your front and watch them bounce with every lash of my whip," he whispered in her ear and smiled when her breathing faltered.

He chuckled and stepped back. The whip cracked again; a tiny whoosh, then snapped against her skin. This time the gasp that escaped her, sounded shocked and the crowd applauded his skill for finally drawing a reaction from her. She was known for her ability to control every scene. Watching her helpless and responsive under the command of the powerful Dom was a new sight for them.

He continued. The lashes started to feel like flames on her skin. They rained over her back, down her ass; a few touched her thighs. The intensity increased and she struggled to keep her body relaxed; to lean into each lash. She felt the heat flow through her skin and her veins.

"Take a deep breath, sub," Kent ordered sternly.

The whip cracked again and she cried out with each sharp stroke that followed. When she trembled, anticipating the next burning lash, he eased to sweet brushing strokes; then without warning—harder again. Stinging ... shocking ... turning her moans into cries of pain, only to switch back to soothing, brushing strokes, eliciting sighs of pleasure. Her mind scrambled to keep up with the changing rhythm, which resulted in a coiled pressure inside her loins.

Kent watched the woman leaning weakly against the cross with a satisfied smile when he lowered the whip. He circled her waist to stroke her breasts, exulting in her nipples which had tightened into hard little stones. He pinched each tip, drawing moans of pleasure from the sub. When he found her clit and stroked it firmly with the pad of his finger, she couldn't contain her pleas.

"Sir ... please," her voice faltered. It was obvious that she wasn't used to begging for anything from a Dom.

Kent wasn't surprised. Not with her history. She was used to forced orgasms, humiliation, and pain.

Her hips orbited in a desperate attempt to gain more pleasure and sobbed when he slapped her clit hard.

"Behave, sub."

He could feel her body tremble as he continued to play with her, until she was a quivering mass of need in his arms.

"Please, Sir. I need to come," she stammered between sobs of pleasure.

"No," he snapped and stroked her clit harder, faster, as he pumped two fingers inside her pussy, deliberately brushing the swollen ganglia inside her vagina.

Her breathing escalated; her hips danced wildly against his hands. "Please, please," she begged weakly as her knees turned rubbery, forcing her to lean against the cross.

"Very well, Sharon, come for me," he ordered brusquely, but softly. He pinched her clit hard.

She tried to bite back the scream but the husky cry still echoed through the dungeon as she thrashed in helpless surrender. The climax flung her straight up, only to yank her down.

Her breathing harsh and uneven, she blinked against the sharpness of the light as he removed the blindfold and kneeled to untie her ankles from the cross.

"How ... how do you know my name?" she managed to gasp, still battling to find her breath after the climax that had weakened her body to a boneless vessel.

He uncuffed her arms and picked her up in his arms. She leaned weakly against his chest and only glanced at his face when he settled with her on his lap in one of the sofas in the lounge area of the dungeon.

"You!" She gasped and struggled to get upright.

"Keep still, Sharon," Kent snapped.

She immediately slumped back in his arms but couldn't keep her heart from thumping wildly against her chest.

Kent didn't say anything as they stared at each other; each with their own set of dark memories of the time when they had first met. It had been the darkest time of her life. When, her husband Roberto Vitale had tried to kill Nolan ... *and her.*

Linzi Basset

CHAPTER TWO

A remote farm in Tecula, Texas—5.6 miles from Jacksonville.

"Keep that brat quiet!" Jay snarled at Carol.

Carol stared at him unblinking—one eyebrow rose upward. She'd been married to Maxwell Powell for thirty-five years. He was as dominant a man as they came, so she wasn't cowed by this younger man glaring at her.

"Correct me if I'm wrong but aren't you a qualified surgeon?"

"What the fuck does—"

"Watch your language, young man. Children are like sponges."

"He won't be around to sponge up anything if he doesn't shut his trap!"

"As an intelligent man, I would've thought you knew why he is so niggly and cried all the time," she baited him.

Jay felt the blush spread over his cheeks. No woman had ever managed to make him feel like a brat—not even his foster mother, when he'd been a child. It didn't sit well with him, at all. He jumped up from the chair and kicked it back, ignoring the clatter. The crack of his fist, when it connected with the table between them, ricocheted through the room.

His anger boiled higher when it had no effect on the attractive older woman but caused the little boy in her lap to jump in fright and he started bawling even louder.

"Shh, my darling. Nana's here," Carol soothed Mason. Her glare incinerated the younger man on the spot. "If you intended to kill this innocent little boy, you wouldn't have bothered to bring me along."

"Don't assume you know what my motivation is, old woman. I—"

"I don't care what drove you to become such a

cruel man, but you will show some respect for your elders. My name is Carol or Mrs. Powell. Best you remember it in future."

Jay simmered in anger, but her hauteur staved his immediate response and he elected to remain quiet. He had a pounding headache due to the constantly crying baby.

"I assume you know who my son-in-law is, but tell me, young man, do you have any idea who my husband is?" Carol decided to plant a seed of insecurity. She had no way of knowing if Colt had been able to trace them yet. He could do with some help from her side.

Jay rubbed his temples, wishing the woman would stop her constant chattering. He already regretted his impulsiveness in taking Damiano's child without having a detailed plan in place.

"No, madam. I have no idea who your husband is," he mumbled half-heartedly.

"Hm, I didn't think so. "You obviously know the Occhipinti crime family and the role my son-in-law plays in it, but do you know about the association between US mafia and Maxwell Powell?"

Jay froze. He stared at Carol through blurry eyes. "Are you saying Maxwell Powell is your husband?"

Carol shrugged. "The Occhipintis made a huge mistake long ago when they tried to destroy my husband because he refused to bend to their rule. They underestimated the power he had and because of that he turned the tables on them. He's now revered and feared by every crime lord in the US."

"I know who he is," Jay managed to hiss through clenched teeth. The situation was going rapidly downhill.

"Then you should know what will happen should he be the one to find us. If for no other reason but self-preservation, you should release us."

"Death doesn't scare me, Mrs. Powell. I've stared it in the face many times."

Carol snorted derisively. "You don't know anything about my Maxwell, it seems. He doesn't kill people, Jay. He makes them pay. For as long as he deems necessary and believe me, hell will be preferable than being left to his—"

"Enough! Keep quiet. You've given me a fucking headache!"

"I'm just trying to—"

"I said, shut up! Or I'll gag you and the brat if he doesn't stop bawling."

"If you quit shouting and scaring him, he might just stop. Come now, young man, you've been in the medical profession. Surely you know all about children?"

"Fuck. Give me strength," Jay bellowed. He stomped toward the door. "I'm going out. Don't bother trying anything, Mrs. Powell. I've rigged the door. Open it and you'll be blown to smithereens."

The door slamming shut frightened the already tense boy and he began crying even harder.

"Shh, Nana's little boy. Daddy's coming, little one."

"Dada?" Mason asked tearfully.

"Yes! Dadda will be here soon."

Carol couldn't keep the tears at bay as Mason's face brightened at the prospect of seeing his father.

Luca's face was cast in gray pallor. He'd been devastated at the loss of Gianni and Giorgio, who had both died at the same time. Watching him, Colt wasn't too convinced that he was being truthful. Not in the emotions he was portraying or the claim that he'd been unaware of Gianni's double life.

"I swear to you, Damiano, I had no contact with Jay Vick. He's acting on his own and if you ask me, because his contact on the inside is dead, this is an act of desperation. He knows his wings have been clipped and he's trying to force our hand."

"He doesn't have to force my hand, Luca. He can have the fucking Don's seat. I never wanted it in the first place."

"Don't be naive, Damiano. Jay wants more than the power this position would give him. He wants the money to control the entire mob." Luca paced in Colt's office, ignoring the other four men sitting around and watching him intently. He was irritated that Damiano had brought them along as if he trusted them more than him.

Colt glanced around, his gaze touching each of them—Nolan, Seth, Parnell, and Kent. The message was clear. He didn't trust a word Luca was saying.

"Money? You mean those fucking bonds that have incited everyone to play God with our lives?"

"Yes. I had no idea Gianni ... well I suppose he thought if he had control of it, he could buy his way—"

"Don't bullshit me, Luca. *Non sono un idiota*! You are as much involved in this fuckup. How else did he know to use a woman who would end up in the same town as mine?" Colt sneered.

"Now you're grasping at straws, Damiano. It was a coincidence—"

"*Non cazzo con*, Luca! You knew me! You knew Ceejay was the kind of woman I would be attracted to. Especially in the condition she was in at the time. You would've stooped to any level to coerce me back."

"*Basta di questo*, Damiano. Beating a dead horse isn't going to help us find your son."

"For your sake, I hope you're not lying to me, Luca, because my wrath at this moment isn't what should be concerning you," Damiano said colloquially.

"What are you talking about?" Luca stopped pacing and looked at him. He could feel a trickle of unease begin at the base of his spine.

"My father-in-law, Luca. How do you think Maxwell Powell reacted to his wife being kidnapped along with his only grandchild? Especially when he realized that the Occhipintis are involved."

"Jay Vick isn't part of this family, Damiano. Maxwell can't blame us for this!"

"I can't?" A gruff voice intervened from the doorway. "Correct me if I'm wrong, Vitale, but isn't Jay Vick your son? The one you initially stole from his mother to be your successor? The same one you now claim to have no connection to?"

Luca's face turned sickly at the sight of his very nightmare entering the office. He'd forced

Damiano to cripple Maxwell Powell years ago. But Luca had underestimated the power Maxwell held. Still did. he had some very elite connections. No one opposed, Maxwell Powell. Not even his daughter's husband. Anger threatened to choke him when he watched his son being clasped in a strong embrace by the other man. The affection between them was unmistakable.

How is this possible? Maxwell promised to destroy Damiano years ago. Dannazione! *He never did. Somehow, they both lied to me.* Tutti questi cazzo anni! *Damiano never did what he was instructed to do. He couldn't have.*

"We'll find Mason, son. That's a promise. We'll find our little man soon," Maxwell said. He could see the devastation and concern in Colt's eyes.

Maxwell faced Luca. His eyes narrowed, all signs of the empathy he'd just shared with Damiano evaporated from his eyes; they turned cold and hard—the damning look of an enemy. The balance of power had subtly shifted in the room and was now centered on the imposing man.

"I hate to waste time. Therefore, I'm not going to ask you where my wife and grandson are—"

"I already told Damiano—"

"What I *am* going to do," Maxwell continued unperturbed, "is give you *one* warning. Because you can deny it all you want, Vitale, I know that you have something to do with this. It's your fucking MO. If anything happens to them, you'll never be safe again, I promise you that. So, if you have any idea where they are, I suggest you start talking."

Maxwell towered over Luca. A tailored black suit, with a striped gray and black tie, fitted his tall frame to perfection. His chiseled jaw lifted and the proud, pleasant smile belied the sharpness of his tone. Luca wasn't fooled. This man never made empty threats and the warning in his voice was unmistakable.

Luca squared his shoulders, irritated that Maxwell had the audacity to threaten him in his own domain. His face portrayed the confidence of a man not accustomed to losing.

"I see my courtesy was wasted," Maxwell

snorted. "Let's go, Colt. I need to see my daughter."

"I suggest you rethink your strategy, Luca, because I promise you, if I find out *you* are behind Mason's disappearance, I will personally put an end to your miserable life." Colt's voice grated on Luca's nerves. Maxwell Powell had the respect and regard from his son. *His son,* who never offered him the same honor.

Luca's shoulders sagged once they all filtered out the door. He sank into the sofa. His mouth was suddenly dry. The camaraderie between Maxwell and Colt infuriated him. He'd lied to him—his own father; at a time when he'd believed Damiano had been completely committed to becoming the Don.

The distress Damiano had shown on his return from Los Angeles all those years ago, at his failure to bring Maxwell Powell to his knees, had been a front. Now, Luca was sure of that. *Gianni would know.* He'd been Damiano's confidant from the first day he'd arrived. He was halfway to Gianni's office when his long strides slowed and realization dawned on him.

Gianni's was gone. So was Giorgio. That left only his half-brother Luigi and they'd never been close.

Luca had never felt this lost and alone.

"I'm Luca Vitale. I don't need anyone. I am feared because of who and what I am. No one can take me down or get the better of me."

He slammed his fist on the wall.

"*Nessuno!* Not Maxwell Powell and certainly not my own son, Damiano."

He lit a cigar and stood in front of the window in his office. He puffed on the fragrant Cuban delicacy. It was his love, his comfort, his companion, and the only consistency in his life. He puffed and blew the smoke in the air carefully, watching the thin trail of smoke twirl upward like a slithering snake.

"Damiano should've realized I don't lay all my cards on the table. If he believes he has the upper hand, he's got a surprise coming. No one walks away from the Occhipinti family. *Nessuno!*"

Luca unlocked the small safe in the secret

compartment of his desk and selected a silver burner phone. He sat chomping on the cigar as he made the call. The Cheshire grin on his lips had turned twice as evil by the time he heard the voice answer.

"We have to meet. *È giunto il momento.*"

Linzi Basset

CHAPTER THREE

"Still nothing. Goddammit! Where is that bastard?" Colt raged as he paced in front of the window in his office. His friends glanced at each other, not surprised at his frustration. He missed his son, but his concern for his safety was the main conduit to the rage that swirled under the surface.

Colt and Ceejay had not been to the club since Mason's abduction. All of them had put their lives on hold to help him look for his son. They were all tired, scouring the surrounding areas day in and out, since the little boy and his grandmother's kidnapping. So far, they've found no trace of them.

"I don't know what to do. For the first time in my life it feels like my hands have been cut off. *Jesus*! He's got my son!"

Colt teetered on the edge. He could feel the

darkness threaten to burst from the depth he'd hidden it in. He was tempted to let go of his restraint and allow it to take over. At least that way he won't feel the pain of loss—of having to look into Ceejay's begging eyes, demanding that he find their son.

His heart rate accelerated while his mind replayed movie scenes of child abduction. How traumatic it was for the child. His biggest fear was that Jay Vick was psychotic enough to act on impulse. He pushed the thought back as soon as it birthed in his mind. He mentally repeated what everyone had been telling him; that Jay Vick needed his son alive to have a hold over him. It was the only hope he could hang onto.

"We won't stop looking. Not until we have the little tyke back," Nolan said. "We are assuming he's in the surrounding area somewhere because Jay knows it so fucking well. This also means he could be hiding under our noses and we wouldn't know."

"Jay is a fucktard, but I don't believe he'd harm Mason, Colt," Kent remarked. "He wouldn't have taken your mother-in-law too if that had been his intention. And you know her; she wouldn't allow him to come near Mason."

"I've been telling myself that, Kent, but I can't help but worry. He's only *two years* old. Two fucking years! How can he . . ." He visible forced himself to calm down.

"Why don't you go home, Colt and try and get some sleep. We've got the club under control."

"Yeah, and I'm grateful for that. I'm glad you didn't cancel the auction. It's for a noble cause and brings in enough money to help destitute women and children who've been abused by some bastard in their lives."

Colt watched them filter out the door one by one. He slumped into his chair with his head in his hands and elbows on the desk.

"Hurt my son, Jay Vick and you will be begging me to kill you."
The promise sounded vicious in the silence of the room, but the red glint in his eyes would have frightened even the most hardened soul.

"Are you telling me that the three of you arranged this evening without discussing it with Kent?" Nolan asked. When the three women glanced at each other, he wasn't surprised to find that his own wife was the forerunner of the group.

"He would've said a very decisive *no* in his derisive tone," Jewel said.

"Yes, for a very good reason. Now isn't the time for such frivolities, Jewel," he berated her.

"Frivolities? Gmphf, ensuring that he finds love is anything but frivolous, my love. He deserves to find happiness as well."

They'd decided to postpone their honeymoon until Mason was found. Jewel was just as upset and lost without Mason. She loved him like her own. Since she'd looked after him for months during the time when Ceejay had been on the run and scared for his life, she'd become very attached to the little munchkin. Her new endeavor was nothing more than something to keep her mind off his abduction. Nolan sighed as she hugged him and stared at him doe-eyed. She knew he couldn't deny her anything when she looked at him like that.

"And you, Kacie? Does Parnell know you're at the club?"

Kacie shifted her weight from one foot to the other and glanced toward Sasha.

"Oh lord, give me strength," Nolan muttered. "You are looking for trouble, Kacie. Parnell can be very grumpy when his orders are ignored."

"Well, then we don't have a problem. He never ordered me to stay away from the club."

Nolan stared at her, not surprised to see a blush reddening her cheeks.

"He didn't? I find that surprising, especially as he told us that the two of you won't be living the BDSM lifestyle," Nolan intoned wryly.

"But that doesn't mean we can't visit the club, does it?"

"Hm, was Parnell party to that decision, Kacie?" Nolan asked, observing another flush of red adorning her cheeks. "Yeah, I didn't think so. I assume he's not back from his mission with Rhone yet?" He sighed when she shook her head. "Then you'll call him. No, don't give me that puppy look. Phone him, *now*. Or wait, I'll do it. I want to talk to him myself."

"Nolan, I'm only here to help with the evening's arrangements. Surely we don't need to bother him with this?" Kacie pleaded. It was too early in their relationship for her to test Parnell's patience.

Nolan ignored her. "Hey Parnell, how's it going? Are you on your way back, yet? You are? Well, I suggest you make the club your first stop." He glanced at Kacie when Parnell cursed in his ear. Kacie winced noticeably. "Yep, she's here. They've decided to arrange an auction—a slave auction I'll have you know—to find Kent a sub."

He chuckled at Parnell's response and agreed to keep an eye on Kacie until he arrived.

"Right. See you soon."

He looked at the three women as he slipped

his phone back into his pocket. "The three of you will find Kent and inform him of his good fortune," he instructed with a snicker.

"Inform me of what?" The man in question asked from behind the three women, who groaned when they heard his guttural voice.

Nolan rocked back on his heels. Side by side the men folded their arms across their wide chests. They looked like two soldiers on a warpath.

"I know everyone is upset about Mason but we all agreed how important the auction event is." Jewel began with a sideway glance at her two cohorts.

"Get to the point, Storm," Kent instructed mildly. It'd been a week since the abduction and his mind had been occupied with hunting Jay. He didn't intend to stay for the auction but would add his financial contribution.

Well, we thought this would be an ideal opportunity to … well … ehm," Jewel said in a rush, "we decided to arrange some extra entertainment for the evening."

Nolan's expression didn't change, but he admired how quickly his wife thought on her feet. *Little imp. She knows Kent will never get angry at her.*

Jewel peered at Kent from beneath her lashes. She deliberately kept her demeanor submissive.

"I see. From what Nolan said, I assume I'm the lucky recipient of the additional entertainment you've arranged?" Kent asked. He was aware that he was being set up by the three women. They were just *too* demure and submissive. His father had always warned him to be careful whenever the word 'too' came to mind. Alarm bells began to ring.

Ah hell! Now that Parnell is hitched with Kacie, I've become Jewel and Sasha's next target for wedded bliss!

"I do appreciate the effort the three of you have made—whatever that may be—but no thanks. This is not the time for something like this, Storm. I'm more concerned with other things at present. Besides, I'm not interested." Kent turned to walk away, only to find his way barred by the three, very determined women.

"I know the timing is bad but we all need something to take our minds off that. Even for a few hours. You, more than anyone, have been searching out there, from dusk to dawn every day." She stared at him and he wasn't surprised that her searching glance summed up his feelings. She squeezed his arm. "You have to take a break, Kent," she said softly. "It's not your fault. You can't take the blame for Jay's deception just because he was your business partner. He was everyone's friend. He screwed all of you over."

"I'm still not interested, Storm," he said gruffly as he unsuccessfully tried to skirt past the three women again.

"But you don't even know what it is! You can't just assume that we've done something you would find repulsive!" Jewel complained vehemently, as she physically tried to prevent him from leaving.

He laughed at her efforts. His eyes twinkled with mirth as he looked at them. He could feel the tension slowly ebb from his shoulders. Maybe she was right. He needed to relax, before he collapsed. He was physically and emotionally drained from worrying about Mason. Supporting Colt was a given, but carrying the strain of regret and guilt, was something he'd been struggling with since Jay had shown his true colors.

"Please, Master Steel, just hear us out. I promise you won't regret it. I assure you, we've taken all your requirements into account," Sasha added her plea.

"My requirements?" He asked with raised eyebrows. This was turning into a very intriguing discussion, notwithstanding the fact that he still wasn't interested in allowing them any leeway.

"Yes, for a slave," Kacie said.

Kent had to keep his jaw from going slack. These women never ceased to amaze him. Their innocent expressions would've been laughable if their manipulation wasn't so apparent.

"You better tell me what's going on ... and quickly, Storm," he growled under his breath.

"Well, we've arranged a ... how shall I put this

... a slave parade, if you'd like, to find you a suitable sub. But, with a little twist," she said and continued quickly before he could voice his protest, "We've combined it with the annual auction to raise funds for abused women and children."

"Fuck! You just couldn't leave it alone, could you, Storm? I'm not in the market for a wife—"

"Who said anything about a wife? We're looking for a slave sub for you. Debauchery isn't going to help you find 'the one' for you," Sasha pressed.

"And exactly how is this going to work? I look at a parade of masked slave subs and pick one from the lot?"

"Ah, no," Jewel replied. "No, wait, let me finish. The ladies in the parade line up have agreed to unmask for you in private before the auction. You'll have the opportunity to interact with them and make your choice. You will have the option to make the first bid for the one you choose. In case you don't bid, the auction will be opened to the floor. See? No one loses. All the participants will have an opportunity of a night with a Master who wishes to spend it with them and who knows, it might even end up meaning something for some of them."

"Yes, and you decide the rules of the agreement with the slave you choose. It's your choice if you only want to spend the night with her or consider something longer. Come on, Master Steel. This is only a slight deviation from the usual auction," Sasha pleaded with him.

"Yeah, of course. They'll all be slave subs. That limits the number of members who will bid. There aren't many members in our club who prefer a Master/slave relationship." Kent mumbled under his breath.

"Ah yes, we took that into consideration. The participants are submissive woman who are open to a slave relationship, so that's not a problem." Jewel said with a broad smile.

"You seem to have thought of everything," he remarked. "Except you have no idea what kind of woman I like," he tried one last time to wriggle out of their claws.

"Oh no, that was easy. Blondes. You prefer blondes. Preferably tall ones, but that's not a deal breaker. Also, their beauty should be more than just skin deep. You'll never be satisfied with a superficial woman."

Kent glared at Jewel, who stared at him with a self-satisfied smile. It didn't help his defense when Nolan laughed and said: "Well, it seems they *do* know you better than you thought."

"It's not fucking funny, Nol."

"No, I agree, but the auction is for a very good cause and you'll gain a slave for the evening, if nothing else."

Kent sighed. "Very well. *But,*" he anointed each woman with a warning glance, "this is the first and last time you attempt something like this. No setting me up. Is that understood?"

"Yes, Master Steel," they readily chorused.

"I know I'm going to regret this," Kent told Nolan as the women trotted off excitedly.

"I have to admit, I expected you to put up more fight."

Kent scoffed. "You know your wife has all of us wrapped around her little finger, Nol. Good thing she's hitched to you now. Maybe you'll be able to keep her out of mischief."

Nolan laughed. "Ah, no, Master Steel. It's that very sassiness that yanked my feet from under me. I wouldn't want her to be anything but exactly who she is."

"Problem is, Nol, I'm not so sure I'm looking for that kind of relationship anymore," Kent admitted with a faraway look in his eyes.

"Meaning?"

"I loved Anthea, very much. We started our relationship as Dom/sub. We were married two years later when she suggested we switch to Master/slave, just to test waters. She fell into the role and pretty soon it became our lifestyle. Twenty-four-seven. I was opposed to it, but it made her happy, so I gave in. I always wondered why though. She was such a strong person. When she died, it was like I lost part of my soul."

"You never told us what happened," Nolan

prodded gently.

Kent was quiet. He remembered the devastation he felt when he opened the door to find two police officers standing there. Instinctively, he'd known.

"Car accident. She lost control over her car going around a bend and went into a tailspin. Her car smashed head-on with a tree and flung her through the window. Her neck was broken on impact." He shook the memory off. "At least she didn't suffer. She died instantly." He took a deep breath. "I struggled for a long while to cope, until I realized I had to take a chance."

"That's when you moved your practice to Dallas and bought the farm here?" Nolan asked.

"Yeah, and it was the best decision I ever made. I've shied away from relationships all these years because I wasn't interested in another permanent arrangement. The memories of our marriage were just too raw."

"And now?"

"I've been thinking for a while it's time to move

on but ... you know that time with Sharon, when she came here and I helped you with her?"

"Yeah. You knew how to handle a slave. If not for that, she would've run circles around me."

"Well, I realized then it's not what I want. Maybe I never did and the only reason I did it was because my wife pushed me into it. Being responsible for someone, day in and out, their emotions, guiding them with every decision? Dealing with Sharon made me realize I don't want that anymore."

"Well, most of the women who've entered the auction are subs, willing to become slaves, because of the formidable Master Steel. All in all, my friend, you'll have the pick of the crop tonight. Even if it's only for tonight," Nolan set his mind at ease.

"And your wife wouldn't offer me any respite. Damn that little spitfire. If she wasn't pregnant, Nol, I would've suggested a good flogging for her trouble."

"Ah, come now," Nolan chuckled. "Who knows, you might just score a jackpot and find your perfect match."

She caught his eye the moment she entered the room—quite aptly named—Pandora's Box, where the 'slave selections' were in progress.

What the fuck is she doing here?

Kent didn't need her to remove the black, oriental bob wig or the black lace mask that covered her eyes, to know who she was.

He subconsciously made his choice the moment he recognized her. This was the sub he wanted for the night. He didn't even need to go through the motion of pretending to choose someone.

Jesus, Gibson, you're asking for trouble. You should just walk out of this goddamned room.

His body chose to ignore the order. The look on his face was brooding, almost angry. He sat in the 'Kings' chair', as Jewel had christened the large wingback chair they'd dragged to the center of the room.

"Smile, Master Steel. You don't want to chase these lovely ladies away by glaring at them, now do you?"

"What they see, is what they get, Storm. Very well, let's get back to the entertainment room for the auction," he said abruptly. He rose from the chair, only to be surrounded by three very determined women who herded him back to the chair.

"We can't! You've not interacted with them yet," Sasha wailed as she tried to press him back into the chair. She shrieked when his hands closed around her waist to bodily move her out his way.

"It's not necessary, ladies." His voice deepened when they continued to protest. Kent was aware their annoyance was because he'd just changed their carefully laid plans for the evening.

"I've made my choice and I will bid on her in the usual fashion, along with the others on the floor."

"But ... hey! Master Steel, come back here!" Jewel cried after him as he walked out the door. She stood gaping as his voice floated from somewhere down the passage at them.

"You better get this circus started, Storm. You've got five minutes, or I go home."

"That was fast," Nolan was puzzled when Kent joined him a few minutes later.

"I know who I'm going to bid on." Kent shrugged. "But then, you knew that, didn't you? Tell me, Nol, does your wife know that *she* is one of the participants? And for that matter, why the hell didn't you warn me?"

"There wasn't time. She arrived thirty minutes ago."

"What? Then how did she end up as one of the participants?"

"When she heard about the auction, she requested me to add her as a late entry." Nolan smirked while sipping his beer. "I guess the fact that it was you, had something to do with it. You didn't tell me you scened with her at the opening of Club

Tiberius."

"It seems the two of you had quite a 'catch-up' chat. I don't know what she told you, but it wasn't a planned scene. I intervened because she was manipulating the Doms. You know how I feel about that."

"Yeah, we all hate it. Anyway, you don't seem too upset that she entered the auction, and besides, you don't have to bid on her. I'm sure there are a few others you feel attracted to."

"I wouldn't know," Kent admitted grudgingly.

"What do you mean?"

"I made my decision the moment I realized who she was. There's something about her, Nol, that found resonance deep inside me; a lost soul in need of saving."

"Kent, I care for Sharon because of our history, but you know how Roberto abused her and turned her into his slave. Do you honestly think she's ready to bow to another Master?"

"That's just it, she never had a proper Master, Nolan. He didn't treat her with the care and respect that should be there in a Master/slave relationship. He abused her; he used her for his own depravities. She might not be ready, you're right; but with me she'll be treated properly and taken care of. Her needs, as well as mine, will be met in this relationship. It's as much a two-way relationship as any other, Nolan."

"Yes, but you just told me you didn't want that kind of relationship again."

"I don't, and to be honest, I don't believe it's what she needs either, but what she *does* need is a way to find herself again. A strong Dom/sub relationship with some aspects of Master/slave might be the way to help her become the person she used to be."

"Maybe it's exactly the reason she was so keen on being here. She told me a while ago how lonely she was. She even considered entering into a slave relationship with one of the Doms who used to be a regular at Club Tiberius during Roberto's time."

"What? And jump right back into the same abuse she was exposed to before?"

"Yeah, but I managed to talk her out of it. Which is the reason for her visit. I told her to get out of Italy and go on a trip. I guess I should've realized she would come here. I am, in all aspects, the only friend she has in her life."

"Well, I'm about to change that. Jewel is right. It's time I moved on in life. Sharon triggered something inside me when we rescued her from that hellhole. I haven't been able to forget it and now that I've scened with her ... I know there is a much deeper connection between us which deserves to be explored."

"I'm glad to hear you say that. As long as you realize it's going to be a long road with her. You're going to have to be patient with her"

"Oh, don't worry about that, Nolan. I've got the patience for the job and Miss Sharon Watts doesn't stand a chance."

Seth, the MC for the evening, made the announcement that the auction proceedings were about to start and they ambled closer.

"One more thing, Nol. You better warn Jewel

about Sharon. You know how she feels about her. If she suddenly comes face to face with the woman her husband was once engaged to—"

"Jesus, Kent! When is everyone going to quit this shit? I don't have feelings for Sharon anymore and I sincerely doubt if she ever loved me in the first place. I was just there for her when she needed help, but that's all."

"You don't have to convince me, Nol, but you know women and you know your fiery wife; especially now that she's pregnant. Warn her before she realizes who that sub is."

"Yeah, you're right. I'll tell her. Well, here we go my friend. Let's go get your slave." Nolan sighed and finished his beer in one gulp.

Kent approached Jewel, who directed him to a special chair in the center of the audience.

"You need to have the best view," she said with an impish smile.

"Storm, I told you I've made my choice. Just continue with the usual bidding process and I'll place my bid when the time comes," he said once he was seated.

"How? It can't be someone you've scened with at the club because then you would've ... oh, no! That's it. You decided on someone you know and picked her to get this over with quickly. Is that it?" Jewel asked. The annoyance was rife in her voice. Kent watched with male appreciation as her breasts bobbed when she slammed her fists on her waist.

"No, miss-know-it-all, that's not it. But, I did recognize the woman I am prepared to take a chance on. So, let's just do this as quickly and painlessly as possible."

"Take a chance on? Really? You're willing to commit to a relationship—"

"Honey, stop badgering Master Steel. You heard him. He's been a Master long enough to know what he wants," Nolan intervened.

"But, I still don't understand. How could he—
"

"Because he scened with her at Club Tiberius' opening," Nolan said quickly.

He saw Jewel's shoulders straighten and her

body tense. She suddenly swung her eyes in Nolan's direction and the temperature dropped a few degrees.

"He scened with her. In Anacapri," she said slowly. "Don't tell me it's *her*, Nolan Shaffer? What the hell is *she* doing here and how did she enter without my knowledge?" she raged at him, keeping her voice low.

"Honey, you know she's been keeping in contact with me. She was on the verge of making another mistake and I suggested she go on a trip to clear her head. That was before the opening of the club. I had no idea that Kent met her there."

"But what is she doing here?"

Nolan shrugged and glanced at Kent who sat slumped in the chair watching them with an amused smile.

"Well honey, at a guess, after that scene, maybe she remembered the connection she felt with Kent when we rescued her from Roberto."

"You invited her here?" Jewel asked with narrowed eyes.

"No, baby. Her arrival was as much a surprise to me, as was her request to enter the auction."

"And you didn't think to warn me beforehand?"

"There wasn't time. You were already in the room for the selection process when she arrived. I told you, Storm. I didn't know she was gonna show up here."

Nolan suffered through the long stare that followed. Then she nodded and stepped closer to hug him.

"I believe you, honey. Thanks for telling me."

"Honey," Nolan said as he tilted her chin up. "You know how much I love you and how elated I am about our baby. You never have to doubt my feelings or devotion to you. Sharon is part of my past; but she is still a friend. Nothing more. You're my heart, my love."

"And you're mine," she whispered just before his lips captured hers in a deep kiss.

"Well, I sure hope you know what you're doing Master Steel. That woman ... I tell you, if she's still as manipulative as she was before … I'm gonna give her a good brush down this time. She's not going to mess with one of my friends," Jewel said decisively.

"I appreciate your candor, dear Storm, but once she agrees, I will be taking her under my wing. None of you will interfere. Let's leave the past in the past and look toward the future. Okay?"
Jewel stared at him intently before she acceded with a nod. "Very well, Master Steel. Let's get your slave for you." She flashed her usual bright smile to reiterate her agreement, before she walked back to Pandora's Box to fetch the participants.

"I've made my choice."

Sharon's heart plummeted to her feet. She'd done some retrospection since the opening of Club Tiberius and the unexpected scene with the powerful Dom that had managed to break through the blankness of her life. He'd made her *feel* again. She shivered at the memory of the sensations that had rushed through her body when he'd touched her; first, with his hands, and then his whip. Both had shattered her superficial equilibrium.

She'd been fighting an inner battle with herself from the moment she booked the flight to the US.

You're going to make a fool of yourself, Sharon. What man would want a damaged woman like you? Better turn around and go back home. At least your parents are there.

Yeah, but what else? Everything on that goddamned island reminds me of the hell I lived through for years.

Every debate ended with the same thoughts. It was time to break the chains of the horrid memories that still kept her awake at night. She *had* to move on. It was the only way to forget the vile things Roberto Vitale had done to her. The things he had made her do, under the influence of the drugs he'd pumped into her without her knowledge.

As she watched Kent walk out of the room, her shoulders slumped. That was it, then. She'd lost before it had even begun. Apart from Nolan, all those years ago, when she'd been young and innocent, Kent was the only man who had managed to reach the part she'd kept hidden from the world. The secret she'd been trying to deny herself.

Yeah, but Roberto knew and he used it to destroy me. Fuck! Stop it, Sharon. You're stronger than this. For once in your life, admit what you are and then go after what you want. Stop being such a goddamned whuss!

She'd treated Nolan abysmally. Only to end up with Roberto Vitale. And why? Because he'd overpowered her with his dominance in such a subtle way that she'd not even realized it until she was completely ensnared and lost.

She might have denied it all those years ago, but it was time to admit it.

I'm a submissive. And because of Roberto, I can be nothing but a slave now. I crave the dominant to control me. That's why I'm here. Because I've found that man in Kent Gibson.

He was the kind of Master she was looking for.

She'd watched him with the subs a few times during her visits to this club, Club Wicked Cove, after they'd rescued her in Anacapri.

He was never mean or cruel. There were times she'd stared in amazement at how lovingly he treated the subs, albeit in a slightly menacing, or vaguely threatening, but always in wickedly pleasurable ways. It wasn't just the expert way he handled impact tools. It was the Dominant energy he'd exuded during their recent scene that had excited Sharon and drawn her to him like a bee to honey.

"Very well, ladies. Master Steel has apparently decided he doesn't need this selection process. We're going straight into the auction and he'll bid on the one he chose. Yes, I know you're disappointed but you never know, it just might be you he's going to bid for."

Sharon caught the eyes of a sub wearing a white wig and silver mask. *Jewel, Nolan's fiancé. Or, no, they're married now.* She suffered a glacial stare from the other woman and realized that Nolan must've told her who she was. She sighed dejectedly.

Will any of them ever forget the mess I was before? Is it possible to start afresh at all? Will they give me the opportunity to show them the real person I am and not the fucked-up bitch Roberto had turned me into?

Sharon started following the rest of the participants out of the door when Jewel barred her way.

"I'm willing to let bygones be bygones, but I'm warning you, Sharon Watts, I *will* be keeping an eye on you." Jewel declared without any preamble.

"I can't blame you for not trusting me, Jewel, but believe me when I say; the woman standing in front of you now, isn't the one you got to know before. All I ask is a chance to show all of you who I really am."

"I don't trust radical changes in people, Sharon. However, I know what you've gone through and I'm prepared to give you a chance. Don't make me regret it."

"You won't. All I want ... I ... since I married

Roberto, I've not had any friends. I just want to forget the colossal mistake I made, which nearly cost me my life. I want to build a new one. Make friends and maybe find happiness. It's not too much to ask for, is it?"

Jewel heard the quiver in her voice and noticed the sincerity in her eyes, even through the black lace mask. She, more than anyone, realized how certain events could change people. Seth, Sasha, and Kacie were perfect examples of that. Who was she to judge this woman? She actually admired her for having the guts to walk away from a man who had been bent on destroying her; more than that, after everything she'd been through, to have the courage, to find a path to a new life.

"Very well, Sharon. Let's shake on it. I know what you meant to Nolan once, so you can't be all bad. He wouldn't have loved you if there wasn't goodness inside your soul."

Sharon took the hand Jewel offered. She swallowed the lump in her throat.

"To building a bridge between us. Maybe we'll

become friends. It's too early to say, but who knows?"

"Thank you, Jewel. You don't know what this means to me."

"Well, let's go. What's your club name, by the way?" Jewel asked as the followed the rest of the subs toward the entertainment room.

"Minx."

Jewel frowned but wasn't too surprised that she'd chosen such a name. "I'm afraid it won't do. You're aiming to start a new life, Sharon. Don't keep a reminder of what you had to endure. The fact that you're here shows how you've risen above what he made of you."

Sharon was shaken that Jewel had immediately made the same association with her club name, like everyone else. A loose woman, a harlot ... everything Roberto had forced her to become.

"Let's see. Hmm, I believe Sapphire will be a much better choice—the color of your eyes, eh?"

"I guess it does sound better," Sharon

conceded.

"It's time to get this show on the road. Before the mighty Master Steel decides to leave without placing any bid."

Chapter Four

"The next sub on the auction block tonight is the delightful, Sapphire. This lady has a preference for a Master/slave relationship and is willing to go through training to please her Master. Who wouldn't love to have such an accommodating slave?" Seth's voice droned over the hum of the audience.

Kent wasn't surprised at the Doms' reaction to Sharon when she stepped on the stage. Even with the disguise of a black wig and lace mask, she looked stunning. Dressed in a tight, black leather body-suit that molded every curve and line of her lithe figure and spiked, black stilettos, she was seduction on steroids. She had legs for days and deliciously rounded buttocks that made Kent's mouth water. Her full breasts pushed enticingly against the leather and her nipples hardened when her eyes met his.

"Who is going to start the bidding for Sapphire, Doms?" Seth prodded the audience.

"Twenty thousand dollars," a voice declared from the back.

"Thirty thousand," from another, closer to the stage.

Kent was close enough to identify the weary look on Sharon's face as her eyes darted between the Doms shouting out their bids. It reached two-hundred thousand in no time. It was a high sum for an unknown sub to achieve with the regulars. At two-hundred-and-fifty thousand the bidding dwindled and Seth looked around.

"I have two-hundred-and-fifty thousand, going once, going—"

"One million," Kent's voice rang clearly across the room. Everyone strained to see who had made such a generous offer. Usually only the Senior Masters made such bids for their subs during the auctions. They were also the biggest supporters of the benevolent cause.

"Well, well. A new bidder. What a pleasant surprise to see Master Steel joining in," Seth said with a crooked smile. Kent gave him a dirty look.

"One million dollars. Going once, going twice ... *gone.* The bid for Sapphire is awarded to Master Steel. Sub, please join your new Master," Seth instructed, before he turned to the next participant.

Sharon could feel his unwavering gaze as she walked closer to him. He showed no flicker of recognition. She was hard pressed not to turn tail and run. Roberto had been a monster—evil, but this man exuded power and control. She wondered worriedly if she was ready for someone like him.

Her eyes met his and became lost in the mahogany orbs that returned her gaze unabashedly. She'd noticed the sorrow in his eyes in Anacapri; a melancholic veil cloaked his eyes even now.

She lowered her gaze when she reached him and waited silently with her hands clasped behind her back. She could feel herself trembling when he didn't say anything at first.

"Unless I tell you to lower your eyes, I want to see them, sub. Is that understood?" Kent told her in a deep voice.

Sharon could feel her legs beginning to wobble when his gaze caught hers with a hint of power. The fear inside her was foreign. She had been degraded, debased, and humiliated to the highest level any human could possibly be, by an abusive monster. Why would she fear a man who had never shown her anything but respect and understanding? But she did.

"Yes, Sir," she responded when he frowned.

"Sir? I thought you offered yourself as a slave. Was I mistaken?"

Sharon shifted her weight. *Damn him. How am I supposed to know what he wants from me?*

"No, you weren't mistaken," she mumbled.

"Hm, lucky for me, you *did* offer to undergo training. It seems you need lessons in proper slave decorum." Kent deliberately pushed her. He wanted to see how far she would let him go before she snapped at him. The full pout of her lips flattened in response. He watched her chest expand when she took a deep calming breath.

Impressive. She has control over her emotions. His gaze sharpened when she began fidgeting. *Did she know the auction was for my benefit? What is she aiming to achieve with this stunt?*

"Let's drop the pretense, Sapphire. We both know each other. So, tell me, what are you doing here?"

This time she couldn't hide her sharp intake of breath.

He'd known it was me when he placed the bid. Her excitement at the thought confused her more than the fear she'd experienced earlier.

"I can ask you the same question, Master Steel. Why did you bid on me?"

"I see we're not off to a good start, Sapphire. You should know better than to answer your Master's question with a question." Kent didn't bother to hide the recrimination in his tone. "I'm not into playing games, so don't even try them with me. The quicker you realize that the better. Now," he snapped as he rose from the chair, "I reserved a room. We'll continue this discussion in private."

As tall as she was, Sharon had to scramble to keep up with his long strides.

She swallowed at the view he offered. Broad shoulders tapered into narrow hips, which were encased in a pair of tight black jeans. His buns were toned, as were his thighs. He was muscular, but not bulky; a lean, contoured form that belied the strength underneath.

He had removed his mask by the time she stepped into the room and was in the process of removing his formfitting black t-shirt. Sharon's stomach clenched at the sight of his bared torso. His muscled chest and washboard pecks drew her eyes. She drooled at the alluring V low on his hips when he unzipped his jeans.

"I know we had chemistry in the dungeon, Sharon, but unless we have seamless sexual energy between us, going into any kind of relationship would be pointless for me," he explained. His eyes dropped to her feet and slowly back up. "Undress, please," he ordered in a gruff voice.

Her eyes snapped to Kent's face. His attractiveness was unmistakable. He'd grown a scruffy beard since she's last seen him, which, along with his chiseled jaw line, gave him a roguish look. He had the naturally tanned, mountain man kind of look that made her knees go weak. His dark brown hair was thick and lustrous and had a tousled look, which at a guess, came from running his hands through them often. His eyes were mesmerizing as he returned her gaze. His usually playful mouth was drawn into a hard line at her hesitation. Sharon licked her lips. She could almost feel those soft lips brushing against her own.

Kent's smile etched its way back onto his face. His body was warm as he pulled her closer, comforting her with his touch. His voice was deep, as his lips brushed her ear, "Do you need my help, Sharon? Or have you forgotten how to behave?"

Sharon forced herself to step out of his

embrace. Her eyes flashed when he removed her mask and with a casual grin, made short work of removing her wig from her head. His hands buried in the luxurious golden tresses that tumbled over her shoulders.

"I wondered if you were wearing a wig at Club Tiberius. Your hair used to be brown."

"He made me color it. He hated my blonde hair."

"*He* was an idiot. So? Are you going to answer me?"

"I have ... you know the life I've lived, Master Steel. Being a slave to Roberto made me nothing more than a plaything for his dementia, which is why I am willing to be trained."

"Is it truly what you want, Sharon? To be someone's slave? Or is it the submissive in you that you're trying to satisfy?"

"I'm here, aren't I?" The words fell from her lips. She'd been recovering from her usual cowered state, slowly but surely. But, as a Dom, he might not appreciate her assertiveness.

She lowered her eyes. Kent was too perceptive.

"Eyes, sub," he growled. "That's better. Don't try and hide your emotions from me, Sharon. I expect full disclosure from you. Always. It goes hand in hand with honesty and trust. Unless you can offer me those three things, we have nowhere to go."

"I understand."

"Good. Now, answer my question," he ordered.

Sharon found it difficult to concentrate with his hands in her hair, still caressing her scalp.

"To be honest, Master Steel—"

"Kent. When we're alone, you will call me Master Kent."

"I don't know if it's only the submissive in me that needs to be satisfied. I do know that I miss being under someone's control. But not someone like *him*," she said quickly at his raised eyebrows, "but I want someone to be there to ... I don't know, Master Kent, what I really want," she admitted dejectedly.

Kent wasn't surprised at Sharon's confusion. The relationship she'd had with Roberto had been anything but a normal M/s one. It'd been abuse; pure and simple. From what he'd witnessed at the opening of Club Tiberius, she'd not been able to rise above the way Roberto had treated her. She still demanded abuse from the Doms she scened with. The way she'd been pushing those two Doms had been aimed at angering them, so they would end up whipping her cruelly.

"Sharon, sexual domination is only a small part of a M/s or D/s relationship. BDSM, as a whole, is an intimate experience. It's an exchange of power that can either be physical, erotic, sexual, psychological, or spiritual. As part of our relationship, we will explore the territory between pleasure and pain by eroticizing the power you give me. *We*, yes, little one, not just you, will experience intense physical sensations and hopefully develop a cerebral connection. But know this—I will push your limits."

"Will you ... be cruel? I mean, will you force me to—"

"Sharon, don't compare me to your dead

husband. *Ever.* And do not confuse being a slave with how he treated you. I know what he made you do. He had a sexual hold over you which he used in the vilest manner. But, he was fucked up, my pet. Sexual dominance is not the heart of a real D/s or M/s relationship; it's just one component of it. You will have your own life and find something to keep yourself busy. If you decide it's what you want with me, you'll surrender yourself to me. But I'm not a micro-managing Master. I will be demanding and controlling, but I'll never abuse your trust."

Kent shook his head as he listened to his own words.

"Fuck, who am I kidding? It's not what I want anymore," he muttered under his breath. He tilted her chin higher to gaze earnestly into her eyes. "To be honest, I've come to realize over the years that I'm not looking for a slave relationship anymore, Sharon. I don't want to control another person's day to day life."

Her eyes sharpened. "Then why did you bother to bid on me if—"

"I'm not done. I prefer sexual domination, Sharon. In other words, a Dom/sub relationship. We might incorporate some aspects of a Master/slave at first, until you adapt to what I want, but then that's it. However, if you commit to a D/s relationship with me, I'll expect it all from you, Sharon, because I would offer it all to you in return."

"What exactly do you expect?"

"Obedience, trust, respect and ... love."

"Love?"

His mouth curved into a half-smile. "Eventually, who knows, especially if we have a deeper connection than just physical attraction for each other. I'm too old to play around. If we're going to commit to each other in a D/s agreement, it might eventually become a permanent one. I've been alone far too long, Sharon and I'm not going to waste my time if you're only interested in a fling."

"I appreciate that, but you know I have a history. It might not be that easy for me."

"I'm aware of that, but it's in the past. Either we move on or we go our separate ways. Which one is it going to be?"

"I'm not going anywhere," she said. Shocked, but elated at the same time that he was willing to take a chance with her.

"But I still need to know whether we're sexually compatible or not. So, get naked, Sharon."

She stared at him without moving. He could see the struggle that ensued inside her. She squared her shoulders and looked into his eyes knowing it wasn't something she could hide.

"You know I have scars. I'm not pretty—naked," she said while the pad of her thumb smoothed over the cicatrix of a scar on her hand. She fought the nervous swirls braiding in her stomach, trying to think about something other than the recollection of how the scars had been inflicted onto her satiny skin. But she couldn't avoid the images that had been permanently embedded in her troubled mind. She was trapped in her own psychosis; a living nightmare for one, tailor made by her own brain, to play on her deepest fears—that he'd find her repulsive.

"I've seen you naked, Sharon and you're beautiful. Those scars are signs of your tremendous courage, to endure what you did. I'll treasure every one of them."

"Could we, perhaps, dim the lights?" Suddenly it was important to Sharon to be beautiful in his eyes, but those scars mapped her humiliation and abuse over the years.

"Look at me, Sharon. I'm a plastic surgeon and have seen many ugly scars in my career. There isn't a part of your body that I find less than perfect. You're a beautiful woman and I daresay it comes from within as much as from the outside."

"Not many people will agree with you."

"Maybe not, but at a guess, I believe that's why you returned here. To show everyone who and what you really are. Very well, I'll turn down the lights but it's not going to be a permanent feature. There'll be no hiding between us, Sharon. Not even those scars."

Kent settled on the bed naked, to watch her undress. She reminded him of a white orchid;

beautiful—yet fragile. Somehow the imperfections that bothered her so much, made her perfect. Her movements were different than before. Not crass and raw, rather feminine, and sensual. It was contrary to the demanding bitch she'd been when he'd first met her. He was enamored by her eyes when she glanced briefly at him. Like a bottomless ocean, they were pools of iridescent blue, like glittering sapphires, radiant and beautiful—perfect jewels to enhance her flawless, creamy skin. Strands of molten gold cascaded down her back and over her rounded, ivory shoulders.

She turned to face him. She brushed a stray tendril of hair behind her ear, gently trailing her fingertips over her high cheekbones. Her plump, cherry lips were caught between perfect set of pearly white teeth.

Sharon struggled to suppress the gloom of chill that began to crystallize across her pinched face. It was her deepest fear that she would fail to please him.

"Come to me, Sharon," Kent ordered in a deep

voice that wrapped around her insecurities like a warm blanket.

He was surprised that the once confident woman now spoke with a tremulous rasp, betraying the anxiety that haunted her voice.

"I'm scared that I'll disappoint you. He managed to change me. In more ways than I care to admit. I want you to know, Master Kent, it's important for me to please you, but I'm afraid that I don't know how."

The raw urgency in her sultry, Italian-inflected voice triggered a blazing heat to prick his loins. Kent felt an unexpected surge of arousal pulse into the head of his cock, engorging and inflaming the veins along his considerable length and girth.

"All you need to remember, my pet, is that I'm your Master now. My word is law and you'll do what I expect of you. There is no need for seductive wiles, Sharon. You enthrall me. I'll tell you what I expect from you. What will you feel and experience? Well, that's for me to deliver and you to find out, now isn't it?"

Sinewy muscles rippled along the curved line of Sharon's back as she felt herself relaxing, set at ease by his words. This, she could do. Follow instructions. It was something Roberto whipped into her during early days.

"No, Sharon. I don't ever want to see the brilliance of your cerulean blue eyes dim because of his thoughts. He will not stand between us. In this relationship, there'll only be room for two people— you and me. Is that understood?" His voice racked over her in reprimand.

"Yes, Master Kent."

"Banish him from your mind, Sharon. This can be a new future for you—for us, but not if your every thought is going to be cloaked by memories of Roberto Vitale."

"It won't be, Master Kent. From this moment, you'll be the only one in my mind."

"That's what I want to hear. Now, come closer and kiss me, my pet."

Sharon leaned forward and kissed him, slowly, reverently; no longer surprised that this was happening; that she wanted him more than her next breath. His lips were soft and warm against hers. Blood surged in her veins, and euphoria unfurled like the mist across a tranquil ocean. She could feel the tension melt away. There was no room for her to withdraw into the memories always lurking in the back of her mind. His arms were around her, as hard as a rock. She felt the rush of helplessness; the surging tide of warmth that left her limp in his proximity. Like he'd done during the scene at Club Tiberius, his touch blurred every troubled memory of Roberto Vitale, until it vanished into nothingness.

"Very good, my pet," he praised against the pulsing vein in her throat, surprising Sharon with his ability to identify the moment she gave over to him completely.

"You make me forget myself, Master Kent."

"That's good to know, love," he praised her honesty.

Their eyes locked and he leaned down to kiss her. Their breaths suspended, for a moment, before fusing as their lips met. The kiss held the promise of tomorrow; of the passion that fired their lust with every brush of their lips. Heat sizzled between them, igniting the tumescence he pressed into her softness.

Sharon was lost in the gentleness of his touch, so contrary to what she was used to. Goosebumps broke out all over her body as he pressed his chest against her. He trailed his fingers over her arms with feather-like touches; then her shoulders, making her catch her breath as he traced a line toward her breasts. She stopped breathing for a moment when he boldly pressed his lower body between her legs with his hard arousal throbbing against her soft belly.

"I'm not going to question that you want me. Not when you make me feel this good," she managed to gasp with pleasure.

"You will learn, my pet, that I don't do anything against my will or just to appease any sub. I *do* want you, Sharon," he growled in a voice that resonated inside her.

Sharon shivered as every nerve in her body

smoldered. Her whisper, "I want you too, my Master," exploded in his mind and engorged his cock to full arousal.

"Mmm, you smell enticing, baby." He breathed in the sweet elixir of her scent that wafted into his nostrils.

She shuddered and surrendered to the moment that would become a crystallized memory in her mind.

Oh God. Please let this be real. Let this be the beginning of something good.

"Grasp the headboard, Sharon and don't let go. I want you to *feel*. No thoughts; just feel my touch and our bodies sliding against each other. I don't suppose I need to tell you this, but you don't come until I say so."

"Yes, Master Kent, but could you stop talking and just fuck—"

"Are you telling me what to do, sub?

Sharon felt the power of his will seep into her skin. She shook her head, weakened by the heated look in his eyes.

"No, my Master. I'm only requesting you to speed up the pace."

"You, my lovely slave, do nothing without my permission. Now, spread your legs and pull your knees up." He waited while she complied. "Beautiful, my pet. All open and ready for me," he murmured as he brushed his hand over her labia. "Very ready; all hot and wet."

Sharon had become adept at hiding her true feelings for so long; she didn't know how to open completely to a man; especially, in intimate situations, where her actions became automated, rather than emotional. The magnetism of this man overwhelmed any motoric action. His warning rang inside her mind. He ensured that she was focused on him, by drowning her mind with sensations.

"Please," she whimpered, feeling lost as she rubbed herself against his cock, grinding her swollen nether parts up and down his length.

Kent responded by tickling her hips with feathery strokes. His fingers dipped and grazed, soothing, and teasing the softness of her skin. His gentleness was deliberate—an opposite of anything she'd experienced during her life with Roberto.

"I see I have a task set out for me. Keep still, my pet. I'll tell you if I want you to move."

Sharon's mind was a scrambled mess, unable to process the pleasure that followed each caress. It felt like her body had been numb and only his touch had the ability to move her.

"Your honeyed nectar is intoxicating." He nibbled on her ear. Kent sighed against her delicate mouth, aware of the conflict raging inside them, if he was honest. *It was time to let go of the past.* He'd loved his wife and they'd had a good life. But she'd been gone for a long time. It was time to move on and find happiness again.

He looked at her, disarmed by her nudity in the dim light. There was vulnerability in her eyes as his gaze travelled over her body. Her breasts were perfectly molded to her form, begging for him to brush a finger across the taut nipples.

"You have beautiful breasts, baby," he murmured as he leaned closer to nibble on one taut nipple while fondling the roundness of the other perky orb. He coasted his palms over her nipples, enjoying the sensual moans from her. Kent lingered just long enough for her to understand how beautiful she was to him.

The club rules required regular medical check-ups. All visitors had to supply a recent medical certificate before acceptance to the club; therefore, Kent was assured they both were safe.

"Now, my lovely, it's time to fuck that pussy of yours," he growled huskily and pressed his swollen shaft against her puffy folds, teasing her, before slowly pushing inside. His heart-rate accelerated as he watched her eyes flare and her breathing increase.

"Kent," she whispered his name as their bodies became one, limbs entwined. Their bodies moved to the rhythmic sounds of Kent's deep murmurs of praises in her ears.

His tongue scored the slopes of her shoulders and throat like an artist painting a masterpiece. His kisses were drugging; aimed at stealing her breath.

Her passionate moans drifted to roof in a rush of pleasure.

He thrust ... *harder* ... he plunged ... *deeper* ... they began the sacred dance of passion. He went faster, gasping for breath as their bodies sparked with heat, demanding more. Their hoarse cries echoed in the quiet room as pleasure washed over them in vociferous waves of ecstasy, drowning them in the climax that took control of their bodies.

A shuddering sigh escaped Kent's lips and expressed his emotional turmoil. He was overwhelmed by their union. It was the first time, in a very long while, that he felt whole. He had this pressing need to give, to hold and to protect. *Her* ... only her.

"Master Kent," she began hesitatingly, still reeling from the rush of sensations that had floored her body and mind.

His fingers on her lips silenced her recurring insecurities.

"This was only the beginning, Sharon. From here on, we will build on our future. Together."

CHAPTER FIVE

"You want me to *what*?"

Jay was annoyed. Not that he had anyone but himself to blame. It came from playing on both sides of the fence. Siding with *this* man had been a stroke of mastery. No one would ever have expected the two of them to get along so well. Not Gianni, not Giorgio and definitely not Luca Vitale.

"You heard me, Jay. Give Damiano's child back to him. As sad as their deaths were, losing Gianni and Giorgio actually paved our way. We don't need another deadly enemy to prevent us from achieving what we want."

"Exactly what is it that *we* want to achieve? I've been the game piece for you, Giorgio, and Gianni for longer than I care for, and I'm fucking tired of being used, with only vague promises coming my way. Even Luca. All of you are using me and I've had it. You know what I want, but I also know you're not just going to stand back and let me have it. So, exactly where does that leave us?"

"*Fanculo*, Jay! Get a grip. Now isn't the time to split hairs. We need to act fast. Maxwell Powell is here, searching for his wife and grandson. Believe me; you don't want to be on the wrong end of that man's wrath."

"I'll lose all *my* leverage, the moment I give up the brat and you know it! What do you think Luca is gonna do when he finds out I'd not just been playing Gianni, but him as well? This is the first time I truly have the upper hand. My dear brother is ripe for picking. He won't think twice before handing over those bonds to me."

"Oh, I know he is. He even said as much to Luca. They're yours for the taking. But see, therein lies the problem. If he just hands it over meekly, we have no guarantee that he'll step down. We'll still have to deal with him. No, we need him to abdicate his role as the Don completely in front of all the crime bosses in the US. It's the only way—"

"He'll fucking step down if I hold his son's safety in balance."

"*Gesù*! Don't you ever listen? I said; give Mason Fargo back to his father. *Do it*, Jay or you'll have me to deal with."

"You? Don't believe, for one moment, that I'm scared of you. You're in no stronger position than me. Actually, I might have one up on you. Luca Vitale hasn't given up on me, just yet. Hahaha, got you with that one, didn't I? You thought you're so clever, but it seems that he wants one of his firstborn sons on the throne."

"You're lying. I've known him all my life. He never backtracks once he comes to a conclusion. He had decided that you're too weak to succeed him. Stop dreaming and do as I—"

"It's no dream. He's more than aware of my movements. We both know what that means, don't we?"

Jay laughed as a string of Italian curses reverberated in his ear.

"Gotta go. I need to feed my prisoners. It won't do to starve them. Not if I want Damiano to bend to my will ... and make *no* fucking mistake. He will bend!"

Jay abruptly ended the call. The smirk on his face turned flat. Luca calling earlier in the day, wanting to meet him, had been unexpected. He had just been trying to unsettle his cohort by goading him, but he wasn't comfortable with the upcoming meeting. Luca didn't do anything without a well thought out plan. Somehow, Jay had a feeling that he was going to be used once again.

"Well, my dear father will soon come to realize that I'm not the same man he spurned years ago. I am more than a match for Damiano, and all those coveting the position of the Don. *Mio cazzo primogenitura!*"

Jay contemplated his next move as he drove back to the remote farmhouse where Carol and Mason were locked up.

He had to be clever. The stories about Maxwell Powell weren't rumors. They were all true. He was a formidable man, feared by everyone in the mob. He was untouchable because of his powerful allies all over the US. Gianni had learned the hard way—the price of opposing MP—as he was known in the crime syndicates. He'd thought he could overpower him by threatening him with his contacts in the LAPD and Government, only to find that MP had an even higher approach. Gianni almost lost every cent he'd owned at the time.

"Yes, I have to be one step ahead of them all the time. And contrary to what *he* says, Damiano's brat is the key. They would do anything to get his son back and I'm gonna cash out on that. My brother is going to bend the knee and *beg* me!"

He ignored the hostile glare the older woman gave him when he entered the house. The little boy was playing with the stuffed toy on the rug in front of the fireplace and for once didn't burst into tears when he noticed him.

Mason stared at him with an unflinching intensity, reminiscent of Damiano's. Jay shuffled uncomfortably.

Jesus. Get a grip, Vick. He's a little boy, for fuck sake!

"How much longer are you going to continue with this farce?" Carol asked coldly.

"Farce? Oh, it's anything but a farce, my dear woman. I have it from a very dependable source that your son-in-law is ready to give me what I want."

"So, what's the hold-up? Or are you playing games?"

Jay snorted. "I brought some food. Feed that brat before he starts bawling again."

Carol eyed the bags he'd placed on the kitchen counter.

"He's too young for junk food. A little child needs proper nutrition. Don't, for one moment, believe that my husband or Damiano would—"

"I'm not a fucking idiot, woman. I bought baby food and fresh produce. Get off your backside and make him something to eat. I'm sick and tired of your constant nagging. *Jesus!* What the hell was I thinking when I took you, of all people? I shudda taken the young girl. At least then I would've had some fun as well," Jay barked. "Make it snappy. We're moving out in an hour."

"Moving out? Why?"

Jay speared a glance at her. "I wasn't born yesterday. Damiano and your husband have sources that can access any satellite or use a facial recognition search to find us. Staying too long in one place is asking for trouble. And don't even think about delaying us. We're leaving in an hour whether or not the brat has been fed," he sneered just before he slammed out of the house.

"It's been a week, Colt. Why haven't you found him yet?" Ceejay asked. She had just passed coffee to him, her father, Parnell, and Kent who sat around the kitchen table. "You know the statistics about missing children. I can't lose him, Colt. I can't lose another child! Please, you have to find him!"

Colt pulled Ceejay onto his lap and hugged her close. He buried his face in her hair when she began to cry quietly, hiding his own tears.

"The statistics don't matter in this case, honey. Jay wouldn't ... he knows Mason is worth more alive to him. Our little boy will be back home soon. I promise," he said in a deep, soothing voice.

"When? Tell me when? He's not used to being away from us for so long. He must be wondering why we've deserted him."

Colt looked at Maxwell. A silent communication passed between them; a vow to redouble their efforts to find their loved ones.

"We're doing everything we can, honey. We've been scouring the surrounding areas every day and we won't stop until we find him. Quade has asked Quinlan Shaw, Bracus' partner to help. He designed a specialized facial recognition program linked to the International Space Station. It was a battle to obtain permission at first, but they're using it now to comb through the surrounding areas. He's going back to the day of the kidnapping and if they're in a hundred-mile radius of Jacksonville at present, he'll find him." Colt explained.

He got up and carried her to their bedroom, with a brief nod to his friends.

"I want you to rest, honey. You've hardly slept this past week and it's not good for the baby. Shh, Ceejay," he placed his fingers against her lips. "I know you're worried, my love, but I promise you, I *will* find our son. For now, you need to take care of Mason's little brother or sister. Okay?"

Ceejay nodded and curled on her side. Colt stroked her back until her breathing slowed and she fell asleep. He knew it wouldn't be more than a short nap, but at least she'll get some rest. Mason's absence hung like a threatening hail-cloud over her peace of mind.

He walked back to the kitchen; his steps heavy. He was concerned that Quade won't been able to find any sign of Jay. He might be lying low or was hiding under their noses and leading them on a wild goose chase.

"Why hasn't he made his demands yet, Colt? What fucking game is the bastard playing?" Kent asked when he walked into the room.

"He's psychotic, Kent. Of course, he's playing a game. He's deriving pleasure by making me sweat."

"How can you be sure he won't hurt them, Colt? From the digging I did about him, I've found him to be ruthless." Maxwell's brow was furrowed with worry.

"Jay might be ruthless but he's not stupid. He knows that if either of them is hurt, he won't get what he wants."

"Yeah, but still, why hasn't he contacted you with his demands? I can't envisage him playing babysitter to a two-year-old boy, Colt. Not the man he's become." Kent paced the kitchen as he spoke. He wanted to wrap his hands around Jay Vick's throat and squeeze the life out of him. "I still can't associate what he is now, to the man I had known and respected for so long."

"He played a part, Kent. According to what Luca told me, he's been coveting the Don's position for years. And who can blame him? Luca stole him at birth specifically for that reason. But the foster family Jay grew up in only wanted the money Luca paid them for his upkeep. He wasn't nurtured and hence, grew up to be cruel and cunning. And he's had years to hone his skills. So much so, that none of us recognized the real person he was."

"Luca Vitale. Now, why am I not surprised that he had a hand in this man's dementia? Are you saying when Jay Vick didn't turn into the man Luca wanted him to be, he spurned him?" Maxwell asked, watching Colt closely.

"Yeah." He got up to stare at the open fields through the back door. "Luca started training him, but the inherent cruelty had taken root the day he burned down his foster mother and her house and became uncontrollable. Luca didn't want that for his successor. He needed someone who could think on his feet, have a balance between cruelty and compassion—"

"What the fuck for? It's the goddamned mafia!" Parnell interceded.

"Luca is shrewd, but unfailingly diplomatic when it suits him. It is a characteristic he uses to throw people off guard. I suppose that's why he set his sights on me. Only he could never get me to see things his way. That's been his Achilles heel—his inherent need to control me."

"But you didn't bend," Maxwell said.

Colt glanced at him. "No, but I came close; until he sent me after you to destroy your empire. It was you who set me back on track, Maxwell, who showed me the way to keep my true persona hidden from Luca and how to survive his rule. If not for that . . ."

"I saw the struggle inside you, Colt. It didn't matter what he'd made you do until that point. You had good parents who gave you the values that define you as a man today—one with integrity, honor, and respect for humanity. Something Luca Vitale will never understand and because of that, he will never be the kind of leader you've become for the Occhipintis, Colt. He knows it and that's why he won't ever give you up."

"Yeah, Maxwell, you're right and we all know what that means," Kent intoned.

"Maxwell and Kent are right, Colt," Parnell continued. "Luca Vitale will never let you go. Only his death will ensure that you're relieved of the burden of the Occhipinti crime family."

"Then so be it. I've had it. Because of that fucking family, our lives have been in turmoil for the past number of years. We will not live like this anymore. Our families deserve to live without any fears."

"What are you saying, Colt? Do you believe Luca has something to do with Mason's kidnapping?" Maxwell asked.

"For his sake, I hope not, but his actions spurred Jay to act; I am sure of that. What Parnell said is true. Luca will never release me willingly and will continue to find ways to force me back into the mafia's fold. I should never have gone back, but it had been the only way to keep Ceejay safe. Now that Gianni is dead, I can cut the cords. I know what I wanted to know."

"I still can't believe that Stephen Caldwell was Gianni's son. It blows my mind how he could have lived a double life for so long, without anyone being wiser. And to use his own son? His *own* fucking son in such a vile way? I'm still battling to come to terms with that. Killing your own child to gain power? It defies reason." Kent raged.

"It does, and to use someone so innocent like Ceejay ... deliberately setting her up for a fall, then killing Stephen and their son. But that wasn't enough. He used her to hide the fucking bonds here ... he sent her as a bait for me. But why would he? Gianni didn't want me back as the Don. Why would he have steered Ceejay back to her uncle—to Jacksonville? Fuck ... I knew he lied. I fucking knew!"

"Who? Colt, if it wasn't Gianni ... shit. Luca. It's been Luca all along, isn't it?" Parnell came to the same realization as Colt.

Although Colt admitted to himself that he'd had the suspicion for a while, he just didn't want to acknowledge it.

"Yes. It's obvious that Luca had known all along what Gianni was up to and he played him like a marionette. He designed the game and used everyone around him to implement it, while he, the fucking bastard, sat back and watched. I thought I had gotten away from him, but he knew where I was all along." Colt was furious; more at himself for not realizing just how devious Luca Vitale was.

Colt grabbed his keys and headed for the door but Maxwell barred his way.

"Colt, calm down. Barging in on Luca and killing him in cold blood isn't going to help us any. And it's not you. You don't want to go down that route, son. It'll haunt you for the rest of your days."

"He fucking deserves to die a slow, painful death!" Colt barked. The fury built higher and higher inside him.

"Yes, he does, but not now. We need him alive, Colt and you know it. You have to calm down and think clearly. We can't afford to let Luca know that we're onto him. Jay Vick is the key. From what I've just heard, I'm relatively sure that the two of them are in cahoots. We need to be clever, son. You know I'm right," Maxwell said colloquially. It was his relaxed manner that calmed Colt down.

"Yeah, I know. But I'm so fucking angry right now. And you're wrong, Maxwell. Killing Luca Vitale won't haunt me; it will release me from this perennial hell I've been living in."

"I am worried about Carol's tracer not working. Either he took it from her or maybe it has malfunctioned. If not for that we'd have found them long ago. I'll fucking kill Vick myself if he hurts her," Maxwell muttered while he checked his smart phone for the umpteenth time to see if the tracer link was active. Suddenly he froze, as realization struck him. "Fuck! I never reactivated her tracer. How could I have been so negligent?" He raged at himself. "I had the clasp repaired and forgot to reactivate it when we got it back."

"Won't she realize it?" Kent asked watching the pacing man.

"Possibly. Even if she does notice it, she'd need a small pin to toggle the 'activate' button. Which, I doubt she has with her." Maxwell sat down with his head in his hands. He'd been optimistic about finding them through Carol's tracer.

Colt's phone started vibrating on the table, which drew their attention. He froze when he read Quade's name on the flashing screen. The conversation was brief, which ended in a curt instruction from Colt, "Text me the coordinates anyway, Quade. Please let me know when you find him again." His jaw was rigid when he slipped his phone in his pocket.

"They tracked them to a farmhouse in Tecula, but Quinlan says he moved them out just as the satellite shifted position. There's a ten-minute delay before he can continue the search." Colt said as he began striding toward his truck.

"Wouldn't it serve us better to wait until he finds them again?" Maxwell asked. They all trailed after Colt.

"No. I want to go to Tecula. I want to see if he left anything behind. Please stay with Ceejay, Maxwell, but don't tell her anything yet. We'll be back soon.

Colt didn't bother to try and stay his two

friends. If Quinlan was lucky enough to pick up on Jay's trail again, at least he'll have them by his side.

"Do you think he knew about the timing of the satellite change?" Parnell speculated as they drove off.

"Yeah. He's too clever not to know we'd be using everything in our power to track him."

"Fuck! That means he might manage to stay under the radar and we could lose them again."

"Yeah, that's what I'm afraid of." Colt replied softly. "But at least now we know he's close by and we can contain our search in a narrower radius." Colt missed his little boy and he could only imagine what Ceejay must be going through; the angst at the possibility that she might never see him again.

It won't happen, my love. I will find him. If it's the last thing I do, I will bring our son home to you.

CHAPTER SIX

"Enough, Sapphire! If you want this relationship to work, you need to forget the kind of life you lived before this. Or is that it? Is that what you crave? To live in fear and crave pain as a means of pleasure?" Kent was annoyed to find her in the whipping chamber in a scene similar to the one he'd interrupted at Club Tiberius.

His mind had been on the discussion about Jay, something that always spurred his anger. He was disappointed to find Sharon still in the grasp of her fears. Maybe he was fooling himself that he was ready to move on. Did he really have the patience to deal with her emotional demons?

He frowned as the questions swirled through his mind. He stared at the shocked look on her face. She didn't even realize what she'd been doing. And that alone, was enough for Kent. She had toggled something loose deep inside his soul and for once, he decided to act upon it; to take the time and effort to work on his future. She might just be the one.

Sharon startled. She'd explored the thoughts Kent had planted in her mind. She'd lived that kind of life for so long, it had become the norm for her. But wasn't that why she'd chosen to come looking for Kent after that scene in Club Tiberius? Where he'd proven how much pleasure she could reach with a hand that was tender, yet firm and powerful.

"No, but it's all I've known. I need to ... I want to forget that time in my life. I honestly do, but I'm afraid I don't know how. I thought I'd be able to put it behind me if I came here ... with you ... and yet, here I am, still acting like—"

"The other night you expressed your desire to become my slave. Was I mistaken, Sapphire?" Kent's lashed at her sharply.

"No, you weren't. But maybe if it felt like I was your slave—"

"First of all, let's get this straight. I told you I

don't want a slave."

"Sub, slave, whatever. I still don't feel like you and I have a specific agreement," Sharon continued. She yanked the cords of her corset tighter with an annoyed glance at him.

"Ah, so that's it. You want the bells and whistles. You need proof of your status as a sub for others' benefit?"

"No. Not just a sub. *Your sub.* If for no other purpose than to keep those subs from drooling over you every time you walk into the dungeon," she said. Her chin tilted in a sign of rebellion, even as she returned his stare.

Kent regarded her silently. She was a beautiful woman. She did something to him that he was still trying to decipher. He knew all about her past; how she'd treated Nolan. More than that, he knew the cruelty she'd been exposed to with Roberto Vitale, which had changed her personality. She'd become a hard, empty shell. But he'd seen the vulnerable side of her when she'd been under his care in the hospital—the side that needed caring.

She needed to understand that submitting to him didn't mean she had to morph into a different woman; least of all, that she needed pain to find pleasure.

Going by her recent actions, he could ascertain that dominance, when exerted over her in a controlled manner, made her inhibitions and fears disappear. Now, it was his turn to guide her. To make her see that all the past pain, the skeletons in her closet and the burden of destroying all those memories, were not just hers to bear, but his as well.

He needed to help her to relieve the painful baggage and heal. Kent admitted to himself that it might just be what he needed to heal as well.

The pain of losing Anthea—his wife—still caught him unawares at times and kept him from moving on. He'd lost her unexpectedly and quite young. Ten years ago, she'd just been twenty-eight; a vibrant woman in her prime. All that changed in a fleeting moment of misjudgment during that fateful accident. She died instantly but Kent had taken much longer to come out of mourning.

It was time to move on. While helping Sharon, he might just pave the way for himself too.

"You don't feel like my sub? Now why is that?"

"You know why," Sharon snapped. Her eyes widened when his face darkened. She lowered her eyes. "My apologies, Master Steel. It wasn't my intention to sound disrespectful."

"Very well, Sharon. Let's get this over with. You want to feel like my sub, so that's what we'll do. We're going to Nolan's office to sign a D/s agreement that I had drawn up. Once signed, there is no turning back for you."

"I won't—"

"Quiet!"

"Yes, Sir." Sharon stared at the floor, feeling his control envelope her soul. This is what she craved—his guidance and trust. Maybe Kent would show her the way out of this quagmire. He might be the one to free her from its tenuous depths.

"Understand one thing, Sharon," Kent said against her temple. He leaned back to capture her gaze. "Our agreement is going to be very different from what you've been exposed to before. It's not going to be just sexual. We will have a relationship outside of the club. In our relationship, you will find intimacy, love, and respect. Not just for yourself, but for me too."

"Permission to speak, Sir," Sharon said.

Kent nodded and watched her eyes lift before she asked, "Outside of the club?"

"My wife passed away ten years ago, my pet, and I've been alone since then. I want to move on too."

"Are you saying that you want us to live together? As Dom and sub?"

Kent studied her carefully. He knew what she had with Vitale, however demented it had been. He needed to tread very carefully if he wanted their relationship to evolve.

"Yes. Our D/s relationship will be based on sexual domination. I have no intention of controlling every aspect of your life. I expect you to rise above the muck your true personality has been hidden under; to build your life once again. Be your own person. Have your own goals. Maybe some kind of career or whatever interests you. But sexually, Sharon, you will be the slave to my desires."

"And you? Will you be the slave to my needs?"

He smirked. "Well, my pet, that remains to be seen."

"And all those other subs?" She dared to ask.

"I don't need others, as long as we're together. Understand one thing, Sapphire. I am very possessive and I'll never share you with another man. *Never*. There will never be a threesome in our future."

Relief washed over her face, like the awakening of spring flowers. It was the thing she'd hated most. How Roberto had shared her with his henchmen.

"Are you beginning to understand, Sapphire? The difference between a true Dom and the demented man who used to be your master?"

"Yes. Thank you, Master Steel. I am looking forward to learning what pleases you."

Kent lifted her chin. "You please me, Sapphire

and I daresay you will continue to do so, provided you embrace this relationship fully. Now, let's go."

"Yes, Master Steel."

Kent noticed that Colt was in his office. It seemed he came here when he needed to think. He held the door of Nolan's office open for Sharon to precede him.

"Wait here, Sapphire, in the middle of the room in the Nadu position with your back to the door. I won't be long."

He turned to go back to Colt's office without waiting to see if she did his bidding. He found Colt behind his desk, staring at a photograph in his hand. Kent didn't need to ask. It was the picture of Mason playing with colorful building blocks and a big plastic tipper truck. They'd found it in the farmhouse in Tecula.

"Colt?"

He glanced up with a wry smile. "He looks so happy, Kent."

"He's got his Nana with him, Colt. He might be thinking they're on an adventure."

"Maybe at first, but it's been more than a week, Kent. He's never been away from us for this long."

"Children are more resilient than we give them credit for, Colt and besides, knowing Carol, she won't allow Jay to hurt Mason."

"I'm more concerned about his emotional state, Kent. Someone like Jay ... he could damage his psyche without even trying."

"Are you worried that ... you know, he might do what Luca did to him? That would be the perfect revenge against you."

Colt's hands fisted. Just the thought that Jay Vick might take his child away and bring him up as his own, caused his body to tremble with anger. His eyes turned as black as a moonless night. He looked at Kent. "I'll fucking kill him. I am going to find him, Kent. He will not destroy my son's life!"

"*We* will find him. We're all beside you every step of the way. We just missed him in Tecula and now that we know he's close, we have a better chance of finding him."

"Yeah. Thanks Kent. I know Jay's deception, over all these years, must hurt you too."

"Fuck him. He doesn't deserve any kind of emotion; not even hate. He's caused enough heartache over the last couple of months for all of us, Colt. He has to pay and it has to be soon. How's Ceejay holding up?"

"She puts up a brave front, but she's suffering. It's her first boy all over again, Kent. She's already preparing herself for the worst. I can't allow that to happen. Not to our son."

"It won't. What say we hit the skies tomorrow in my chopper? Between Nolan, Parnell, and Seth, we can scout the area once again. We might find some kind of clue that we missed before."

"That sounds like a brilliant idea, Kent. Thanks. I'll chat with the other guys." He ran his hand over his eyes. "I saw you with Sharon. Are you serious about her?"

Kent shrugged as he got up and sauntered toward the door.

"It's time for me to move on. I've mourned my

wife for too long and I've realized that I'm turning into a recluse. I want to start living again."

"She's broken, Kent, you know that."

"Yes, she is. But underneath that exterior is a woman who needs someone to understand her. To tap into the softness that she lost during her years with Roberto. She might be broken, Colt, but together, we might just be the glue she needs to become whole again."

"It's not going to be easy to break the bad habits that he ingrained into her over the years. You're brave, Kent."

"Maybe so, but don't forget that he forced it on her. He was uncaring and cruel. I'm not that kind of Dom, Colt. You know my style. I will overwhelm her by being lovingly menacing, vaguely threatening, and of course wickedly suggestive. I'll keep her on her toes all the time. She won't know what to expect. But one thing she'll never experience again is cruelty."

"Well, if there's one person who can guide her out of her personal hell, it's you. Good luck, Kent."

Sharon fiddled with her fingers behind her back. Sitting there quietly felt uncomfortable at first, until she allowed her mind to wander back to the scene with Kent at Club Tiberius. Remembering how his hands had felt when he caressed her skin before the sting of the whip had connected. She breathed in deeply. Then there was the aftercare. It had been a first for her. That was why Sharon had longed for a true Master and slave relationship.

The night of the auction had been surreal. Sharon experienced a rush of heat every time she thought back to their time together. His control—the power he'd exerted over her in such a strong, yet tender way, had completely overwhelmed her.

She knew most people disapproved and judged her based on her prior life. But what was she supposed to have done? There'd been no escape for her then. But all that has changed. She's been given a second chance at life. Every person needed a harbor, a security.

Kent was her savior. Sharon could easily see herself becoming addicted to him, but for all the right reasons. He would offer her safety and love, an anchor she could hold onto; because this time, it was what *she* wanted.

So, for those who judged me; who have never experienced the brutal sting of abuse, could take their opinions, and shove it up theirs.

Nolan had been her one consolation in a world of pain. He had been empathetic through it all, offering her warmth and patience. That was what had carried her through the months after Roberto's death. If not for Nolan, she'd have given up and taken her own life. But he'd talked her out of it many times. Assured her there would be a shining light one day. His positivity had helped her to heal partially. He was the one who had made way for a miracle in her life. The one she was kneeling for.

A feeling of serenity flowed through her. Peace and acceptance. This was where she wanted to be, where she belonged. She trusted Kent Gibson to take her into the light and help her find herself again. She cleared her mind and calmed her breathing as she waited. Finally, at peace with the direction her life was taking.

She felt his presence when he entered the room silently. His warmth permeated into her skin as he stood behind her. He brushed her hair back over her shoulder and traced her cheek.

"Such a lovely view, my pet. This is what I'd like to see every day when I arrive home—you, in the Nadu position. Naked and waiting for me in my house."

"Yes, Master Steel," Sharon agreed, already envisioning herself in his home.

"The real beauty of life is partly in its unpredictability. Nothing is permanent; everything changes. This is part of the change we're going to experience together, Sharon. The question I have for you, my pet, is if you have the ability to truly accept what I have to offer."

Her eyes lifted to gaze into his. What she found there soothed her troubled soul—obliterated the small remnants of doubt that still resided in her mind. He was opening his heart and soul to her, thereby offering her the ax to sever the invisible chains that kept her tied to the past.

He held out his hand. She didn't hesitate in reaching for it. His fingers curled around hers. The smile on his face drew her in and her lips curved up in gentle acceptance.

"Yes, Master Steel. I accept and will embrace our lives together."

"Very well, Sharon. Come; let's finalize the paperwork so we can celebrate our union with a scene in the examination room."

Sharon felt a thrill run down her spine. This was new to her and it scared her as much as it excited her. She sat down next to him and dutifully read through the detailed agreement. She hesitated when she reached the end.

"What's wrong, Sharon? Is there something in the contract that bothers you?"

"Not really. But from what it says here, you expect this relationship to develop into something as permanent as marriage?" She queried tentatively.

"Eventually, maybe. Who knows, but I do want you to realize that a committed D/s relationship here in the club, is with the intention to look toward the future and what it might bring us. It might take years, but I am willing to walk the distance. Are you going to meet me halfway?"

"I desire nothing more, but I might not be able to give you what you want."

"I don't understand, Sharon."

"You know what he did to me ... the condition I was in after ... after he gave me to his men. The truth is—I don't know if I would be able to give you any children—if things work out for us and we get that far."

Kent cupped her face. He traced her lips with his thumbs. "We'll cross that bridge when we get to it, Sharon. For now, let's concentrate on us. You and me. Okay? Everything else is irrelevant in this moment."

She nodded and smiled sweetly. He leaned forward and kissed her—slowly, reverently, accepting the change in his life. That he was committing to a woman who everyone hated and had pushed away not so long ago. He was surprised how badly he wanted her. Not just physically, but the desire to connect with her emotionally. Maybe it was her broken soul which enticed him so strongly. He stopped questioning it when she pressed her body closer and tilted her head for a deeper kiss.

Kent obliged willingly, drinking from the sweetness that she offered shyly. His mouth became urgent, roving across her face with rough kisses that stung her cheek, her chin, her forehead. She panted when he licked her lips with his tongue, demanding entry.

His hand shifted to hold her hips in a firm grasp, moving her against his rising shaft. He nipped at her lips, hungry for more. Her soft moan mingled with his growl when he grinded his hips against hers. She dazzled him with her passionate response and he wanted more.

"You shouldn't have done this, sub," he growled against her lips.

"Done what, Sir?"

"Arouse me. Now you'll have to feed my hunger. On your knees, Sharon. Show me how much you want to appease my lust with nothing but your mouth. Hands behind your back."

Sharon kneeled between his legs with no reservations as he took out his already aroused cock from his pants. There were no thoughts of past, or future. All she could think of was how desperately she wanted to please this man, who was willing to offer her a second chance at life and love.

She decided to grasp this opportunity with both hands. A door had finally opened for her, offering her more than she had hoped for when she'd boarded the plane to Jacksonville.

"It'll be my pleasure," she acceded and leaned forward, flicking her tongue over the soft spot where his balls and shaft met. She licked the base of his shaft and then hungrily sucked and licked her way up to his bulbous head.

"Beautiful, my pet. Now take my cock into your mouth. I want to feel your heat surrounding me," Kent instructed as he guided his tip past her lips.

She pulled back to poke her tongue out as far as she could, allowing his cockhead to rest on her tongue. She kept her eyes locked with his as she pulled her tongue back into her mouth, taking his cock in at the same time.

"Fuck, that looks hot, baby."

Kent dragged in a deep breath. The sight of her hot pink tongue caressing and slurping at his shaft had him on the verge of combusting. When she traced the slit on the tip of his cock with her tongue, a roaring moan sidled out from the back of his throat. He pushed his swollen cock into her throat and pumped into her mouth forcefully, watching as viscous strands of saliva hung languidly from her chin.

"I love the taste of you, Master Steel," she murmured briefly before sucking him back into her mouth.

Every part of his body ached and pulsated, howling for a release. He fisted his hand around a tuft of her hair, pushing into the hilt inside her throat. He couldn't stop and repeatedly impaled her. Their eyes met. He watched tears running down her cheeks. Her throat spasmed around his cock, making him lose the last fragments of his control. A first for him. With his body quivering, he pushed himself down her throat again with fevered need.

"You know just how to please me, little one," he grunted, his voice raw.

Reaching down, he pinched her nipples through her corset, wanting to give her some pleasure too. Sharon twitched in response, her eyes pleading, as her clit thrummed eagerly in response.

Kent grunted with satisfaction at her immediate reaction to his touch. His world fell away when he ejaculated.

"Oh, fuck!"

Kent erupted in the back of her throat. He cupped her head to hold her still as he emptied himself with short quick thrusts.

Sharon continued to milk his cock with her mouth, keeping his cock at the back of her throat while she sucked and licked him clean of any remnants of his release.

Their breathing harsh, he pulled her into his arms and nestled her against his chest. He closed his eyes and held her, feeling her essence flowing unbridled into him.

Tilting her head back, he used wet wipes that Nolan kept in his desk, to clean her face. He studied her expression with a quiet intensity that unsettled Sharon. Then he kissed her slowly, in an engagement of warmth, passion and need; a need that was growing stronger with each intimate encounter they had.

"Come, I wish to see how you submit to me in a scene."

"I've never been in a proper scene, Master Steel," Sharon admitted. The fact that she might fail at the test was a concern.

"I'm aware of that, my pet, which is why I want to test your resilience and submissiveness. I just want to ascertain if you are open to new experiences and how you react to them."

Sharon nodded and followed him.

"How long have you been a Dom?" she asked on the way there.

"Eighteen years. I started young, but my parents lived a D/s lifestyle so it wasn't a foreign concept for me. Most men in our family have been Dominants."

"Dominant or alpha males?" she asked teasingly.

Kent glanced at her and smiled, happy that she seemed so at ease in his presence.

"Is there a difference between the two, my pet?" He teased back gently.

They entered the examination room and Kent flattened the OB chair to turn it into a bed. "Strip, please. Everything, but those fuck-me shoes you seem to love so much."

He chuckled at the pink blush that bloomed over her cheeks. She always wore stilettos to the club. She loved the way they elevated her posture and made her legs appear longer.

"Sapphire, remember what I told you. Every

inch of your body is beautiful to me. Your scars make it even more so because they are proof of your strength and survival." Kent assured her when she hesitated. The lights in the examination room were bright and every scar would be visible to his eyes.

Once she undressed, he caressed her arms and legs while he tied her to the chair.

"Hmm. I'm gonna need some assistance with this scene. I think Master Wolf would do perfectly," he said as he turned to the club coordinator.

"No! Permission to speak, Sir," Sharon interrupted quickly.

"Yes?" The warning in his tone didn't escape her attention. He watched as she licked her bottom lip; agitation was clear on her face.

"Not Master Wolf, please."

"Why not? You know him well enough to be comfortable with him."

"Please, Sir. My relationship with Je ... I mean Storm, is tenuous at best. She's just beginning to accept my presence here. I don't want to jinx it."

"I understand. Very well. I'll ask Master Zeus

to assist." He nodded the instruction to the waiting coordinator who immediately darted away to go and fetch him.

"Wouldn't his wife mind? They've not been married very long, isn't that right?"

"No, but he is the Training Master here. His wife understands his role in the club. She would most probably be in attendance during the scene as well. She's relatively new to BDSM herself and might even help your transition into your new role here." Kent traced the curve of her breasts as he spoke, watching her nipples shrivel into hard little stones. "Do you like that, my pet?"

"Yes, Sir," she said through clenched teeth. She could feel the effect of his feather soft touch all the way to her loins. She caught her breath when he pinched her nipples. "Ooh," she moaned as a shard of pleasure shot to her clit, setting it to throb in reaction.

"You need my assistance, Master Steel?" Seth asked from the doorway, Sasha by his side.

"Yes, please, Master Zeus and Miss Sassy,

you might be of help as well. My sub isn't used to the proper conduct of a submissive and might learn something with your guidance through the scene."

"Oh, it will be my pleasure, Master Steel. Although, I'm not exactly sure how much help I'd be. She's been in the lifestyle longer than me." Sasha said with a gentle smile at Sharon.

"Oh, I daresay, you would be. Just help her to focus on her emotions and feelings throughout. You'll know what I mean once we begin." Kent directed Sasha to stand beside the examination chair.

"So, what do you want me to do, Master Steel?" Seth asked as he took the small stool at the foot of the reclining chair.

"This scene is all about awakening sensations. Something that is completely foreign to my sub. For now, you need to do nothing. When I give you the sign, I need you to use the G-spot vibrator inside her pussy."

Kent smiled at Sharon when she looked at him questioningly.

"I'm going to awaken sensations that you've never experienced before, my pet, and once I do, Master Zeus is going to escalate your arousal. I have to warn you, he's quite masterful with that specific tool. Here's the catch, sub. You will not climax. Not until I tell you to. Is that understood?"

"Yes, Master Steel."

"Good. You agreed by signing the contract that you trust me enough to allow me to decide what is best for you during our scenes. Are you comfortable with that?"

"Yes, Sir."

"And you've chosen to forgo the use of a safeword when we're together. I do appreciate the trust, but if anything overwhelms or hurts you, you will tell me. Is that clear?"

"I won't need—"

"Sapphire, when we scene, the intention is not for you to suffer through any kind of pain to please me. That's something I never want. A scene is for your pleasure, as much as mine. You *will* tell me. Is that clear?"

"Yes, Master Steel."

"Good. I'm going to play with your senses, my pet and to ensure you concentrate on that, I'm going to blindfold you. Okay?"

Their eyes met for a fraction of a moment before the world went black behind the blindfold that he pulled over her head. Her breathing increased and her chest shuddered in anticipation. His fingers against her cheek quieted her.

"Easy, love. I'll be here the entire time. No one else will touch you but me and Master Zeus. Now, relax your body, clear your mind, and concentrate on the sensations on your skin," he instructed close to her ear. Her body sagged into the chair and her fists unfurled slowly. "Beautiful, that's what I want to see, Sapphire—expectation, willingness and above all, trust."

Kent picked up the tool he'd set down in preparation for the scene on the side table.

"You have experienced the Wartenberg wheel before, haven't you, sub?"

Sharon stiffened. "I have, Sir, but it was much

more than a prick. It was … I have scars in … internally from one of those," she managed to say. Her bottom lip turned blue as she bit into it.

"Sapphire, one thing I learned from my Master is to forget about the past and concentrate on the future. Don't let memories destroy what you could be now. When used properly, this toy can blow your circuits. I can personally attest to that." Sasha assured her in gentle voice.

Sharon swallowed. "Thank you, Miss Sassy."

"No more hurt for you, my pet. Nothing I ever do to you will result in anything but pleasure. So, give me your trust, little one and let's begin," Kent coaxed her gently. She nodded and relaxed. "Do you trust me, Sapphire?" He asked softly.

The answer sprang to her lips, but she bit it back when another voice from her past flashed through her mind, asking her the same question. How naive she'd been then. It was such a loaded question. Back then, she'd believed herself in love and hadn't hesitated in responding.

Now, she carefully listened to the tone of his

voice. It was warm, wickedly suggestive, and somewhat playful. She'd seen the way he acted and treated his friends and the subs in the club. She'd given him her trust when she signed the contract. In here, at his mercy, she didn't feel the same fear and revulsion she used to, with Roberto. The only feelings that swirled inside her were excitement and wonder. This time it was a conscious decision.

"Yes, Sir. I trust you," she whispered against his cheek.

"Ah, now that's what I want to hear, sub. I love the sound of that, my pet."

Kent gently tested the wheel over his palm. It was a seven-row pinwheel and when used correctly, it offered intense stimulation. Each of the seven wheels was detailed with twenty-two spikes. When they rotated over satiny skin, no sub could avoid the increased awareness of their nerve endings and the excitement it brought to them.

He'd deliberately chosen it for their first scene. He'd seen the scars on the inside of her labia, caused by the ruthless use of something similar, during his treatment of her. He still recalled how shocked he'd been at her condition when she'd been brought to the hospital. Roberto had given her to his army of men to use and abuse nonstop for days. She'd required intensive surgery.

This scene was a calculated move. Trust was the driver in a Dom/sub relationship. She needed to know he would never physically hurt her, no matter what tool he had in his hand.

"This is more than just a normal Wartenberg wheel. It's an ElectraStim Uni-Polar Wartenberg Wheel," he stated. "It's connected to a stimulator charged with electricity. With this little electric tool, you will experience tingling electro sensations on top of the spikes pricking your skin."

"Pricking only?"

"Yes, love, nothing more than some stinging sensations to awaken the juices deep within your core." While he spoke, he gently lowered the pinwheel to her stomach. Her back lifted and she jerked in reaction. "Easy, sub," he ordered and waited until she calmed down before he wheeled it around her bellybutton with a light pressure. She jerked again, but relaxed when all she felt was little pinpricks.

He continued over the curve of her belly to linger across her thighs, the electro sensations surprisingly set her clitoris throbbing. She whimpered as he wheeled the pinwheel all over her body, causing pleasurable shivers in its wake. Her mind was frayed with the anticipation of where he was headed next. Prickling and electric charges forced her brain to focus on each body part he graced with the wheel. Sometimes it was no more than a tickle; others stung, but the zing of the electrodes sizzling across her nerve endings, set her entire body ablaze with need.

She relaxed her muscles completely and gave herself over to the tingles. It was what Kent had been waiting for and slowly edged the wheel over her pussy mound, to draw circles around her clit. Her breathing spiked and her stomach rolled like the stormy waves in the ocean. But this time, it wasn't with fear and he knew it. She was already on a cloud of euphoria and could do nothing but moan huskily when he wheeled the pin over her spread labia.

"Now, don't move, Sapphire. I would hate to hurt your moist, puffy lips with these spikes."

Sharon only whimpered and felt her body melting into the chair, as he wheeled the pin closer to her slit. The electro sensations caused her pussy to go into overdrive and her thighs began to quiver.

"Fuck, Master Steel! Stop. Please."

Kent brought the wheel back, pulled her labia open.

"No! Please!" She begged fearfully, the painful memory resurfacing inside her mind.

"Relax, my pet. This is me and you assured me that you trust me," Kent soothed her gently as he rolled the wheel ever so gently—a mere prick, just on the inside her of slit, following the line of the scar that was barely noticeable.

Sharon became so lost in the rapture that flushed her body; she couldn't even comprehend what was happening. All that mattered was the awareness that flooded her mind.

"I'm warning you, Sapphire, do not come."

Kent nodded at Seth, who curled his hands around her hips and held her still. Kent wheeled the pin back and forth a few times while Sharon wailed and begged him to stop. Juices dripped from her throbbing pussy, weeping for release.

"I need to come. *Please.*"

Kent didn't respond, just continued to concentrate on gently wheeling the pin over her tender flesh. She cried out and moaned nonstop. The pressure inside her loins was unbearable and every nerve in her body crackled with need.

"Hmm, I love your scent, my pet; very enticing indeed. Now, behave, Sapphire. Master Zeus is going to find the swollen ganglia inside your pussy while I continue with my quest. Do. Not. Come."

"I hate you," she whimpered.

Kent was aware how devastating the sensations must feel to her. She'd never been exposed to arousal such as this. This must be blowing her mind.

"I'm proud of you, love. You're holding out

longer than I'd anticipated."

Her cry echoed against the ceiling when Seth gently pushed the G-spot vibrator inside her and switched it on, while Kent simultaneously rolled the wheel across her breasts.

The sharp edges stung her aureole as he moved it closer to her nipples. Her breath hitched in her throat. The gentle vibration inside her pussy and the sharp sting on her taut nubs caused a flush of juices to dribble from her pussy.

"Remember that you are not allowed to come, my pet."

Then he wheeled the pins directly over her nipple. Her back arched off the chair and she cried out as the movement pressed her nipple harder into the sharp spikes of the wheel, causing pleasure to zing directly to her clit. She panted, even as Kent leisurely continued his quest on the other nipple.

"Please, I beg you ... it's too much."

"Ah, sweetie. I love to hear those words from your lips."

Kent removed the blindfold and stood

watching her. Her eyes rolled back in their sockets as Seth masterfully maneuvered the vibrator inside her.

Sharon had never felt like this. The sensations that he had elicited on the inside of her labia with the spikes still sizzled, intensified by the gentle vibrations of the tool gently probing against her G-spot.

"Now, my pet. Come for me," Kent ordered as he gently pressed the wheel against her clit and rolled it back and forth.

Sharon screamed and bucked wildly as a surge of warm liquid erupted from her pussy. Her eyes blazed as she stared into his face. She choked out another scream as streams of cum showered the vibrator and spilled from her pussy.

"Now, *that*, Master Steel, is one hell of a climax." Seth declared.

Sharon sat on the small balcony of the hotel room

having breakfast. She preferred to eat in, rather than going down to the dining room. Especially when one of the male guests pounced on her every time she walked downstairs.

"I wonder if the daft man has radar or something to know when I leave my room."

That was the thing about being a woman alone. She got to make the choices about her own life. No more commands of what to wear or how to act.

Her mind wandered to the conversation with Kent when he'd driven her back to the hotel the previous evening.

"Where do you intend to stay, Sharon? Now that you've committed to me, I assume that you're moving to Jacksonville permanently?"

"I haven't given it that much thought, in all honesty. Things have happened quicker than I expected." Her voice turned husky. His hand was resting on her thigh and his thumb drew lazy circles on her skin. She wondered if he realized the effect his touch had on her. Even now, after the scene at the

club.

"Do you plan on going back to Anacapri first?"

"No. I don't want to see that place again. Not for a long time at least. Now that I've had the courage to leave, I'm going to concentrate on starting a new life."

"And your parents? I don't believe the mighty Simon Watts will be too happy losing his little princess." Kent slanted a sideward glance at her, a small smile to indicate that he meant nothing harsh.

Her tingling laugh filled the car. It was a sound of pleasure and companionship. Her gasp at the end told him she hadn't laughed in a long time.

"I'm not ashamed to admit that my father has always spoiled me. Mom too, for that matter. I am an only child but they understand my reasons for leaving. Dad is still trying to overcome the guilt for what Roberto had done to me."

"His guilt? Oh, yes, he refused to help you at the time to get away from Roberto."

"Yes, and that's what I believed. More proof that one should never make assumptions based on *appearance. Dad never knew about anything. He never liked Roberto and the only reason he did business with him was to keep a close eye on him. Since his death, Mom and Dad have been trying to make up for their ignorance. Not that I expected them to, but I realized it's something they needed to do. You know? To find peace in their own mind that I actually survived the ordeal."*

The silence that followed was peaceful, apart from the music that played softly in the background.

"How would they feel if you moved in with me?"

Sharon looked at him and he met her glance briefly before his attention was drawn back to the road.

"Or does the prospect of living with me spook you?"

Sharon mulled it over. His question caught her unaware, not that it was unexpected. He'd left a couple of hints during the evening that it would be easier if they saw more of each other to transition into their relationship. The thought of living with him filled her with a feeling of comfort and excitement. Kent didn't scare her and she believed he was the kind of man she could trust. With her body and her heart.

"No, it doesn't. You've proven to me that I can trust you with my body. But wouldn't your friends find it strange? You know, with my history and how I acted before? Maybe it's too soon to take such a step?"

"Sharon, neither of us is getting younger and my life belongs to me. I make my own choices and decisions. Besides, if we find we're not compatible living together, you can always move out. You're not going to be locked up in a room, you know."

She giggled when he snorted and it was so infectious, he laughed with her.

"It will solve the problem of where to live and like you've said earlier tonight, we need to see more of each other to get to know the people we are now and give our relationship a chance. I do want that, Master Kent. To make our relationship work."

"So that's it then. You'll move in with me."

A knock on the door yanked her from her

thoughts and she went to answer it.

"Jewel? What are you doing here?" She was too shocked to hide her surprise at the smiling woman standing in the hallway.

"Good morning to you too, Sharon. Well? Aren't you gonna invite me in?" She asked with an impish smile.

Sharon stepped back and held the door open. "Of course, please come in."

"I've often wondered what this old heritage hotel looked like inside. I have to say, I'm pleasantly surprised." Jewel said looking around.

"Yes, I was too. They've modernized the interior of all the rooms but the downstairs and dining areas maintained the original look and feel."

"Oh, you're having breakfast. Please, don't let me interrupt you. I'll just sit with you on the balcony."

"I'm done, but there's some extra tea if you'd like some," Sharon said, joining Jewel at the small table.

Jewel groaned, eyeing the pot of tea. "Oh, how

I miss my early morning tea," she wailed and glanced at Sharon. "I've developed an aversion to tea. It makes me nauseous."

"Oh, yes, Kent told me you're pregnant. Congratulations."

"We're so excited." She giggled. "Imagine that, we'll probably go on honeymoon with a little baby."

"I'm sure you won't mind."

"No, it'll be wonderful." She rubbed her hands and smiled. "So, are you packed and ready to go?"

Sharon frowned. "I don't understand?"

"I'm taking you to Kent's ranch, silly. He phoned early this morning to tell us that he'd asked you to move in with him."

"And you don't mind? I know you don't like me, Jewel and that you might not be too happy about him and me ... our relationship—"

"I didn't like the person you were before, Sharon. Since you've come back, you're a changed person. I would like us to become friends. Also, Kent's been alone for too long. It's time he found happiness again."

Sharon blinked back the tears. She cleared her throat. "Thanks, Jewel. You don't know how much that means to me."

"Well, then, what are we waiting for? Let's get you and Kent settled, shall we?"

CHAPTER SEVEN

"Fuck!" Carol cursed as she watched Jay Vick pace in front of the window. He'd moved them to another remote farm, not far from the previous one.

"Ooee! Nanna fuk!" Mason said with eyes as wide as saucers.

"I'm sorry, little man. That was naughty of me," she cooed at the baby, annoyed with herself. She'd been doing her best to remain calm and not upset Mason. But the excitement of the 'adventure' was slowly waning and he was becoming more and more fretful. He missed his parents and had been asking to for them nonstop.

"Mase wants Dada," he wailed as he hurled the blocks Jay had bought for him, across the floor. They rolled to a stop against his scruffy boots.

"He better not start with his tantrum again,

woman," he growled.

"What do you expect, genius? He's bored and he misses his parents. These toys will only keep him occupied so long. He's a two-year old boy for heaven sake!"

"I don't care. Keep him busy; play a game. Just keep his trap shut!"

Carol fingered the bracelet on her arm. She'd realized on the second day of their abduction that the slight vibrations, when signals were sent out from her tracer, were missing. She hadn't the opportunity to check the tracer to see what was wrong. It was the only link Maxwell and Colt had to them and it wasn't working. Because of his wealth and the threats his position posed to her, he'd insisted on the tracer to keep a tab on Carol at all times.

"We need food. I'm hungry and I imagine he is too. You better get some fruit and veggies this time. And some of those baby crackers and milk too. He's used to nibbling on them during the day."

Jay slanted an irritated look at her. "What do

you think this is? Tinsel town? There aren't big grocery shops around here, Mrs. Powell. You'll have to make do with what you get!"

Carol shrugged. "Well, it's your ears he'll be howling into when he becomes irritated."

"Oh, for fuck sakes!"

"Oooe! fuk! Noty man!" Mason piped up, pointing a finger at Jay.

"I better get out of here before I lose it. What kind of fruit?" He growled as he grabbed his keys.

"Bananas, apples, oranges and peaches—if you can find any. Don't forget the crackers and nuts for me, please."

Jay didn't bother to respond. He stomped outside, slamming the door, and locking it behind him.

Carol ran toward the window and watched the car disappear around the bend. She sat down and removed the bracelet. Maxwell had had the link repaired couple of weeks ago and must've forgotten to reactivate the tracer.

"Damnit! It *is* off," Carol muttered as she

peered at the small emerald covering the tracer. It wasn't blinking. She'd become so used wearing it, she didn't even feel the vibrations anymore. "Now how the devil am I supposed to ... ah, yes, there it is. But how do I switch it on?"

She jumped up and began searching through drawers for something small and pointed.

"Please, a pin or a needle. I need something! Anything!"

The tracer could be turned on by pressing a tiny button that was hidden in a very narrow opening on one side of the emerald. She had a little tool in her purse that Maxwell had given her, but of course, she hadn't had the opportunity to grab her bag when Jay had kidnapped them.

Fifteen minutes later she slumped into the sofa, next to where Mason was playing on the carpet. She'd frantically searched every inch of the house but couldn't find anything thin enough to fit into the opening. She'd even taken the time to try and bang against the burglar proofing to see if there was any way to escape. It was useless.

Her eyes fell on the one small plastic truck Mason had just thrown aside. She pounced on it.

"Yes!" she cried out excitedly and immediately yanked on the small wheels, to pull them off the axle that was made of a very thin steel wire.

"Nanna! Bweak!" Mason shrieked. His eyes were wide as he stared at her. "Mommy angwy!"

"Ehm ... no, Nanna's not breaking your truck. We're gonna play mechanic. Yes! We're going to build the truck again." Carol said as she finally managed to pull the small wire from the plastic toy.

Mason shuffled closer and stood next to her, watching her with a frown. Carol brushed her fingers over his forehead and smiled to put him at ease

"Kanik?" He asked; his face scrunching up again.

"Yes, we're gonna fix ... come on, Carol! Get the damn thing ... in! Yes!" she cried out, startling Mason, who jumped back and stared at her in wonder.

Carol counted the seconds and sighed with

relief when she noticed the flicker of light behind the emerald. If you didn't look close enough, you wouldn't notice it. She snapped the bracelet back on her wrist and hugged Mason tight.

"Nana! Kanik?" he asked, pushing her away.

"Yes, see ... we're going to fix—"

"What the devil is going on here?" Jay asked behind them. Carol startled. She'd not heard him return.

"Kanik. Nana, kanik," Mason offered with a wide smile.

"Come, let's see what's next. Hmm ... where do you think this goes?" Carol asked Mason. She glanced at Jay over her shoulder. "You told me to keep him busy, didn't you?"

Jay glowered at her for a few seconds longer but couldn't find anything out of place. He retreated to the kitchen to unpack the groceries he'd bought.

He muttered to himself. "Fuck, Vick. You should've waited a couple of hours for the satellite movement. Now, they might've picked you up."

He shoved his concerns to the back of his

mind. He kept an eye on the woman and child, who seemed engrossed in rebuilding the plastic truck. Yet, Jay couldn't shake the feeling of doom that was bearing down on him.

He reached into his duffle bag and took out his gun—a German-built 10mm Glock Automatic. He made sure it was loaded and slipped it into the waistband of his trousers, underneath his shirt. It was better to be prepared than sorry. No one was going to get the slip on him.

It was time to make his demands and then, they would have to move again. He needed to find a more secure location, so that he could leave for two days, to meet Luca Vitale. His negligence today could be the end of this endeavor, but he refused to give up now. Damiano Vitale needed to suffer. One week wasn't nearly enough to be without his child. Or the child without his parents.

"I've been without mine, my entire miserable life, while he basked in their love. Luca Vitale even *doted* on him. The fucking bastard has no idea how lucky he'd been."

Carol glanced his way. "What did you say?"

"I said, come and fix lunch. We have to move in three hours."

"Not again! You can't keep—"

"Shut up, Mrs. Powell. I can do what the fuck—" The sight of Mason looking at him wide-eyed, made him swallow the word and he cursed under his breath, before he continued, "Whatever I want. You just do as you're told and everything will be fine. Continue to yap and I'm gonna gag you. I'm getting tired of your constant complaining."

Carol complied meekly. She had no idea how far away they were from Jacksonville but prayed that Maxwell was keeping an eye on his smart phone's app and would find them before they moved again.

"Goddamnit! We've circled the entire Tecula area three times now and nothing! Have Seth, Nolan or Parnell picked up anything?" Colt asked Kent as he circled back to the original hideout.

Kent checked with the other three, but none of them have noticed any anomalies.

"He could be hiding in any of these remote farms. Many of them are rentals," Kent said.

"Wait!" Maxwell cried from the back of the chopper. At the same time, Colt's phone rang.

"Quinlan? Tell me you found something," Colt snapped into his phone, looking toward Maxwell who was pointing excitedly at his own phone.

"Carol's tracer! It's on! They're at ... lemme find the coordinates . . ." he said, scrolling frantically around his phone.

"We spotted him at a greengrocer, Colt and from there followed him back to a farmhouse north of the previous location," Quinlan informed Colt.

"Head north, Kent. Maxwell, do you have the coordinates yet?" Once Maxwell rattled off the coordinates, Colt relayed them to Quinlan, who confirmed that it was the same location where they'd found Jay.

Kent gave the coordinates to Parnell, Nolan, and Seth. They agreed to land the choppers just south of the farm and approach on foot.

"We need to surprise him. If he sees us coming, I wouldn't put it past him to hurt Mason or Carol," Colt said to Maxwell. "And this time, that motherfucker better not get the better of us. It's time to snuff his fucking lights out for good," he said into the microphone. "I'm done being manipulated by all of them. Those fucking bonds have brought us nothing but devastation and death. It's time to end it. Once and for all."

"You should donate the fucking money to charity, Colt and fuck the mob. That way, they'll have nothing—"

"No, Kent. I don't want to give them any reason to keep coming after me for the rest of my life. I'm going to take the fucking lot back to the mob coffers and then, I'm walking away."

"Far be it for me to be the prophet of doom, Colt but you know as well as I do that Luca Vitale will never let you go."

"I told you, Maxwell. I'm done with them. They've manipulated my life enough. We've been stranded on an island of fear and uncertainty, without any rafts of hope of a better life, for too long. It's time to end the war; for our future; for the hopes and dreams of my family. If Luca Vitale knows what's good for him, he'll stay out of my way."

It didn't take long to reach the rendezvous point. The other three choppers were already winding down; their rotors slowing to a stop by the time Kent landed his chopper.

Parnell pointed north. "The house is about a quarter mile in that direction, just past this section of trees. At least it will give us adequate cover."

"Yeah, I doubt he's expecting anyone to find him this soon, so let's hope we can get inside the house undetected." Nolan said as they began jogging toward the grove of trees. Everyone fell in a single line formation behind Parnell, who automatically took the lead. As the one most experienced in stealth operations in the field, they trusted his guidance.

They huddled, watching the house in the distance, when they reached the edge of the grove. It was silent all around, apart from the chirping birds.

The house was the color of unfinished wood, weathered for years by harsh elements and baked by the hot summer sun—a deep, rich copper striped with hearty gold. The wood itself was cracked, warped, and twisted by shrinking grain here and there and was stained sporadically. The windows were burglar proofed—a modern addition to an old relic of a farmhouse.

"Seems unreal that such a serene view holds so much evil inside it," Seth murmured. He cocked his gun, as did others, in readiness.

"No shooting unless you're absolutely sure you won't hit Mason or Carol. I'd prefer no shooting at all. Mason's been through enough, he doesn't need that emotional stress added to his young life." Colt said gruffly.

"Agreed," Parnell agreed immediately. "If not for that, I could've gotten him easily through the window."

"I know. Maybe you should stay under cover of the trees, Parnell. If Jay manages to evade us, don't hesitate to kill that fucker," Colt ordered.

Parnell was a sharpshooter and the best equipped to be on point.

"Got it."

"Let's move out. Maxwell, stay with me. Seth, you and Nol take the front. Whatever you do, get Mason and Carol out of there first."

Colt stopped, resting one hand on the gate that blocked the yard, briefly considering what awaited them inside—his son and his biggest enemy. For one—he would die protecting, the other—he would kill without blinking. Love and hate, two opposing emotions, yet both equally strong. The desire to extract vengeance from the man who had so little regard for innocence, trembled through his body.

"Let's go," he said and carefully pushed open the gate, wincing when it made a loud squeaking noise. The four men froze and stared at the house. No one appeared in the windows. With a silent gesture, they trailed through the gate, each splitting in a different direction.

Colt's satisfaction, when he kicked open the back door to see Jay's face turn ashen, was short lived. In an instant, Jay's skin turned gray, his mouth hung open and his eyes widened. Then they turned cold as he turned to Mason, violent intent in his gaze.

"Dada! Dada!" Mason screamed when he noticed Colt and jumping up from the floor, he charged toward his father. Carol intercepted him and picking him up, she ducked under Jay's grasping hands.

"No! You motherfucker! You won't get your hands on him," she cried and ran for the door. Her eyes widened as she almost collided with her husband, Maxwell who'd followed Colt inside.

"Nana, fuk!" Mason piped and catching a glimpse of Colt chasing after Jay, who was still trying to catch Carol, screamed again, "Dada!"

Carol managed to evade Jay and slipped through the door that Colt and Maxwell had just kicked down. She ignored the sound of a gunshot and the hoarse cry that sounded like it came from her husband but didn't wait to find out and simply ran. Carol's heart was thudding wildly and the trees in the distance seemed to be swimming in her vision. She clutched Mason tighter to her chest as she ran. She couldn't breathe, her lungs were crying out for mercy. But she couldn't stop.

"Nana! Mase wants Dada!" Mason cried and pointed back to the house over her shoulder.

Carol ignored him, straining her ears. She could hear him behind her; his footsteps, almost as loud as her own heartbeat. She forced her screaming muscles forward, trying to coerce her trembling legs to keep running. But they faltered and twitched, ready to go under.

In a desperate attempt to get away, she pumped her legs harder and headed toward the small gate, slamming it closed behind her. Jay's curse was vicious as the little lock slipped into place. She ignored the zings she heard in the air and ran for the cover of trees.

Jay cursed as he felt the bullet burn into his upper arm. "Fuck! They left one in the trees!" He spun around and headed for the back of the house, cursing when he caught sight of Damiano tearing out of the house after him.

Colt had been delayed when Jay had shot Maxwell. He'd waited until Kent and Seth had charged inside.

"You motherfucker!" Jay screamed at Colt as he ran. He managed one shot in his direction but knew that trying to shoot with his injured arm was a waste. But he'd be damned if he gave in without a fight.

His feet slipped on the wet autumn leaves as he rounded the corner of the farmhouse. The sudden humid midday air choked his throat and lungs. He inhaled deeper—faster. With each footfall, a jarring pain shot from his ankle to knee.

The goddamned fall from that rock! I should've had my leg fixed already!

Jay kept running, realizing he wasn't as quick as before. His heart beat frantically, all or nothing. Fail—and he would pay the price. Damiano Vitale was ruthless in his pursuit.

Hell no! He smells like vengeance and he won't stop until I'm fucking dead!"

But if Damiano thought Jay was completely unprepared, he didn't know him well enough. He'd scouted an escape route on the day they'd arrived here. *Catching me won't be that easy, you mofo!*

He'd seen that Damiano was armed with a Kahr P9 double-action semi-automatic. He had one of those too. Six inches long, made from stainless steel and polymer, it was a lightweight weapon and wouldn't slow him down. But if he did catch him, Jay had no doubt that Damiano would shoot him. He won't aim to wound him. Damiano was out to kill him. It had been there in his eyes when he'd seen him reach for Mason.

But, Jay knew him well enough to know that he'd never shoot him in the back. For that matter, Damiano wanted to get his hands on him. Shooting him wasn't going to give him the satisfaction he was after. Jay pumped his legs harder and managed to run faster.

Just a couple of yards to the rock pool.

Jay smirked when he reached the dense cover of trees and shrubs surrounding a pond. He turned and snickered when he realized that he'd managed to put distance between him and Damiano. He slowed down and hunkered low to keep the noise level down as he slipped silently into the cool, muddy water. He did it so smoothly the surface hardly made a ripple. He settled on his back in the stagnant water, disguised by the dark mud. He slipped a hollow reed into his mouth to breathe through and just lay there, still as a corpse.

He heard the distant sounds of cursing and added voices as Damiano's cohorts joined him in the search. Jay kept his eyes closed and barely breathed as they came to stand on the bank of the pond, a couple of yards from where he was hiding. He prayed that the blood from his wound wouldn't be visible in the dark murky water.

Their garbled voices were barely discernible under the water.

"How the fuck did he manage to get away? I was behind him all the time! *Fanculo! Gesù!*"

Colt looked around, anger swirling inside him.

"We'll tell Quinlan to keep vigil on this area, Colt. Let's take Mason home. Maxwell needs to get to the hospital. Kent says the wound is serious and he's battling to stop the bleeding."

"Yeah, let's go," Colt concurred and with a final look around, he turned to follow Nolan and Seth.

"Dada!" Mason screamed and tore across the lawn the moment he saw him. Parnell ran beside him, his eyes scanning their surroundings nonstop.

Colt caught the little boy in his arms and clutched him against his chest until Mason protested from being held too tight.

"Mase wants Mommy," he began to whimper; suddenly overcome with all the tension he could feel emanating from the men around him.

"We're going home, Son. Mommy is waiting for you," Colt soothed him.
"Mase wants Mommy," he repeated tearfully, but clutched Colt around his neck, pressing his face into his throat.

Ceejay was lying back on the hammock, swinging for a while before coming to a stop. In the distance, the soft chirping birds soothed her soul. She thought of her cell phone, sitting on the kitchen counter. She'd left it there before going for a walk to calm her nerves. Waiting for it to ring with any news of Mason was driving her insane. She closed her eyes and drew in a lung full of fresh air. The day stretched out like an eternity. If only wishes had wings. But, she'd learned over time, wishing didn't bring any solace.

She felt a shiver run down her spine when her mind filled with the vision of her first son, Dean. He'd been the same age as Mason when he ... "Oh, God! Not again. Please. I can't lose another child!"

Her voice sounded hoarse as tears pressed through her scrunched eyelids. She saw his little mangled body and the blood ... "Oh lord, there was so much blood," she whimpered. He'd been lying in a pool of his own blood—his blond hair matted and stained red.

In quiet contemplation, she tried to turn her mind to love, the people she cherished and what was right in her life. Finding Colt had been her absolution. He'd been her savior and he'd taught her how to live with those memories. She'd banned them and had concentrated only on the happy ones. And then they'd had their own little bundle of joy. *Mason.* So different from Dean, but so much like his father—Colt. In them, she'd found her happiness, a path to a bright future.

Until, that bastard Jay Vick, took her little boy. She contemplated the man she'd met years ago and felt sad that the carefree spirit she'd come to know, had been fake. He'd been loved then—by all of them. How could his thinking have changed so much?

Power, Ceejay. Power changed people. That's what made Jay Vick the bastard he'd become.

She peered toward the sky through the treetops when the purring sound of a chopper drew her attention. She watched the black and red Augst Grand chopper circle overhead. She knew it was Kent's.

She watched it listlessly as the chopper was enveloped in a cloud of dust when it lowered to the ground a few yards away. The blades sliced through the air imitating a small tornado. As it came lower Ceejay held her breath as the blades came to a standstill.

She didn't bother to rise and meet them. One thing she'd learned over the years was to never have any expectations. Jay Vick was cunning and the chances that they'd found Mason, were scarce.

"Shh, Mommy doodoos."

Ceejay heard the loud whisper. Her mind struggled to decipher whether it was wishful thinking or reality. Just hearing his familiar baby voice caused tears to trickle from under her lashes and run down her temples.

"Aaw, Mommy cwying. Mommy sad."

This time it was too real, too close and her eyes popped open. To be caught by the onyx colored warmth of the only man she could never keep her eyes off of. As always, power radiated from his huge muscular body. In his arms, he held the wriggling boy who was looking at her with his head askew and a frown similar to his father's. His was looking at Ceejay intently and she knew that behind those dark irises, his mind was fiercely active. His tousled blonde hair fell into his eyes and a huge gap-toothed smile broke on his cherubic face. The dimples on the corner of his mouth deepened as the smile widened to light up his entire face.

"Mason? Oh my god!" Ceejay whimpered as she struggled to get up from the hammock without falling on her face.

"Moommmyy! Mase wants Mommy!" he began to wail when she took too long to get to him. He frowned at Colt when he chuckled. Ceejay couldn't stop her own tinkling laugh, which lead the little boy to howl. "Mooommy!"

The two grown-ups couldn't stop laughing. Relief washed over Ceejay as she reached the two men who meant the world to her. Mason fell into her arms and she cuddled him tight against her chest as his arms wrapped around her neck in a strangling hold. Colt folded his arms around them and didn't bother to hide his tears from his wife when she lifted her swimming eyes to his.

"You found him. Oh, my love, you brought our little boy home!"

"He used my son as a sacrifice—a two-year-old innocent baby as a pawn in his sick games. He made a grave mistake by coming after my family. He's hurt Ceejay once before. Now he took the game to a completely different level. Using my son, *mio figlio*, just destroyed any compassion I might have had toward him for the life he'd been forced to live. There'll be no forgiveness this time. *Fucking none.* He's proven that he has no integrity. There is no redeeming him. *Il cazzo di bastardo!* He's less than a sentient being in my eyes. I love my wife and son. There is no value that can be placed on that."

"Calm down, Colt. Find your focus. You know anger leads to destruction. You need a clear mind to deal with Jay Vick in the right way."

"Fuck that, Seth! The only way to deal with that motherfucker, is death!" Kent sneered.

"What are you planning to do, Colt? Give the money to Luca? Is that your plan? To play Luca and Jay off against each other and let them fight over it?" Parnell asked, having picked up on what Colt had been alluding to.

"Jesus. Of course! You're fucking brilliant, Colt," Nolan said.

"Jay is after the Don's position and I'm going to give it to him on a platter. Luca has to realize he has no collateral against me, especially now that his cohorts are dead. But we must never forget just how cunning he is. He has always been one step ahead of everyone and I still have a suspicion that he's the one who has been playing the fiddle, controlling how our lives have evolved over the past years—mine and Ceejay's. Gianni might have been the one putting it into play, but under whose direction?"

"Does it really matter now, Colt? Do you really want to waste more energy on Luca Vitale and the Occhipinti crime family? I, for one, am tired of looking over my shoulder. I want my kids home. It's time to walk away, Colt. For all our sakes," Seth said.

He sounded tired. Colt could see the longing in his gaze. He missed the twins and after Mason's kidnapping, he'd vowed to keep them away until the danger had been eliminated.

"You're right. You all are, and it's ending now. I'm going to publicly announce my retirement from the mob at the global meet next week and then hand the bonds over to Luca in front of everyone."

"Isn't that taking your life in your own hands, Colt? How do you know they will allow you to walk out of that room? No one just walks away from the mafia. You know that, as well as we do. It's not just Luca you pose a danger too; it's all the mob bosses," Kent cautioned.

"I'm aware of that," Colt said. He sighed deeply. "I need to find something to give them;

something that would appease them enough to let me walk away."

"A two-way sword, so to speak." Nolan said.

"Exactly. Now, I only have to find it."

"How is Ceejay doing?" Kent asked.

"She's ecstatic that Mason is back but she's become obsessive. She refuses to let him out of her sight and if he doesn't sleep in our bed, she sleeps with him. Nol and I discussed it and decided to send her and Jewel to New York. Quade and Maxine invited them to stay with them at the farm he'd bought in Jefferson last year. Of course, she refuses to leave until Maxwell is well and out of danger. He'll be moved out of ICU within a day or two."

"Yeah, with Jewel pregnant, I don't want to take chances of her losing our baby. And she knows how to console Ceejay," Nolan concluded.

"I'm sorry that this has fucked up your honeymoon, Nol. You and Jewel deserved to have one after the harrowing episode with Roberto Vitale," Colt said.

"It's not your fault, Colt. No matter how much

you'd like to take the blame. You can't be held accountable for other's greed. Besides, once all this is over, we'll be able to go on a long honeymoon."

"One way or other, this will be over soon, I promise you this. I'm done with the Occhipintis. I am done being a puppet for Luca Vitale. The two fuckers can fight for the throne. I don't want it. I *never* did."

CHAPTER EIGHT

Kent pondered over their conversation on his way home. He and Jay had made a connection the first day Jay had stepped foot into his office, almost eight years ago. A year after Colt had arrived in Jacksonville. Jay had been easy going, relaxed and easy to befriend. He hadn't thought twice about offering him to buy shares in his clinic at the time. Together, they'd turned it into one of the most successful plastic surgery practices in Dallas.

"What a fucking waste. I suppose it's time to start looking for a new partner," he muttered as he got out of his SUV and strolled up the steps to unlock the front door of his house on the farm that bordered Seth's. This was his haven over weekends and sometimes during the week. It was also where he'd left Sharon when he left for Dallas three days ago.

Whatever he'd expected to find when he opened the door, it wasn't the sight that beheld his eyes.

She sat in the middle of the foyer in the Nadu position. Her head was lowered and her eyes were closed. She had peaceful expression on her face. Her body glowed with sensuality in the sunlight pouring through the French windows that overlooked the backyard.

The only thing that kept her from being naked was a diaphanous, dark blue chiffon cape draped over her shoulders.

He didn't move and stood staring at her. Kent didn't understand the intensity of attraction he felt for this woman. She had such a checkered past.

The day he'd come across her in Club Tiberius, he'd noticed the change in her and it was there he'd felt the invisible pull of her allure. A kind of carnal magnetism that he couldn't resist and if he was honest with himself, didn't *want* to resist. He'd known then that he wanted Sharon Watts.

Not just to fuck, but as his.

His sub.

His to love.

Was it love? Fuck no, it was too soon but it could turn into love. Do I want it to?

He'd been struggling with these questions for a while now.

When he found her like this; waiting for him, offering herself freely and without reservations, then the answer was yes. Everyone deserved a second chance in life and maybe this would be theirs.

That's what pulled him to her. The glimpse of a loving woman behind her eyes when she gazed at him. That was the woman he wanted to release from the prison her circumstances had locked her in. The one he wanted to love.

"What's this, sub?" he asked, lifting the cape from her shoulders.

Her eyes rose to his and he was surprised to notice a blush coloring her cheeks.

"You know why, Master Kent," she responded in a soft voice.

"I'll not have it, Sharon. No." He snapped when she opened her mouth to defend herself. He took her hand and pulled her to her feet. His palms cupped her cheeks as he tilted her head back to stare into her eyes. "I told you before, you are beautiful to me. Those scars are part of you and the road you have travelled in life. They don't define the person you are. Do you know what I see when I look into your eyes, Sharon?" It was a rhetorical question, but she still shook her head in response. "I see a beautiful soul, broken and begging to be healed. I see the beauty of a woman who should be cherished and honored. I see all that because it's what you deserve. Do not hide your beauty, little one. Not from me. Not ever. Is that understood?"

"Yes, Sir."

"Now, drop this cape, Sharon."

"May I speak, Master Kent?"

"Sharon, this is not a M/s relationship. You never need to ask for permission, except when we're in a scene. In our house, you'll always have the freedom to be you."

"Thank you." She was still coming to grips with the differences from her prior life to what he was offering.

"Tell me."

"The scars, I . . ."

"They don't bother me, Sharon," he assured her once more.

"And I appreciate it, but I *hate* them. I do! Don't you understand? It's not just their ugliness, I abhor; it's a constant reminder of what *he* did to me. What he made *me* do! They keep pulling me down. I'm afraid I'll never be able to overcome this feeling, Kent. And I want to—for you. I *have* to because I want to have a future with you. You're the only man since ... not even Nolan could make me feel like this, you know?"

Kent traced the scars on her back, her breasts and lower stomach and felt a shudder run through her body with every stroke. *She really did hate them.* He realized then, no matter how much he tried to convince her that they were only skin deep, to her they were reminders of a bloody war—her war with

199

Roberto. She would always be burdened down by them.

"I'm sorry to disappoint you, Master Kent, but you have to know, every one of these scars feels like chains, binding me to his memory. When you ... stroke them, no matter how much ever I try to concentrate on the sensations you evoke with your touch, all I see is—how I earned that scar."

Tears were now running down her cheeks. Kent knew he could remove all her physical scars surgically, but he kept it to himself. Most importantly, he had to help her heal the scars from inside. Until she learned to cope emotionally with her past and accept what the future held, healing the physical ones would be pointless.

"I understand, love, but I want you to learn to compartmentalize your emotions. Like a little box inside your mind. Memories of Roberto go into a little iron box. Eventually, over time, you need to let it go. We cannot undo what's been done. You had no control then. But you *can* control what happens next, to an extent. As we evolve together, and create new memories, new experiences, and new dreams for the future; there won't be any room for Roberto in your mind. Because one thing you need to understand, Sharon, is that in our relationship, there is place for two people only and Roberto Vitale isn't one of them."

She deliberated for long minutes before answering him. "I understand and I will do my best to lock every single flash of memory away, like you suggested."

"There is a concept that Japanese use—it's called *Kintsukuroi*. It is the art of repairing pottery with gold lacquer. Every time a piece chips away, they put gold in its place. Every time it breaks, they glue it together. Can you guess why, my pet?"

Sharon shook her head. She'd heard of the term before but was too enamored by the glow in his eyes to try and think.

"In their eyes, a piece of pottery is more beautiful after having been broken. You, my pet, have been broken so many times, but you've managed to emerge from your past, more beautiful than ever—*you're all gold.* Your scars are nothing to be ashamed about. They are your badges of honor, for the wars you've waged, inside and out."

She stared at him, amazed that he saw such strength in her when she battled to rise above her past.

"You humble me, you truly do. I've never thought about it like that. In fact, over the years ... but, you're right. It's time to let it go and I will. With you by my side, I will overcome my insecurities."

"Very good. Now, take the first inspection position, slave. I want to see if you've been taking care of my property."

Sharon smiled brightly. She liked being referred to as his property.

Yes, that's the woman I've seen lurking behind those shadowed eyes. That's the one I need to give the strength to bury Vitale's memories.

He waited until she stood with her legs spread, hands behind her neck and her breasts pushed forward. He ran his hand over the curve of her buttocks.

"Perfect. I didn't expect to find such beauty when I walked through the door. How did you know I was coming home?" He asked and slowly walked around her, brushing a finger on the underside of her arm.

"I didn't know, I just had a feeling," she admitted.

"How long have you been sitting here, waiting?"

"Not too long. About an hour."

"That pleases me, Sharon. It pleases me tremendously and because of that, I believe I will reward you today."

Her face brightened, but she kept her eyes lowered respectfully. Another shy smile graced her lips. "Reward, Master Kent?"

"Yes, my pet. I will take great pleasure feasting on your charms. *All of them*. One by one, and take my time doing so. Would you like that, slave?"

"Yes. Please, my Master."

It was the first time she'd called him that. *Her Master.* He looked at her, startled. He hadn't pushed for it because it was something she should feel on her own. The fact that she already did, was an achievement on its own. It was proof that she was trying to overcome the emotional clusterfuck Roberto had put her through.

"Hm, your under-arms and legs are nice and smooth, slave. Did you shave or wax them?"

"Wax, Sir."

"Very good. I'll make a standing appointment for you at a spa in town. I want you to go there and have it done regularly."

"That's not necessary. I can do it myself."

She twitched under his sharp look but refused to back down.

He cupped her breasts and squeezed them. "Are you saying you refuse my offer?" Kent asked in a deceptively soft voice.

"I'm not ready to expose myself to others," she dared quietly. As his slave, she knew he had the power to make decisions about how her body was maintained, but since their relationship was different now, she hoped he wouldn't force this issue.

But you can refuse, Sharon. That's what he's been telling you. You have the control over your own body and mind in this relationship.

Sharon smiled to herself when she realized her renewed power.

Kent cursed. He'd thought he'd be doing her a favor, give her a treat and instead he'd reminded her, once again, of her scars. He'd noticed that she usually avoided being completely naked at the club. Her legs were always covered with sheer stockings.

"Very well. For now, you may continue to do it yourself, but make sure that your skin is always smooth for me. Is that clear?"

"Yes, my Master."

"Good. Second inspect position."

He waited until she spread her legs wider and bent over, with her legs straight, to clasp her ankles. It was an extremely vulnerable position for any sub, but perfect for the Dom to inspect her body.

Kent ran his palm over the curve of her buttocks before he pulled her cheeks apart. He ran the tip of his finger over her tight rosette. His lips flattened when he noticed the faint scar between her cheeks. How she survived such an ordeal, he still didn't know.

He knew what he would find when he traced the slit of her labia. He'd seen the scars on the creases of inner thighs and labia when he'd sewn her up then.

Roberto Vitale had been more than demented. He'd been a cruel, fucked up monster who had tried to destroy something as beautiful as this woman. He knew it was also the reason she didn't shave her pussy.

"Sharon? What's this?" he asked tugging on the soft curls covering her pussy.

"Please, I—"

"Didn't I give you explicit instructions about the hair on your body?"

"Yes Sir, but—"

"But nothing. We just had this discussion. Bury *him*, Sharon. This," he murmured, "will not do. It has to go."

He stepped back from her. "Get up."

She straightened. Her gaze was weary when she returned his determined look.

"I know it will take some time to overcome the emotional scars he left you with, but you will not hide your body from me. Not even an inch of it. Do you know why?"

"Because it belongs to you," she said, tilting back her chin just a tad. The fire was slowly returning to her eyes.

That's what Kent wanted. He didn't want her to turn into a whimpering 'yes Sir', 'no Sir', kind of a sub. He wanted to see life in her eyes. Anger, elation, wonder, and most of all, pleasure.

"Yes, it does and what does that mean, sub?"

"That it's yours to do with, as you please."

"Correct. And it pleases me to look at your naked skin. *All over*. Is that clear?"

"I understand, but Master Kent, as your *sub*, it's my choice whether or not I'll allow you control over *every* aspect of my body," she said. It was a good time to assert herself.

Kent smiled secretly. He was elated that she had enough confidence in their relationship to cross him.

Her hands curled into fists when he didn't respond. Kent knew this would be the ultimate test of her trust in him as her Dom. She needed to trust him, so that eventually, she could trust herself. If she couldn't find the confidence in this moment for something as simple as baring her pussy to him, then the road ahead would be long and winding for them.

"I'll go and shave now, Master."

"No. Go and wait for me on the back porch. Don't worry, Sharon. There's no one around this time of day. Nobody will see you," he assured her when she hesitated. "But, even if they were, I would still expect you to wait for me. You belong to me and everyone knows it. No one will touch you and I, for one, am very proud to call you my sub."

She turned away and walked toward the sliding doors, but not before he saw the pleasure flare in her eyes at his words.

Sharon stared at the countryside around her; spread out like a divine fingerprint; curving and changing, no two parts the same. She breathed in the fresh air. This view was unique—the dip and sway of the land; the patterns and flora; the ever-changing sky and wind. The landscape was painted in myriad of colors. Every day was a new snapshot in time. Gradually, the seasons would bring more changes.

Her mind wandered back to the far-away island of Capri.

"Anacapri," she whispered softly. Where, she'd lived for many years. It was a place of never ending summer vacations and the winter festivals. It had its rhythm too, but it was vastly different. Yet looking out now, she was reminded that here, she wasn't just looking at the nature as a snapshot; she was *in* one.

So much beauty; such tranquility. I could come

to love it here so easily.

She'd found it extremely peaceful for the last couple of days. It was easy to forget about the travails of life when you were surrounded by so much beauty.

Her mind was still reeling from the effects of Wartenberg wheel that Kent had used on her. How gentle he'd been and how he'd completely shattered her control. A testament of the promise that he would never hurt her.

She started to second guess that when he appeared on the porch. At first, she was stumped mute by his muscled body clad only in pair of jeans, which were unbuttoned, much to her fascination. His chest rippled, dusted with dark hair, drawing her hungry eyes to his insanely hot abs. She swallowed hard.

Then she noticed what he was carrying in his hand. Her audible gasp drew his attention. She stood frozen, staring at the shaving kit he'd placed on top of the patio table.

Kent placed it on top of a small white towel

while she tried to settle her breathing. He continued to lay out the shaving tools. Finally, he laid out a fluffy towel on the table.

"Get on top of the towel, Sharon. I'll be right back," he said in a low voice, but he didn't wait to see if she followed his order and left to fetch a bowl of hot water.

He found her lying on the table when he returned. She was stiff as a plank. But he felt a sense of accomplishment at her compliance.

"When was the last time you shaved your pussy, Sharon?"

"Ehm ... I haven't. Not since the surgery," she admitted. Her hands were still fisted next to her hips.

"Hmm, are you cold?" He asked. He brushed his palm over her nipples which were hard and pebbled.

She sucked in a breath at the feather-like touch. "No, it's actually quite warm here."

"Hmm," was his only response, which caused her eyes to pop open, only to find him watching her closely. "Would you be able to keep still or do I need to tie you, love?" He wanted the choice to be hers and waited patiently while she struggled with the decision.

"I will do my best not to move, but if you feel it's necessary, you may tie me up." The smile she offered him was tremulous at best. Her smile filled his heart with warmth.

"I love your smile. I'd like to see it more often." His smile was warm and engaging and her lips widened in a sweet response. "Ah, yes, there's the little dimple I love so much," he muttered. He leaned closer and placed his lips at the corner of her mouth to kiss her softly. He moved his head to whisper against her lips, "Ready, love?"

"Yes, Sir." Her breathless response caused his smile to widen.

He walked to the end of the table. He took her ankles and gently pulled her closer to the edge.

"Spread your legs wide, my pet. It might be best if you hold onto your knees. I don't want to nick your juicy, silky lips."

She followed his instructions blindly, her eyes on him all the time, watching as he dipped a washcloth into the bowl of hot water.

"This is hot, but it isn't scalding," he said, placing it gently over her pubic area. "Let's leave it there for a couple of minutes." He brushed his hand over the area he'd just covered and repeated it when the cloth cooled down.

She hissed when he squirted some shaving gel on his palm and lathered her vulva.

"At least you kept it neat and trimmed. There's not that much to shave. Ok love, keep still for me," he ordered, picking up the razor.

Sharon's hands tightened around her knees; her eyes were glued on the razor in his hand as he leaned closer. He gently pulled her skin tight before he moved the razor over it. He did it with such care and precision that she hardly felt the glide of the sharp blade. He rinsed the blade and glanced at her before lowering it again.

"What kinds of music do you like, my pet?"

The question took Sharon off guard, especially

as she'd been struggling with the ripples of pleasure shuddering through her at his touch. His gentleness aroused her without any effort.

"I like all kinds of music, except rap, but I'm more partial to classical music."

"Oh? Well, what do you know? Me too. Who is your favorite artist?"

Kent concentrated on the task at hand but the spicy smell of her arousal didn't go unnoticed. He could see her labia puffing up as he shaved her. His own body reacted in a rush of heat that shot into the veins of his cock, slowly engorging him.

"I've become quite attached to the work of John Luther Adams. He's a wonderful naturalist composer and is inspired by natural landscapes. I love nature and that might be why his compositions draw me in. Do you know his work?" Sharon's voice sounded breathless. Her hands clamped tighter around her knees. She could feel the moisture gather in her pussy and prayed it wouldn't trickle past her lips.

"Hmmm, I believe his, 'Become Ocean' won a

Pulitzer Prize a few years ago, am I right?" He asked while he gently pulled her outer labia open to shave the folds in between.

"Yes! Hmm," she moaned when he leaned closer and placed a soft kiss on her pelvis. She cleared her throat before she continued, "He did. He also composed 'The Place Where You Go to Listen'. It's absolutely magical; using computers that translate data from magnetic, seismic, and meteorological data into music. I've always felt that he writes the music of the planet," she shared excitedly; her breathing had become erratic from the kisses Kent continued to place on her thighs and stomach. Almost hypnotically, like he couldn't help himself.

"I heard that piece on the flight back from Italy. It was in a compilation of the best composers I bought from a classical music site. It's quite a phenomenal piece, you're right."

His voice sounded gruff and she realized he was also affected by the intimate act he was performing.

"And yours? Who do you like?"

"Ah well, love, I'm old school. Beethoven's Symphony No. 5 in C Minor and Bach's Orchestral Suite No. 3 in D major are my favorites. But I also enjoy a variety of more contemporary composers. And, like you, anything but rap. I even have a collection of most rock bands in my collection."

His finger slipped in past her lips to twirl in a slow circle deep inside her pussy. Her eyes met his. They glowed like embers. It was becoming difficult to keep her hips from moving.

"Oohmm." She licked her lips and had to find her train of thought. "Really? I would never have guessed you to be rocker," she said with a small laugh.

The sound was like the softest tingle of heavenly bells.

"No? Well, remind me one day to show you my head banging technique."

That elicited another delighted laugh from her, enveloping his mind with her charm. She was completely relaxed now. He quickly rinsed her mound and began soothing some balm all over her skin. It triggered another rush of moistness to flush her pussy. Kent watched her deliciously plump bottom lip disappear between her teeth. He was tempted to dip his finger inside her honeyed sweetness again but decided against it.

"Oh, my goodness. You're done already?" She looked at his large hand rubbing the cooling gel onto her skin with such gentleness; it triggered something deep inside her.

"Yes, we're done. Come, let me help you down."

Kent took her hand and pulled her upright. Her hands palmed his cheeks. She brought his face closer to her and gave him tiny, little pecks on the lips.

"Thank you," she whispered against his lips.

"What for, love?"

"For being so patient with me; for giving me such gentle care and for taking a chance on me. Not many men would."

"You underestimate your allure, love. I'm glad

you chose me too."

Sharon blushed at his words.

"Ah love, you're a sight for the sore eyes. Come, I have to prepare for a surgery scheduled for tomorrow morning. You can choose some music and sit with me while I work. Would you like that?"

She beamed at him; her smile brightened his entire day. It stayed on her lips during the course of the afternoon while she lounged in a loveseat in his den, reading a book, her head on his lap.

Sharon was in seventh heaven. He kept running his fingers through her hair and circled her throat to rest his fingers on her neck; gently claiming her while he worked.

Kent relaxed completely for the first time in months. Her serene presence brought calmness to his soul. He did his final drawing before he sat back with a sigh. The final step in his preparation was envisioning that first carefully placed cut. Reconstructive surgery was his passion and he excelled at it.

Sharon had disappeared a while ago and he

went looking for her. He found her in the kitchen, busy preparing dinner. She smiled at him when she noticed him standing there. She looked beautiful in a breezy, lavender summer dress.

"Thank you for letting me use your kitchen. I didn't realize how much I missed cooking."

"Sharon, this is your house now. You don't need my permission to do anything you want. And besides, I love your efforts. You're a fantastic cook. It does mean, however, that I'm gonna have to start exercising more if I don't want to get fat."

Her eyes took a lazy gander up and down his tall frame. She tsked. "You won't get fat. You exercise, have a great metabolism and besides, they do say that sex burns a lot of energy."

He laughed at the red tint that bloomed over her cheeks when she realized what she'd just said.

"Ah baby, I love that you've become so comfortable with me. So, what're we having?" He asked looking over her shoulder as he wrapped his arms around her waist.

He watched her rub a clove of garlic into a

teak wood salad bowl. The smell of roasted pine nuts and fresh wild arugula was mouthwatering. She had sliced red onions sautéing and added some balsamic vinegar to caramelize them.

"I'm making broiled salmon steaks prepared with olive oil and a squeeze of lemon and freshly baked soda bread."

"Hmm, sounds delicious."

He tilted her head back. Their eyes locked as he leaned down to kiss her. This time, their kiss held the promise of tomorrow, of the tenderness of their growing affection and of the passion that fired their lust every time they made love.

They smiled against each other's lips, completely lost to the world around them. Sharon leaned back, reached up and traced his lips with a finger. Her eyes were hooded and bluer than the early morning sky.

"Thank you, Master Kent, for taking a chance on me. I love it here. I can't tell you how much."

"I love having you here, my pet. You've brought me back to life."

She hugged him before extracting herself from his arms.

"I need to finish the fish. Why don't you fetch us a bottle of Sauvignon Blanc from your cellar? It'll go well with the fish. I've set the table on the back patio for us."

Kent smiled as he walked into the cellar. He was more than content with how his life was shaping. She was on the mend. This new side of her was exhilarating.

Linzi Basset

CHAPTER NINE

Initially Jay was surprised when Luca wanted to meet him at the Occhipinti head office. Until he realized that Damiano wouldn't be there. Not with the threat to his family.

He did expect Luca to make him wait a while before he strolled into his office and waved him to a chair.

"*Perché cazzo hai sparato* Maxwell Powell? *Sei pazzo?*"

"I didn't have a choice!"

"You always have a choice, Jayanni, which is something you still can't comprehend, after all these years. *Responsabilità,* Jayanni, that's what you lack." Luca chastised him. With a snort, he lit a customary cigar.

Luca's eyes narrowed on his belligerent son.

"That's the difference between you and your brother. Right from the beginning, he took accountability for his actions. When he did something wrong, he fixed it. He didn't belabor or deny it; he stood tall and did better. *Cazzo ho scelto quello sbagliato!*"

"You know what, Father? I'm fucking tired hearing how much better Damiano is than me. *Cazzo fuoco. Mi senti?* All my life it has been 'Damiano this, Damiano that', 'Why can't you be more like Damiano?' *Fanculo quella*! I am Jayanni Vitale. The name you gave me, and I accepted. Now you need to accept it, too. Live with it! And stop fucking comparing me to him. If you weren't so sold on him as your successor, you would've realized long ago that I am as good as he is. *Se non è meglio.*"

"If not better? Well, my son, if that's the case, you better step up and prove it to me. Because nothing you've done to date has—"

"Nothing? *Non cazzo niente*! I protected you from Gianni! If not for that, he would've ousted you long ago and he would be the one at the helm now. He was ready to take—"

"*Basta di questo*! Gianni didn't have the balls to face me directly. Why do you think he appointed you as his strong arm? Gianni never did anything himself. Not because he was cunning, oh no, my dear son. It was because he was nothing but a fucking coward. And if he has rubbed off on you ... well, that leaves us with a problem, now doesn't it? You couldn't even successfully kidnap a two-year-old child! You managed to botch up that too!"

"Because of you! I told you it was too quick; that I didn't have a well laid plan. You were the one who ordered me to go in blind!"

"There it is again. Not taking accountability. Do you think as the Don you only act once you have a carefully laid out plan, Jayanni? No! *Non lo fa*! Most times you have to make a decision quickly and act right off the cuff. Damiano learned that within the first year he was under my tutelage. It's been what, twenty years and you still don't get it. You think you're ready to be the Don of the Occhipintis, Jayanni? If you do, you're naive and stupid."

"Don't call me stupid, Father. You know I hate

that."

"Yes, but then, you can't hide from the truth, now can you?"

"This is bullshit! He's become a liability! You know that. He refuses to bend to your rule and everyone is aware of it. He's making a fucking fool out of you. He has to die. It's time for me—"

"To what? Become the Don? Think, Jayanni and don't be a fool. We need him. He's become the power that makes us the most feared family in the mob circles. If you're as clever as you claim to be, you'll get on his better side. Yes, don't glare at me like that. You need to learn how to control your emotions and you might just learn something from Damiano. Play your cards right and you'll be ready to take over from him sooner than you think."

"You're the fool, Father. Me get on his better side? The only thing Damiano wants is me—six feet under."

"That may very well be true but once he realizes it might be the only way I will let him walk away from the Occhipinti family, he will do as he's told. He won't have a choice. Oh no, my son, I have your brother just where I want him. The beast inside him is slowly slipping his leash."

"*Gesù!* That's why you pushed Gianni to kidnap Seth's sister again. And Giorgio? You deliberately brought him back here. You knew Damiano wouldn't let them walk away alive. You're slowly but surely eliminating all your threats, aren't you?"

"Ah, at long last, you're catching on."

"And the kidnapping? You want him to go dark again. But why? Wouldn't that make him a bigger danger to us?"

"Of course not. You have to understand the darkness inside him and what drives it, Jayanni. Once you do, that's what you need to tap in, to gain control over him."

Luca kept a vigil over Jay. He needed to keep him flustered. He would never be as strong a leader as Damiano, but he needed him to keep Damiano unsettled and on guard. That way, he would concentrate on Jay and allow Luca the time to get past his guard to force his hand. His son needed to learn that no one refused Luca Vitale. Not even his own children.

"Me? Gain control over Damiano? Now, you're delusional, Father. I'm not a fool. I might believe I have what it takes to be the Don, but controlling him? No fucking way."

"O ye, of little faith. *Vergognatevi*, Jayanni. Damiano's darkness is power—*ultimate power*. He's been able to suppress it, but I've seen him slipping. It's so slight, I don't think he even realizes it, but it's there. He's ripe for picking. We just need to give him the final nudge in the right direction."

Luca removed a small square box from his drawer and lifted the lid. He stared at the black leather bracelet before he slid the box across the desk toward Jay.

"And *that* is going to be the weapon that will bring Damiano back in line. Mark my words, Jayanni, soon, I will have both my sons in control of the Occhipinti family, just as it should have always been." Luca lied seamlessly.

"You mean your three sons, don't you?" Jay asked as he examined the bracelet.

"Of course. Vito is already so entrenched here; I tend to forget about him."

Jay glanced up with a wry smile. Just another one of Luca Vitale's brood who didn't make the cut. It wasn't easy to live up to this man's expectations. Vito, more so than Jay, had been living in Damiano's shadow all his life.

"It's a small wonder Vito doesn't hate Damiano, Father—the way he'd been forced to submit to his rule over the years."

Luca puffed on his cigar. The woody smoke entered his blood stream and he exhaled the smoke in a swirl that danced toward the ceiling. He considered Jay's comment for a moment and then shrugged.

"Strangely enough, Vito is quite fond of his half-brother. They've always gotten along splendidly and unlike you, Vito was clever enough to tap into Damiano's strength of character and intelligence. He observed and learned a tremendous amount from him." He took another calming puff. "I have to admit, if not for Damiano, Vito would be more than capable of running this family."

Luca reached over the desk to retrieve the little box and its contents, replaced the cover, and locked it back into his drawer.

Jay watched him. Contrary to what everyone believed, Luca had taken him under his wing after the death of his foster mother and had been mentoring him since he turned ten. He'd been an angry child and had resented Luca for taking him away from his real mother, at first. He'd only found out that Damiano was his twin much later.

Whether or not Luca wanted to admit it, Jay was more like him, than Damiano would ever be. He had the same cunning, the same desire for power that Luca did and most of all, he had the same insight in how little life meant.

Jay was living for the day when Luca would come to realize it and finally admit to the world that he'd been mentoring his son on the sly for over twenty years. That day, his life would come full circle. Then, he'd know that all the pain, hate and sacrifices had been worth it.

Jay had made many sacrifices. Not that it meant anything because he was the only one who knew what they'd been. But the one he'd come to regret the most, over time, was Amelia Cooper. The beautiful black-haired angel he'd fallen in love with at varsity. Something, Luca put an end to, the moment it was brought to his attention.

"I don't understand, Jay. Why are you being so cruel? Doesn't my love mean anything to you?"

Those were the last words she'd uttered to him. He'd been heartless with her.

"Love? Lust, you mean. You were a good fuck, Amelia. Nothing more. Now, it's time for me to conquer the world and I can't afford to be pulled down by a meek little mouse like you."

Those words had hounded him for years. Some days, the shocked expression on her face woke him from his nightmares. *Yeah, I destroyed her love. The sweetest love any man could ask for.*

And for what? To become a pawn for the

Occhipintis, instead of the Don? He snorted to himself. Some of it had been his doing. He'd ingrained himself in Gianni's life. He'd wanted something he could hold over Luca's head one day, as a proof, of how he'd been the ultimate protector of the Vitale rule. And then, of course, there was the other one. *The one,* who, over the past couple of years, had given him more trust and guidance than either Luca or Gianni ever did. *He* was the one who would ultimately be Jay's final trophy. The one who would make Luca stand back and realize just how well he'd been played.

And the time is nigh. I'm fucking tired of this double life I've been living.

"What do you intend to do with that, Father?" He queried when Luca slipped the small key in his pocket, once he'd locked the little box away. "Something you don't need to concern yourself with, Jayanni. Now, I want you to listen very carefully. *This* is what I need you to do . . ."

"I suppose you're calling to gloat?"

Silence followed Jay's abrupt greeting when he answered his cell phone. He sighed to calm himself. Luca always managed to upset him, but he had no intention of apologizing for his rudeness to *this* man.

"Contrary to what you may believe, Jay, I wish you no ill. Like you, I just want what's best for the Occhipintis."

"For the Occhipintis or for yourself?

"Come now, Jay, *enough*. Do we really have to be at loggerheads? Now that we're so close to winning?"

"What makes you think *we're* close to anything?"

"The bonds are in our hands, so to speak. Damiano is ready to hand them over and I'll be sure to be around when he does. Luca won't trust just anyone with their safekeeping. He learned his lesson with Stephen Caldwell and Gianni."

"Of course, and when he does, you'll *safeguard* it in your own special way, which I assume, isn't the family coffers?"

"I am getting a distinct impression that you don't trust me, Jay. Have I ever given you reason to doubt my sincerity?"

"No, you haven't, but ultimately both of us are after the same thing and if you're the one with the bonds, I lose. Again. I'm tired of being the follower."

"Ah yes, but that's where I am different from the rest, who've only used you to get ahead."

"Of course you are. Care to enlighten me as well?"

"Power share, my dear Jay. We each have our own special strengths and weaknesses, but if we take the helm together ... just imagine the combined force we'll be."

Jay didn't respond but simmered silently. Once again, Luca had been right. Others were always one step ahead of him. *Power share.* Not something he'd even thought about, let alone considered. *But, damn, he was right. Together they would be invincible! Damiano and Luca Vitale wouldn't stand a chance.*

"Jay?"

"You have a point. I imagine you have a plan?" It grated on him to ask the question, but he'd not had the time to formulate a new plan of action since the foiled kidnapping and his narrow escape.

"I believe you were shot? Are you okay?"

"I'm fine. It was a flesh wound."

"Good, we can't afford to slack now. We need to hit and hit hard. Damiano is angry ... upset, and that makes him vulnerable."

"We are talking about Damiano Vitale, right? None of those emotions would make him vulnerable. It'll make him more alert."

"Exactly, and we're going to give him what he needs."

"And what is that?"

"A diversion. He's on his way to the annual meet in LA. Here's what I need you to do."

Jay listened intently as a sinister smile lighted

on his lips. This was going to be too easy. Funny, how this man's vision was so similar to Luca's. This time, he had no need to split himself in two. He was going to do the bidding of two men, with one act. For once, he was looking forward to returning to Jacksonville. He already had his disguise planned. No one would recognize him. Especially, not his target—his own brother.

"Fancy that. Luca asking me to unsettle the high and mighty Damiano Vitale. Now, I only have to come up with a plan to remain incognito until the perfect moment to take the shot." He snorted. "Pity they only want him wounded. I would've loved to finish him for good."

He got into his rental car and whistling jauntily, he headed in the direction of JFK airport. *'I'll arrive in Jacksonville in style this time'*, he thought wryly as he purchased a first-class plane ticket to Dallas.

CHAPTER TEN

"As often as the two of you visit our dungeon, I'm beginning to wonder if you're not considering moving to Jacksonville," Kent joked as he shook hands with Rhone Greer and Keon LeLuc. They'd assisted Parnell in rescuing Seth's sister, Kacie, when she'd been kidnapped a couple of months ago.

Keon laughed. "Nope, not gonna happen. Club Devil's Cove is beginning to shape up and we should be opening our doors pretty soon. We've already signed up close to a hundred members."

"In the meantime, this place offers us a little break, away from city life," Rhone explained.

"I hope that doesn't mean we'll never see you once your club opens?" Nolan asked, having overheard Keon's response as he joined the group.

"No, we like these trips and of course, we

expect to see all of you at our club as well," Rhone said.

"What a surprise, Masters Razor and Blade," Jewel smiled, as she and Sharon joined them.

Sharon took the hand Kent held out to her. He pulled her under his arm and kissed her on the forehead.

"You look lovely tonight, my pet. Dare I believe it is for my benefit?"

"Well, I have to do something to keep your wandering eyes at bay. Did it work?" She teased with the endearing dimple showing in her cheek. She'd noticed how the subs perked up when Kent walked into the club.

"When your eyes shoot daggers at me, I can't help but say, 'of course it did, dear.'" He laughed at her expression. His arms wrapped around her. "You take my breath away and you're gonna be awarded for it later, love."

Sharon was surprised when she felt a blush blossom over her cheeks but she couldn't help it. She wasn't used to honest compliments, especially when they came with a promise of endless delights.

"This is my sub, Sapphire," Kent told Rhone and Keon who were eyeing her appreciatively.

She looked beautiful in a long, white sheath dress with side slits all the way to her waist. The dress was molded to every curve of her body. Underneath, a gold thong peeked out when she moved. Her dainty feet were adorned in gold stilettos, a perfect foil to the blonde hair cascading in loose curls down her back. With a gold lace mask, she looked like a seductive mythical creature.

"Sapphire, this is Masters Razor and Blade from Washington DC. They visit us quite often. Albeit, I daresay, not for our company, if the looks the subs are giving them is anything to go by."

"Do I detect a twinge of jealousy?" Keon teased. His eyes moved over Sharon as he spoke. There was melancholy in her eyes that belied the seductive picture she presented. He wondered about it but shook it off when his eyes met Kent's.

She was his sub and obviously in a D/s relationship. Something he didn't covet. Give him a variety of sassy subs and he was happy.

"I've had my turn, Master Blade. More than enough, thanks. Now, I have this lovely sub who keeps me more than content."

Kent was aware of the glances between Sharon and Keon. It didn't worry him because he trusted the bond between them as a couple. She would never cuckold him. But, he had been a Dom long enough to read the signs. Sharon had become used to threesomes. Hell, foursomes, and orgies for that matter. From the tautness of her body, he detected that she was thinking about it while looking at Keon.

"Master Wolf, I'm starving. Can we please go and get something to eat in the restaurant?" Jewel pouted with a tug on her husband's arm.

"Again? We ate less than two hours ago, baby."

"That might be so, Master Wolf, but you do remember she's eating for two now, right?" Sharon said with a teasing smile. Her friendship with Jewel had grown since she'd moved in with Kent and the two of them visited each other often.

The kiss Nolan shared with Jewel was one of loving indulgence. He shook his head but wrapped his arms around her waist.

"Well, excuse us. I need to feed my two loved ones. Luckily, she craves carrots and grapes most of the time, so I don't need to go running around in the middle of the night."

Kent watched them leave—Nolan's hand protectively covering his wife's belly. Part of the reason he'd decided to move on with his life was because of that—children. His gaze shifted to Sharon who was also watching the couple with a yearning look in her eyes. Kent accurately identified it as a longing to be in Jewel's shoes; to have her own baby.

He'd told her it wasn't an issue and they would deal with it when the time came, but it was obviously something that was on both their minds. They wanted children. Would he be satisfied adopting someone else's child? Would she be willing to accept a surrogate to have their child?

You're putting the cart in front of the horse, Gibson.

Rhone had drifted off in the direction of the subs. Kent turned to Keon. "How about it, Master Blade, care to join us in a scene?"

Sharon glanced up at him with a mixture of weariness and surprise. His look darkened when he detected a slight tremble in her body. He locked his fingers around her throat, squeezed gently in warning and she obeyed instantly by lifting her chin.

"Do you trust me, Sapphire?"

There it was again—the loaded question. She did trust him, explicitly, but she couldn't deny the warning that flashed inside her mind when something like this triggered the hateful memories.

"Yes, my Master, I do, but I have to be honest, I don't understand. You said you'll never allow another ... you know?" She whispered with a glance toward Keon who stood waiting patiently.

"Yes, but then you have needs too, my pet and for now, I'm happy to allow some indulgence to those needs. Later, I might not. It would be wise to prepare yourself for that day."

"I appreciate your offer, Master Steel, but it's not necessary. I don't need a third party in our relationship." Her voice had turned raw as a memory slipped into her mind which she immediately banned from her thoughts.

"*This* is for your benefit and whether you wish to admit it or not, your body craves it. But, believe me, love, it'll be nothing like your past experiences. You're going to feel nothing but pleasure."

"Master Blade?" Kent prodded Keon again.

His eyes were still trained on Sharon. She was a little agitated but seemed to have calmed down and offered him a tremulous smile.

"Don't mind if I do, Master Steel. What did you have in mind?"

"Did you do as I instructed before we left home, Sapphire?" Kent looked at her, smiling when her cheeks reddened. She was still adapting to his gentle way of controlling her. It was all virgin territory for her.

She'd hated doing the enema, but the reason

he'd asked her to do it, had made the excitement override her embarrassment. A frown marred her cheek.

Had he intended on having a threesome all along? Or did he only decide it when he noticed me ... oh god! I hope he doesn't think I'm attracted to Master Blade.

She was able to read Kent's thoughts most of the time but there were times she couldn't. Like now, and it frustrated her. She needed to know what spurred him to change his mind about not sharing her. The worry, that he was already tired of her emotional instability, sat heavy on her shoulders.

Kent shared a look with Keon, who immediately drifted toward the bar, affording them some privacy for a chat. "Sapphire, I've told you numerous times if you're unsure about something, ask me. Don't make your own assumptions."

"Was this what you'd intended when you asked me to ... do what you asked me to?" She couldn't bring herself to voice it out loud.

Kent searched her expression. It was easy to

identify the vulnerability and insecurity she felt. He couldn't blame her, but it angered him, nevertheless. He'd made a clear commitment to her and yet, she still questioned his motives.

"No, my pet, it wasn't."

"Then I don't want you to do this. I don't need it, Master Steel. Or are you . . ."

"Or am I what?"

Sharon heard the warning in his voice but blurted, "Already tired of me?"

"It's amazing that a woman, who once exuded so much confidence, even in a demoralizing relationship, is now so insecure. Why is that, Sharon? Why don't you trust and believe in what I have to offer?"

"Because I'm scared it's too good to be true. I know I'm damaged goods. I know I'm not the kind of woman or sub you are usually attracted to and I know I'm not good enough for you. But, knowing all of that, I still want it. I need it because I think that I . . ." She gulped back her words and looked down, clamping her fingers together in front of her.

"That you what?" Kent waited patiently. The flash in her eyes, when she hesitated, was the most honest expression he'd seen from her to date.

He cupped her cheek and smiled gently. It would be so easy to order her to continue and she would—immediately, but he needed her to be at ease; to have the freedom to open her heart.

"I think I'm falling in love with you."

God, yes! I am. I'm in love with him.

Hearing the words aloud made them real for Sharon. He never left her mind, he was always there; mentally, if not physically, since he'd taken care of her in the hospital so many months ago. She found it incomprehensible that this man had become her stable force—her *only* stability in a world filled with chaos.

God, yes. I love him so much and I can't believe I've only just realized it.

The feeling was overwhelming yet made her feel complete. She'd never experienced such emotional intensity before. Not even with Nolan all those years ago. This had no boundaries—it was limitless. Kent had given her the thing she'd been searching for years. *Peace.* It felt like her heart was dancing around in her chest—joyously, filling the void inside her after for so long.

Kent didn't expect those words to affect him as deeply as they did. It's been years since he'd felt love. It was strange—frightening; how she went from being a complete stranger, to becoming an integral part of his life. He was excited to come home every night, knowing she would be there, waiting for him. He loved waking up in the morning with her luscious curves in his arms.

"Let me make this clear, love. You are a beautiful woman. The fact that you've overcome so many travails in life and are striving to put it behind you, makes you a stronger person. I believe I'm falling in love with you too."

Sharon's gaze widened. "Really?" Joy filled her heart and tears welled up in her eyes.

"Yes, my pet and one more thing. I never want to hear you say that you're not good enough for me. Is that understood?"

"Yes, my Master." Her smile brightened the room. "May I ask a boon, Master Steel?"

"A boon?" He chuckled. "I haven't heard that word in a while. Yes, my pet, what do you want?"

"A hug. May I please hug you?"

"Yes, love, you may."

He opened his arms and Sharon didn't hesitate to walk into them. His body was familiar to her now. In a short while, living with him, she'd learned the way he moved, the comforting smell of his subtle aftershave, even the sound of his heart beating during those quiet moments before they fell asleep. But this was the first time she really *felt* him—his essence.

Keon strolled back to them and cleared his throat, having understood the tender moment between them. "Are you sure you want an addition to your scene, Master Steel? I wouldn't be offended if you retracted the offer."

"No. My sub needs this. If only to realize how much her pleasure means to me." Kent moved her to his side. "Are you up for a threesome, Master

Blade?

"I can't think of a better way to spend the evening. Of course, only if your sub is comfortable with me," Keon said, looking at Sharon.

"Well, my pet? Do you object to Master Blade as our third?"

Sharon glanced at Kent, secure in the knowledge that he did care for her. She even understood why he believed she needed a threesome and maybe he was right. She'd been floored by the tender and gentle way he made love to her; loved it when he got rough and wild and turned her body inside out; without hurting her.

Maybe sexual need was like a drug and certain things became a must have. If she was honest with herself, she did miss the rapturous sensation of double penetration—experiencing the ultimate pleasure of being fucked from both sides.

"No, my Master. I'll be comfortable with Master Blade."

"Very well. I've booked the Pandora's Box room for us. Sapphire, you know where it is. Why don't you take Master Blade there and I'll join you in a couple of minutes? I need to have a quick word with Colt."

Sharon nodded. Strangely enough, she wasn't spooked by his instruction. Master Blade's eyes were warm and kind, which had set her at ease.

"Master Blade, why don't you prepare my sub in the meantime? Nothing zealous; just heat her blood."

This made Sharon's footsteps falter. Their eyes met. His bore no expression, but Sharon knew this was a test. He wouldn't have given the instruction to Master Blade if he thought he would take advantage of the situation.

She smiled at him. "Don't be too long, my Master."

His taut body relaxed at her words. "I won't, my pet." The smile stayed on his lips as he watched them disappear into the dungeon. He suppressed the possessiveness that urged him to follow them; to be there when Keon began caressing her gorgeous curves.

Damn! What is this woman doing to me?

Kent stomped upstairs to Colt's office. Sharon needed this to finally realize the difference between his control and Roberto's way. He longed for the time when there would be no shadows left in her eyes. That day, he would know that she'd buried her past and trusted him completely.

Colt wasn't in his office, which didn't surprise Kent. He'd not been to the club too often lately. Not since Mason's kidnapping. Kent suspected they wouldn't see much of him until Ceejay and his son left to visit Quade. His thoughts swirled around Jay Vick, wondering for the umpteenth time, how he'd managed to fool him for so long.

He went to the bar and ordered a single shot of Macallan—the special stash of scotch that Nolan kept for them behind the bar. He swirled the whiskey in his glass, listening to the clinking of the ice cubes, breathing in the woody fragrance of his drink, resulting from years of aging in oak barrels. Watching the vortex of the liquid in his hand was hypnotizing. The aged single-malt, imported directly from Scotland was his one vice and as always, he intended to make a virtue of it; savor it, not race to the bottom of the glass. When the liquid settled he brought it to his lips and let the amber fluid sit in his mouth a while, before swallowing. He closed his eyes, dwelling only on the flavor.

God, it was good.

He bantered a little with the subs, who'd joined him for a chat, before he excused himself and made his way to the Pandora Box room.

"Please undress, sub."

Sharon stiffened at the order but she didn't hesitate. The commanding presence of this man teased at the submissive inside her and she reacted instinctively. At least the lighting in the room was dim and wouldn't make her scars appear grotesque. He might not even notice if he didn't look too closely.

She was startled to realize it didn't bother her as much anymore—being naked in front of others.

All because of Kent.

Keon removed his shirt and kicked off his shoes in easy masculine moves, waiting patiently for her to undress. She glanced in his direction. He was a delicious specimen of manhood with his bulging muscles and broad chest that tapered into narrow hips. His abs rippled with every movement he made. His long hair touched his shoulders and made her think of Conan, the Barbarian. She had to suppress the urge to giggle.

Sharon undressed and straightened. With her hands behind her back, she waited. He circled her, tracing a finger over her skin. Here and there, he tracked her scars.

"You wear the signs of a cruel master. I trust it's not Master Steel?"

"No! He's the kindest Dom any sub could ask for. We haven't been together very long. I used to be married to ... he died a while ago. It wasn't a ... good marriage."

"It's good that you're moving on. Some memories are best forgotten, my pet. Don't dwell on them and allow them to stand between you and happiness. It's something I learned the hard way."

"I'm trying to, Sir."

Keon pressed his hard body against her back. His arms circled her waist to cup her breasts.

"You're trembling, Sapphire. Are you scared of me?"

"No, Master Blade, it's just ... like you said, I have some memories I need to bury."

"You're a beautiful woman—very enticing. You have the kind of beauty that sets a man's blood afire without any effort and yet, even with the story those scars tell, there's an innocence about you. I can imagine why some people would take advantage of that."

He squeezed her breasts and trailed his palms with feathered lightness over her nipples. His deep voice relaxed her. She leaned back against his hard body, feeling the heat of his touch penetrate her skin. She bit her lip as arousal slowly unfurled inside her loins.

"Do you want me to stop and wait for your

Master, Sapphire?"

Sharon was tempted to say yes, but something told her Kent would be disappointed if she did.

"No, Sir. It's what he wanted and I'm comfortable with you but thank you for offering."

"Very well."

He nibbled on her earlobe while he continued to play with her nipples. Squeezing, pinching, and tugging gently. Every action aimed to spike her arousal. And it did, at an alarming rate as she closed her eyes and imagined what it would feel like to be at the mercy of two such gentle giants.

And then *he* was there, pressing his naked chest against hers, stealing her breath away at the unexpectedness of it.

"Are you doing ok, sub?" Kent asked, examining her expression and eyes for signs of discomfort or fear.

"Yes, my Master, even better, now that you're here." Her soft confession tugged at his heart and not for the first time he wondered just how

demented Roberto Vitale had been, to have not to
see the purity and love this woman had to offer. But
maybe he *had* and it was what had fed his demented
desire to demonize her.

"Hm, I see you're wearing that rosy hue of
arousal I like so much, my pet.

"Master Blade has magic hands, my Master,
but you have the master touch," she hissed when he
leaned down to nibble and suck on her taut nipples.
"I'm sorry. I should keep quiet," she mumbled when
she realized she'd unwittingly broken one of his
rules. No talking during a scene.

"For this scene, you're free to talk, my pet.
Had I wanted your silence, I would've told you."

"Thank you, Master."

Kent moved them toward the bed without her
noticing, until he gently pushed her back onto it.

"Scoot over to the middle, love," he instructed
as he and Keon followed her, one on each side.

Sharon could feel the trembling in her thighs,
the slow burn of warmth that ignited inside her core.
Just the thought of their cocks rubbing against each

other deep inside her, caused her pussy to tingle in anticipation.

"We're about to give you a mind-blowing experience, my pet. One that will make you realize what BDSM is all about. What being *my* sub means. From this point on there'll only be pleasure on your mind."

The two men removed their pants and she could feel their hard tumescence press against her thighs. Kent was big, but from the hardness pressed on her left, she ascertained that Master Blade was huge. Her past experiences in a ménage à trois had never been tender, or with any foreplay. Sharon felt a wave of trepidation wash over her, hoping she wasn't about to make a complete fool of herself.

Keon traced his hand over her stomach, while Kent pressed his lips against hers in a warm, tender kiss that promised sensual delights. She whimpered as their hands closed around her breasts, gently kneading, and flicking their thumbs over the taut tips. Kent feasted on her mouth with a skill that made her forget the past. Her breath hissed from her mouth as Keon trailed his lips over her collarbone to kiss the curve of her throat.

She hung onto Kent's neck and returned his kiss with urgency, arching her back to press her breasts deeper into their hands. The experience flung her onto a cloud of euphoria. She moaned when the two men licked a slow path over her chest to kiss the underside of her breasts.

"Oh lord," Sharon whimpered, not used to such tender caresses from two men at the same time. She'd never realized how sensitive her breasts were to touch. Gentle touch, not painful twists, and pinches. Now, with both of them nibbling and kissing the slope of her breasts, she craved more. Their lips tugged on the needy tips and then sucked them into their mouths with evident lust.

They were gentle, until Keon sucked harder and stretched her nipple, clamping his teeth around the tip.

"Aahhh … fuck!" Sharon cried out in surprise as she felt her pussy flush with her essence. He returned to soft and deep sucking, while Kent bit down on her nipple and repeated the same action.

"How does that feel, my pet?" Kent asked, his gaze searching hers.

Sharon was spellbound by the sudden rawness in his voice and the lusty look on his face. His desire was apparent in the rigidity of his muscled frame.

"Better than I dreamed it would, my Master ... oooh!" Her eyes widened as she felt Keon spreading her labia to spear his tongue deep inside her, lapping at the honeyed juices he found there. He kissed a path on the inside of her thigh toward her knee, allowing Kent to lean closer and swirl his tongue around her clitoris, sucking it gently into his mouth.

Ohhhh, shit!

Her body shook and her heart hammered wildly inside her chest. She panted, desperate to slow down her heartbeat. Her fingers curled into the sheets beneath her.

God, I've never felt anything like this! Not ever.

She couldn't find a word to describe her

feelings. There was excitement, loads of heat and expectation, but no fear. In the past, during such a scene, she would be terrified, lost in a helpless cage between two men who enjoyed hurting her and didn't have a care for her pleasure.

Now, she trembled in desire and need. She caught their eyes and was overwhelmed by the coalescence of joy and triumph flooding her mind, because she realized then, that they were as excited and aroused as she was, entranced by her reaction to them.

"I love how responsive your sub's body is, Master Steel," Keon said against her pussy, rubbing her clit with his thumb which caused her stomach to roll in reaction.

"Yes, it is. She looks like a wood nymph—an ethereal beauty." Kent kissed a circle around her nipple before he sucked on it.

"My Master, you make me feel beautiful. Oooh, I ... please, I need . . ."

Kent pulled her into his body and settled on his back, taking her with him. Both the men were already aroused and more than ready to culminate this scene. He didn't need to tease her any further.

Sharon sat up and stared into Kent's eyes as she felt Keon behind her. His hands closed around her hips to lift her over Kent. She hissed a breath as Kent guided his cock to her pussy.

"Ah, my pet, I love that you're always so hot and ready for me. Take it slow, Keon. I want to savor every inch of those satiny petals as they wrap around my cock."

Keon lowered her slowly, kissing her behind her ear when her head rolled back on his shoulder, as Kent's large cock speared into her.

"Master, I can't tell you how wonderful it feels every time you enter my body. I love it when you pulse inside me."

"You really are a treasure, my sweet, more than you'll ever realize," Kent responded. He nodded to Keon while he caressed her nipples.

Kent pulled her closer, to wrap his lips around a taut nub and suckled like a baby. Sharon gasped at the unexpected squirt of lube on her puckered hole. Her body tingled with anticipation as Keon spread the gel inside.

"Master Blade will wear a condom, love, just relax and let us take care of you and your pleasures."

Keon lifted her off Kent's cock until only the tip remained inside, while Kent continued to suck her nipples, lazily tweaking, and pinching the other between his fingers.

Keon slowly pushed the spongy, bulbous tip of his cock forward, while Sharon instinctively bore back until he entered her rosette. He was huge and left her panting as he kept pushing until he was past her sphincter. He stopped to caress her soft cheeks with gentle strokes.

"You okay, little pet?"

Sharon was completely relaxed as she stared at Kent. His gaze offered her reassurance and a promise of untold rapture. Now was the time to show him how much she trusted him. She surrendered her body and her soul into his hands.

Kent smiled as he read her expression.

"Thank you, my pet," he said against her lips.

"No. Thank *you*, my Master. You have shown me there can be pleasure without pain; love without demoralization and most of all, peace, with you by my side."

He kissed her and reaching down, he pulled her ass cheeks apart, an invitation for Keon to go hilt deep inside her. Her moan puffed into his mouth, a sign of the pleasure they were offering her.

Keon dragged his cock back slowly, ensuring that every nerve ending inside her ass and pussy flared to life. Kent pushed back in and they set a slow rhythm—plunging in and out, in opposite directions.

She tossed and turned in pure undiluted ecstasy. Catching her open mouth with his, Kent plunged his tongue in, sucking and chewing on her top lip.

"You are so beautiful, baby," he murmured through short bursts of breath.

Sharon's body was on fire. She gulped as their velvety steel rods plunged deep inside her with long rhythmic strokes. The thrust of their turgid lengths built the pressure inside her loins to a height previously unknown to her; something she'd never experienced before; filling every inch of her and flooding her mind with bliss.

"I need more. Please, my Master," she pleaded.

Kent was elated at her surrender. They increased the tempo but continued the gently rocking rhythm. Sharon could feel the pressure inside her building, like a coil tightening with every thrust. She knew the end was near when Keon reached down to rub her clit.

"Please, Masters. I need to come," she cried, her nails digging into Kent's chest.

"Yes, my pet, come for us. *Now*." Kent urged her.

It was all her body needed and she bucked wildly as a surge of warm liquid erupted from inside her. Her blazing eyes were locked on Kent's face. She choked out a scream and streams of her juices showered their cocks.

"Fuck me, now that's what I call a threesome climax," Keon said with his face drawn into a tortured expression, as he pinched back his orgasm, wanting to pleasure her first.

Keon pulled back and watched as Kent powered into her with strong, upward thrusts. The hot spurt of his ejaculate triggered another climax for Sharon. Her cries and his growl echoed through the room.

Keon thrust home and plunged inside her with fierce strength, to drive her to an uncontrollable climax that rippled through her and tossed her high into the cloud of blissful ecstasy. He kept plowing her body until the familiar flashes of heat flared in his chest; wave upon wave drowning him in a state of rapturous elation. His eyelids fluttered and twitched as the dam inside him burst. He roared when the world around him came to a grinding halt and all his energy was concentrated on that rush of heat, from deep inside his loins, which erupted deep inside her bowels. Pulsating streams of hot viscous semen spewed out, his body shuddering with the intensity of his release.

Keon slumped on the bed next to them. The sound of their breathing harsh in the room, as all three battled to find their breath. Sharon fell onto Kent's chest, purring when his arms wrapped around her to hold her tight.

"I lied to you earlier, my Master," she whispered in his ear. His body immediately stiffened, but she ignored it and kissed him in his neck. "I'm not falling in love with you; *I love you*, Kent Gibson. More than I ever thought possible."

Kent pushed her upright and stared at her. The truth of what she'd said was there, shallow in her gaze, laid bare for all to see. He brushed back her hair to tumble over her shoulders. Neither of them noticed that Keon had silently left the room.

"You are more than I had hoped to find, Sharon. *This*—the woman I see in front of me know, is the one I have been waiting for. Love, I trust you with my heart."

Sharon beamed at him. She wasn't disappointed when he didn't return her declaration of love. He'd told her he was falling in love with her, but after what he'd just said, she understood why he was holding back. He needed to know that she had overcome her past and the demons that had been swirling deep in her mind.

Now, there was hope. For a future filled with love and joy.

Linzi Basset

CHAPTER ELEVEN

"Luca, it's good to see you, my friend."

Colt watched expressionlessly, as one crime boss after the other fell over their feet to greet Luca when he walked into the private conference hall, where their annual meeting was to be held. He'd known that Luca Vitale had always commanded reverence as the ultimate leader of the mob. In early years of his forced acceptance into the world of crime, he'd thought that it was Luca's instinctive cruelty that made others respect him—or rather, fear him. He never made direct threats, but those who swore allegiance to him knew that if they didn't do what was expected, they'd end up in the emergency room, or worse, pushing daisies. Luca had a menacing passive-aggressive streak.

As Damiano, Colt had ruled with an iron fist;

His word was rule. He'd made his mark and was as feared as his father. The sigh that escaped his lips was wrought with frustration. Colt knew, better than anyone, that there was no leaving the gang. The gang was for life—long or short of it.

I should never have come back here. I eluded them for eight years! I should've just kept Ceejay safe and let the fuckers kill each other.

If anyone tried to leave the mob, Luca didn't just go after them, he went after their loved ones too. That's the kind of leader Luca was—no morals, no conscience, and no compassion. He'd reveled in the belief that he'd modeled Colt after himself.

Yeah, Luca was the king of all and no one dared to question his orders; except Damiano Vitale. He opposed him on a daily basis.

"Shall we begin," Damiano's voice boomed across the large room, drawing attention.

He suppressed a smirk at the disbelief he encountered around him. They stared at him like he'd just unveiled a ticking bomb.

No one but Luca Vitale was supposed to be in

charge of this meeting; had always been ... always would be. Even Luca glowered at him from beneath his heavy brows.

"Damiano, what is the meaning of this?" he grated under his breath.

Damiano ignored him, grinning to himself as he boldly took the seat at the head of the table. The one meant for Luca. That earned him a furious growl. Again, he ignored it. He looked around the room, noticing how the men carefully avoided locking eyes with him. They might fear Luca, but they respected Damiano more.

While everyone took their seats, Damiano inconspicuously scanned the room. Luca's muscle, Tony, stood in one corner, whittling away at a piece of softwood. His knife was always in his hand, carving wood was just an excuse. Damiano knew that it was the same knife that he's used to carve out a poor bar owner's eye a week ago. Failure to pay, apparently. Tony took his job seriously and could morph from a gentle giant into someone no one wanted to cross. He had no moral boundaries, no sense of right or wrong, good, or bad. He just followed Luca's orders. Blindly.

He was the one Damiano had to look out for when he left this room.

If *I manage to leave alive.*

"First order of business," Damiano brought order to the murmurs around the table. His deep voice silenced the room. All eyes turned to him; some peeked at Luca to ascertain his reaction to his son taking charge of *his* meeting.

Colt was aware of Luca's eyes on him. The sharp, calculating look warned that he was onto him. Their gazes clashed. Luca was the first to back down and look away. Frustration was rife in his tense body. He couldn't fathom Damiano's motives, but it sharpened his guard.

His son was deliberately trying to unsettle him. It was a warning that he was up to something. Luca knew him well enough to expect the unexpected.

Luca's mouth flattened into a grim line. Damiano still didn't understand that there was no way out for him. Luca had allowed him rope, to rule from a distance. Now, Luca realized it was time to tighten the noose. His son would learn not to toy with him. No one has ever gotten the better of him. His own son was not going to be the first.

The meeting dragged on for the majority of the day. Damiano was frustrated. He wanted to get this over and done with. He'd had it with the menial inconsequential crap he had to sit through for the entire day.

"Now, I have two more points to bring to the table. Neither of them is up for discussion nor debate."

He looked around the table and let his words sink in. Luca sat straighter in his chair. His look turned glacial. A warning flashed across the distance, which Damiano answered with a smile.

The time of intimidating me is long gone, Luca Vitale.

"As you all know I've kept the Occhipinti bonds in safekeeping since I managed to recover it a year ago. The reason is of no consequence. What does matter . . ." He got up to retrieve the silver hard-shelled case that he'd brought with him. He coded in the unlock key and opened it. With a shove, the case skidded across the table to be caught by a startled Luca. "Is that I am now giving them back to the mafia's coffers."

"Are you telling us that Luca is holding the hundred million bonds?" Joey Russo, the boss of the north region asked. His eyes bulged in shock and then began to glitter with greed.

"Yes." Damiano glanced at Vito, who doubled up as the mob's treasurer since Stephen Caldwell had been killed. "I trust you will ensure that these bonds are returned to the family vault?" The mob had a vault they referred to as the 'family vault' where all shared funds were kept.

"Of course," Vito muttered, glancing at Luca. They were both flabbergasted, like everyone else. Handing over the bonds to them in full view of the entire mob congregation left them with no choice but to return it to the vault. If they didn't, everyone would know, since they all received a notification from the bank as soon as there was any movement, in or out of the vault. It was a safety that Damiano had affected a year ago.

Luca was livid. Damiano didn't need to look at him to know that. He'd just effectively put a stop to his plan to create a biochemical weapon with the pox virus. Without the bonds, he wouldn't have the financial backing to see it through.

"Finally, I am formally denouncing my position as the Don of the Occhipinti family and my association with the mob."

The room erupted with noise as everyone began talking at once. The corner of his mouth raised in a smirk. So slight that no one noticed. He appeared as coolly detached as always. Silently, he savored the moment. Luca's reaction was the most satisfying. He jumped up, the chair clattering to the floor as he pushed it back hard. He appeared to be on the verge of having a catalytic fit.

"*Non andrai da nessuna parte,*" His voice grated. Everyone had fallen silent, waiting with bated breath for the showdown to commence.

Except, Damiano had prepared for this. He ignored Luca and addressed everyone in the room.

"I've done more than my share over the past two years to ensure a smooth continuance of the mob's business. And Tony, I urge you to keep that knife in check. No one is going cold in this room today; least of all me."

"You know you can't walk away from us, Damiano. No one leaves the mafia. *Nessuno!*" Joey smirked at him. "You should know that better than anyone."

"And yet, I intend to. *Basta di questo*, Luca," Damiano sneered when Luca began talking once more. "I have made my decision. No one is going to stop me. *Ti sto avvertendo, non cazzo con!*"

Damiano's warning stayed Tony and Carlo, Luca's two henchmen from taking a step farther. They glanced toward Luca, who held up his hand. They didn't move.

"And just how do you propose to walk out of here alive, my son? I might be able to talk them out of killing you, if you admit that this was all a joke …

otherwise, I'm afraid—"

"No threats, Luca. I suggest all of you listen very carefully to what I have to say, because this will affect each and everyone around this table. I will walk out that door and no one will come after me. Not now and not ten years from now. I am done! *Ho finito* and that's the end of it." His face was deadpan but his eyes were black with a twinge of red that glowed like lava.

"I know everything about you and can sink everyone here. No, zip it, Luca. I am talking now. Do you honestly think I would walk in here unprepared? I know how you operate—all of you. I have detailed files on all of you in safekeeping, for that matter, in numerous hands. If I don't walk out of here today or should anything happen to me or anyone in my family of friends, that information would be released to the FBI. You will all be fucked; not just the one who comes after me."

He held up his hand for silence.

"I also have a discussion on tape that points to the mob's intention to create a biochemical weapon, to overthrow the Government."

Luca sank into the chair that Tony had picked up. His face was ashen, but his eyes glowed like beacons of hatred at Damiano, as the entire room rumbled in discontent; especially, in light of a fact that no one but Luca knew about.

"*Cazzate!*" Joey erupted. His voice boomed over the noise and everyone became quiet. "We will never become involved in biochemical warfare! You're bluffing."

"I assure you; I am not. And it matters not if you're not aware of it, Joey Russo, it's a fact. And I will make sure that all of you are implicated. I will forget about your existence once I leave this place unharmed and none of my people come to any harm. So, call off your dogs, Luca. *I am done.* You are once more the Don of the Occhipinti. *Ho finito.*"

He got up and strolled toward the door, expecting a knife in his back at any moment. He turned to run his searing gaze over each man watching him.

None of them got to be where they were today

without the morals of a sewer rat. For all the 'code' they always bandied about, the only ones who counted were the most barbaric, scum-bag rules. Be loyal or be savage, that's the way it was in the mob. "At the first sign of any of you in my territory, I'll release that file. *Non provare la mia pazienza.* You will lose. *That's a promise.*"

With that final warning, he walked through the door and out of the Plaza Hotel.

Jacksonville - 2 days later

"I won't be offended if any of you refuse to keep these files under safeguard. Luca might get it in his demented head to come after all of you, but I did imply that it's kept by an outsider, which it is. I gave a set to Quade as well."

"No problem, Colt. I won't think twice about using this file should anything happen to you or any of us." Kent said, to which Seth, Parnell and Nolan added their agreement.

"Is Ceejay ready for the trip? I believe Maxwell has been moved to a private room." Seth wanted to know.

"Yes, he's on the mend and she agreed to leave with Jewel in the morning. Rhone and Keon are picking us up at Parnell's farm. Even if anyone follows us there, they won't be able to track us once we leave there. Not in that chopper," Colt explained.

"That's a relief. Now, we only need to find Jay Vick and get rid of him so that the twins can come back home. I miss those two like crazy." Seth didn't bother to hide his feelings from his friends.

"Quade and Quinlan are searching for him but he's clever. I have a suspicion that he's using a disguise, which is why they can't find him through the face recognition system. That worries me. I have a feeling that he's involved with someone else in the mob." Colt paced the office while he talked.

"Luca?" Kent asked.

"I don't think so." Colt frowned, thinking over the possibility. "Or if it is, it means Luca has lied to me—again. If that is the case, Luca Vitale better tread carefully."

"When are you going to realize that he won't back down, Colt? You might have put him on the back foot during the meeting but you know he's gonna bounce back. And he's going to do it when you least expect it," Seth cautioned him with a frown marring his brow.

Colt considered what Seth had said on his way home. He'd known he was taking a risk in denouncing the Don's position publicly, but he *had* to do it that way, to register any impact. He sighed as he parked next to an unknown vehicle in front of their house.

He could hear Mason shriek excitedly from the den. He headed that way only to shock to a halt at the scene he walked into.

Luca Vitale was sitting on the carpet, playing cars with Mason. It almost seemed surreal.

Grandfather playing with his grandson; how suburban.

Mason saw him first and jumped up to run into his arms.

"Dada, see!"

He held out his arm to show off the woven black leather bracelet with a silver geometric tribal clasp on his arm. He pointed at Luca and said with a wide toothy grin, "Grampa pressie!"

"*Quello che cazzo vuoi*, Luca?" Colt sneered. The anger swirled in red turbulent flashes in his eyes. The warning was visible to the older man as he stood up from the floor.

"I'm sorry, Colt. He forced his way past me when I opened the door," Ceejay informed him. She stood pressed against his side and he could feel the tension emanating from her body. He squeezed her hand in reassurance.

Luca straightened to his full height, shrugged, and smiled at Mason. "It was time I met my grandson, don't you agree? He's a split image of you as a child. Amazing how the human DNA works, isn't it, little lady?" Luca asked Ceejay.

Colt watched with concern as Ceejay's complexion turned gray. Her eyes darkened like they always did that when she was highly emotional.

"I think it's time you leave." Colt's voice warned Luca. The smile Luca offered was one of satisfaction. Colt couldn't help but be concerned.

What exactly did Luca come here for? He was furious at his audacity.

"Very well. It seems I have worn out my welcome. Enjoy the toys, Mason. And don't forget— don't take off your armband. Remember? Your bond to Grampa," he said to Mason with an undertone of enjoyment in his voice.

Mason nodded and covered the bracelet with his small hand. "Grampa prezie," he said with a beaming smile.

"Get the fuck out, Luca. *Now*," Colt gritted through clenched teeth. This time, Luca turned and walked outside, Colt close on his heels.

"I never want to see you here ever again, Luca, is that clear?"

"Come now, son. All I wanted to do was meet my grandson. You know ... your successor at the Occhipintis." He took great pleasure in pointing it out to Colt.

"My son will never come anywhere near that fucking family, Luca. Let me make this clear. You're nothing to my son. No relation. Fucking nothing! Stay away from my family. Stay away from Jacksonville. There's nothing here for you."

"Nothing? Well, that's a matter of opinion, my boy. As long as I breathe air and you're alive, there will always be something here for me." He got into the rental car and the window rolled down with the press of a button. "I have tried for years to make you see reason, but you're too hardheaded to accept your fate. So, my son, you leave me with no choice."

Luca had no time for losers. People who thought he was callous were bleeding hearts and do-gooder losers themselves; they just didn't make the cut for a better life. While mentoring Colt, he'd told him about the dumb wastrels who needed to learn about the dog–eat-dog in this world; winner takes all. There were thousands of starving mouths all around the world. They weren't his problem. Luca Vitale didn't give a fuck for those people. He felt … zilch.

"Remember what I told you, my son. I'm not callous; I'm successful. Anyone who says otherwise is jealous. And you'll be me. Soon."

Those words came back to Colt now. Luca had been wrong. He wasn't just callous, he was cruel. Fuck being successful; killing and destroying another human didn't make him a success. It made him a murderer.

"Are you threatening me, Luca? Did you forget my warning so quickly?"

"No, I didn't, but let me give you one of my own. You *will* be at the head of the Occhipintis, Damiano. I want you there and you were born for it. Remember that when the people you love start dying one by one."

"Fuck you, Luca. I won't let you anywhere near my family or friends!"

"No? Look how easily I invaded your home

today, even with all the additional security, to bring my grandson a gift. What's in store for your minions if you continue to defy me? Well, let's just say, I don't need to be near them."

"What the fuck are you talking about?" Colt was struggling to hold on to his anger. All those months with the monks were dwindling away with every passing second.

"Certain gifts aren't what they seem, Damiano. They might even be ... lethal. Others are ... airborne."

He drove off with Colt staring after him.

Airborne? Lethal? What the fuck was he—

"*Gesù!* The pox virus! He's planning to—" Colt bit off his words.

His phone rang while he stood staring after the disappearing car.

"One more thing, son. Do not remove that bracelet I gave your son. If you do, he will die within two hours."

"Luca, what the fuck did you do?" He shouted over the phone.

"I secured your future, my son. Make *no* mistake. You *will* rule until the day I breathe my last breath. This is how it works. If you try and remove it, a thin needle hidden inside the bracelet will inject the pox virus directly into his bloodstream. If you defy me, I'll trigger the needle remotely with a click of a button."

"You forget that I have the formula for the antidote, Luca. What fucking game—"

Luca's laughter was like a punch into his solar plexus.

"I find it amazing that you, of all the people, still underestimate me, my boy. The formulas on the drive I gave you are for the common flu. No, Damiano, I still have my trump cards and this is only the first one I played."

Colt tore inside the house, just in time, to find Ceejay trying to pry the bracelet off Mason's arm.

"*Stop*! Leave it."

She looked at him. She was deathly pale.

"Why? I don't want my son wearing anything from that fucking monster!"

"Honey, please just leave it. I'll explain later."

"No, Colt, you don't understand. He called me *little lady*! The moment he said it, I knew it was him. He's the one, Colt. Don't you see? He lied and used all of you! All of us!"

"Ceejay, baby, you're talking in circles."

"Goddamnit, Colt, you aren't *listening*. The man who controlled me all those years ago with threats about the bonds; we assumed it was Gianni when you caught him—but it *wasn't*. Those phone calls … *that man* … he always called me *little lady* in the same condescending tone he just used on me. *He*, Luca Vitale, is the one who was behind it all."

"He's a fucking *dead* man."

CHAPTER TWELVE

"I'm sorry, Colt, but I'm afraid, it's not good news."

Kent looked up. He was unconsciously tracing the vein in Sharon's wrist gently with his thumb. He was concerned with the devastation on Colt's face.

"What did you find, Quade?" Colt rasped. He was finding it more difficult with each passing day to keep the darkness at bay. Rage had been his companion for the past two days. He kept his gaze lowered. Kent was too astute not to notice the struggle within him.

Quade cleared his throat. He could feel the battle his cousin was waging. *But fuck! I won't blame him if he lets the darkness out.* Any man would, in such circumstances. He met Kent's eyes. He and Sharon had accompanied Colt, Nolan, Ceejay and Jewel for the visit. The concern in his gaze set

Quade's mind at rest. Kent had seen it too.

"The ultra-scanner Bracus had used showed the needle secured inside the clasp on the bracelet. It is triggered the moment the link begins to open. There's no way to get it off without the needle pricking his arm. I'm afraid, unless you have the antidote on hand, that thing has to stay on Mason's arm."

"Is there any way they can ascertain what's in that needle, Quade?" Kent asked. "How sure are you that it's even pox virus, Colt? You said yourself that he doesn't have the money to follow through with his plans now."

Colt had to clear his throat. Fear for his son's safety threatened to break him. "He might not be able to embark on biochemical warfare, Kent, but he has enough money to pay off a rotten scientist to develop the virus from the formula. For all we know, what's in that needle might be the prototype of the virus."

"Or it might be a fluke to keep you dancing to his tune. It takes months, years to develop a virus, even with a formula at hand. There are many components to consider and test. It's not something that falls into place with the first try." Kent explained. "There's no way any scientist could have prepared a sample already, in such a short period of time."

"You might be right." Colt ran his fingers through his hair. "But it's a chance I'm not willing to take. Not with my son's life. If that bracelet was on my arm, I wouldn't think twice about testing it. But he's a two-year old child. I can't ... I can't . . ." Colt choked up and with a curse, walked outside.

Sharon squeezed Kent's hand when she noticed him tearing up along with the rest of the people in the room. She didn't know the little boy, but she felt the burning sensation behind her eyelids. Using a small boy, as bait, was incomprehensible. Another sign of Vitale's cruelty.

"I think it's time for something sweet. Jewel, shall we bake some of my famous poppy seed muffins?" Sharon asked and Jewel eagerly joined her and Maxine in the kitchen, leaving the men to compose themselves.

Colt found Ceejay on the banks of the river a short distance from the house. It lay across the land in smooth seductive curves, beautiful in sunlight, cool and innocuous. The water was green, darker in the shadows and pale in the light, but still green. Along with chirping birds that were welcoming the midday heat, the gentle rush of the water was barely audible.

She sat staring at the water and didn't move when he sat down next to her. He could feel her despair resonating deep inside his soul.

"The circle of life is so pronounced out here in nature, isn't it?" It was a rhetorical question but it was a broken cry of a mother fearing for her child. "We die and the planet dies too. Earth will spring back and reboot in a few million years, but it will start from scratch again. Life comes from *nothing* and goes back to *nothing*."

Ceejay reached for Colt's hand. He wrapped it within both of his and kissed her palm.

"He's a baby, Colt. He hasn't experienced the

joys of life yet. He hasn't felt the challenge of being a teenager or the angst of his first kiss."

"Honey, we'll—"

"You have to go back. I know. I've seen the darkness in your eyes when you think nobody's watching. But it's different this time."

"Baby, don't—"

She turned to face him and press her fingers against his lips.

"That's his mistake, my love. He *wanted* it to happen. It's how he managed to control you for so long but he didn't factor *love* into the equation. This time your darkness has direction and it's aimed at him."

Colt stared at her. He shouldn't be surprised that she had figured it out. She knew him better than he did himself. He hadn't consciously thought about what the beast inside him was raging to do. He'd been terrified that once he allowed it to surface, he would become Damiano again. Now, his sweet wife has shown him the error of his ways.

"I know what it means when you go back

there, honey. What you'll have to ... do, to make them believe the dark Damiano is back for good."

"Ceejay, baby, I'll never—"

"You won't have a choice, Colt. You'll have to. I hate just thinking about it, but all I ask is that you never ... never speak to me about it."

She jumped up with a sob and ran back to the house. He stared after her. A muscle ticked rhythmically in his cheek.

"*Dannazione*! I'll go back, but there is no way I'm going to fuck other women just to prove something to Luca Vitale!"

He followed in Ceejay's footstep at a snail's pace, his brow furrowed in thought. She was wrong about one thing. She believed his intention was to go back and rule as the Don to pacify Luca.
"No, my sweet love, the only reason I'm going back to the Occhipinti rule is to ensure our son is safe and once I have achieved it, Luca Vitale is a dead man."

"Keep your eyes and ears open," Kent said to Parnell and Seth, who had him on speakerphone. He was driving back to the hotel he'd booked for the weekend. He didn't want to impose on Quade and Maxine; especially as they hadn't been expecting them. It had been a last-minute decision. He thought it would be good for him and Sharon to break away from the monotony.

He caught Sharon's eye and recognized the concern flaring in their depths. For Mason, but also for the emotional impact it had on him—her Dom. He loved that she was so in tune with his feelings. He reached for her hand and placed it on his thigh.

"What's worrying you, Kent?" Seth queried.

"With everything going on with Colt and Mason I'm worried that we all lose sight of Jay Vick. That man is dangerous and he's somewhere out there. I have a feeling in my gut, which makes me weary. I don't trust him. I have a feeling he's in

Jacksonville."

"I second your feeling," Parnell said. "He might be a fuck-up, but he has a sharp mind."

"Yeah, combine that with the psychotic bastard he's turned into and we have a bomb waiting to explode in our faces. One, I'm afraid, we might not see coming." Kent's said sharply.

"Which makes me wonder why he's become the lackey to others? Gianni, Giorgio and who the fuck knows who else."

"Don't forget that he has his own agenda as well, Seth. He hates Colt. Whether or not Luca realizes it, Jay's only aim is to kill Colt for taking the thing that he covets most."

"I know. Be careful out there, Kent. We've been working with Bracus' team to increase the security around the club."

They spent a couple of minutes discussing security measures before ending the call. Kent parked in front of the hotel.

"I need to meet Quinlan, love, as we discussed. I know you're tired, so why don't you go and take a nap. I shouldn't be longer than two hours."

"Are you sure? I don't mind coming with you," Sharon said. She loved spending time with him away from home. He was more relaxed and touched her all the time. It made her feel special and loved.

"Yes, I am sure, love. Let's go."

Kent walked her to the room, looking around cautiously all the time. He didn't think that Jay would know where they were but he had learned to be wary.

He kissed her at the door and tapped her on the nose. "Now, go and take that nap. Do not leave the room and don't open the door for anyone."

The meeting was shorter than Kent had expected, Quinlan had all the information Quade had asked for ready by the time he arrived. He was back at the hotel in an hour and parked the rental in the hotel's underground parking area. Once again, he glanced around as he jogged toward the elevator. He couldn't afford to drop his guard until Jay Vick was behind bars or preferably, dead.

Sharon wasn't in the room when he arrived. He looked around but found no note or indication of where she'd gone.

"I fucking told her to wait for me in the room. Jesus, doesn't she realize the danger?" He rasped while he tried calling her cell.

The call went to voicemail and Kent cursed. His anger had always been a silent huntress looming in the night, ready to strike when there was enough provocation. He'd never allow it to cloud his judgment. He'd learned years ago that regrets always came too late. Now, he felt the fury bubble inside him with each passing minute.

He wasn't surprised that it was aimed at Sharon's disregard of his order and not on the belief that she might have decided to leave. It wasn't even a consideration. Not since they'd declared their feelings for each other. No matter her past, he was secure in the sincerity of her feelings for him.

The door opened and the clicking of her heels on the wooden floor drew his attention. His shoulders sagged as relief flooded his system.

She was safe.

"Oh! You're back earlier than I expected, honey."

He could discern the concern in her voice when he didn't turn around to face her. The anger was still swirling under the surface, although more controlled.

"What was my instruction to you before I left this room, Sharon?" He snapped at her, still facing the window. Dusk was falling outside and painted the earth in hues of blues, purples, and gold.

"They have the most wonderful spa here. I didn't think you would mind if I went for a massage. I didn't leave the . . ." Her voice faded when he finally turned.

His eyes were narrowed, body rigid and hard. There was no sign of the earlier mirth. His customary warmth had become colder than the South Pole. His lethal stare was piercing, like his glare alone could punish her for her disobedience.

"I asked you a question."

"You told me to stay in the room. I'm sorry, I didn't—"

"Enough. You've been living with me for weeks now, Sharon. You know how I feel about your safety."

"But you said we would be safe here."

"I also said nothing is guaranteed. Goddammit, Sharon!"

"I'm sorry, Kent! But that guy, Jay Vick? He doesn't know who I am. Least of all that you and I are—"

"Never underestimate someone like Jay Vick, Sharon. He's dangerous and he will aim for where it hurts the most. It's why he targeted Ceejay before, and now Mason. You're with me now, which puts you in danger too. No! Keep quiet. I will not stand for this. Get yourself to the bedroom. Ten minutes. I want to find you naked, in punishment position, with your hands on the bed."

"Kent—"

His closed look silenced her. She couldn't prevent the shudder of concern at his anger. He'd never punished her before and she hated that he had to now. She wasn't worried about the pain, because she was used to the worst, but it was the disappointment in his gaze that shook her.

"Yes, Sir," she said softly and walked toward the room with his gaze following every step.

Kent was aware that corporal punishment didn't scare her. But he was different. She needed to understand and accept responsibility for her actions. It was his duty as a Dom to make her understand.

He dragged in his breath when he walked into the room. Sharon was in position, as instructed. Her beauty struck him smack in the chest. From where he stood, he had the perfect view from behind. Her heart shaped buttocks stuck in the air with her legs spread wide and toes pointed inward.

"I don't suppose I need to gag you, do I, sub?"

"No, Master. I won't scream," she said softly.

He could hear the agitation in her voice.

"Are you sure, Sharon?" he asked in a gentler tone. "Punishment from me will be different to what you're used to and no, there will be no erotic stimulation. Make no mistake, this is going to be punishment and it might hurt more than you've ever experienced."

"I doubt that. He was a cruel bastard and he didn't stop until I screamed, bled or passed out."

"There is a difference between receiving punishment from an abuser and the Dom you love, my pet. Don't say I didn't warn you."

Sharon looked over her shoulder. He pulled his belt from his pants and wrapped the leather around his fisted hand while he walked closer.

"Do you know why you're being punished?"

"I disobeyed your instruction, Master."

"And why does it anger me?"

"Because you're concerned for my safety and … and because I disappointed you."

"Keep your legs apart and don't move."

Kent snapped the belt a few times against his leg, building up her anticipation for the first strike.

The swishing belt sounded threatening as he swung it back and forth, and then began to slap her inner thighs with it. The first couple of lashes were light, but they became progressively harder.

Left and right.

Right and left.

He kept switching, catching her unaware. Her silence was broken with soft gasps as he found a rhythm, the sound of leather slapping her skin interposed by her gasps that turned into distressed moans.

"You will never endanger what belongs to me, is that understood?"

"Yes, I'm sorry, my Master." Her voice had a husky undertone and Kent was sure he detected a hint of tears.

"I go to great lengths to care for you and protect you. You will honor the regard I have for you as my sub."

"Yes, Master Kent." This time the tears were clearly discernible in her thickening voice.

"The next twenty will be on your ass, Sharon.

Count them."

Sharon's voice was hoarse, but she followed his command with every strike that connected with her buttocks. His strokes were smooth, even and without any hesitation. First one cheek, then the other and then both. Her skin heated and then burned, as the intensity increased. Her voice turned thin until eventually she was sobbing out the counts.

Kent continued, but took note of every wince, gasp, and cry, ensuring that every impact settled deep into the tissue of her tender skin before the next one landed.

"I'm sorry, my Master. Please! Oh god, please. It hurts," she sobbed on the twelfth strike.

"It's supposed to. Push your ass out, sub. Don't anger me further," he snapped when her buttocks lowered with her knees bending. She straightened immediately and buried her face in the duvet. Her cries turned into smothered screams in the thick cover. Kent's mouth flattened into a straight line, but he didn't relent until the promised count was done.

Her muffled voice was still echoing twenty when he pulled his hand back and snapped his wrist five times in quick succession. Hoarse cries rang in the room as he landed them on her pussy and clit. Her legs gave in and she crumbled to the floor, sobbing.

"I'm sorry, my Master. Please forgive me," she begged in a strangled voice. Her teary eyes pleaded with him.

"You are forgiven, love."

He lifted her in his arms and sat down on the bed. With a tenderness that astounded Sharon, he traced the outline of her face with his fingertips. A small, satisfied smile curved his lips when she sighed and leaned into his hand.

"Do you understand the difference now, Sharon?"

She nodded; trying, but failing to smile at him, the tears were still flowing too freely. He cuddled her against his chest.

"I've never felt the pain to this degree before,

but it was more than the physical pain. Knowing I disappointed you; *that* hurt more than anything. It will never happen again, my Master."

Kent chuckled and brushed his lips over hers. "Ah, my little innocent sub. Trust me, love, it *will* happen and often, however unintended. Life happens and we're only human, but I do expect you to try. I would hate to have to punish you for the same disobedience twice."

"Never again. I swear."

"Very well. Get dressed, my pet. We're going downstairs for dinner."

"Do we have to? Can't we eat here?" She asked with round eyes. Her buttocks, thighs and pussy hurt like the devil and she could only imagine the torture it would be to sit through a five-course meal.

"Yes, we have to."

The sharp glint in his eyes warned her that it was part of her punishment.

"And, Sharon," he called after her as she walked into the en-suite bathroom.

"Yes, Master."

"Don't bother with panties."

Oh lord.

She did as instructed but not with the same trepidation she used to in her past life.

Kent maintained a light atmosphere throughout the dinner. He asked questions about her life before she got married and she rejoiced in how relaxed he made her feel. They even joked about some of the tales she told of her shenanigans as a teenager.

They had just placed the order for dessert when she felt his hand on her thigh, gently squeezing as he trailed his fingers upward. She glanced around furtively but the booth was relatively secluded behind some potted plants.

"Spread your legs, love," he ordered. She complied, feeling her thighs tremble in reaction at his warm touch.

"Oh, what are you ... mmm," she moaned as his fingers found her throbbing clitoris and toggled it playfully. Her mind reeled with how easily he aroused her.

"How does this little nub feel, my pet? Still sore?"

"A little," she whimpered because of his continuously exploring fingers that trailed lower to dip briefly between her swollen vulvae.

"Hm, I can feel the heat on your satiny lips from the strikes. Maybe we should cool them down a little."

Sharon looked into his glimmering eyes. He pushed one finger inside her pussy and twirled it around in a slow rotation while he pressed his thumb on her clit—hard and insistently. She was stumped by the unexpected sensations that floored her brain and she arched in desperate subjugation to their maneuver. His other hand was busy fishing out some ice cubes from his water glass.

"Aah, fuck!" Sharon cried softly. She desperately sucked in air into her lungs as spasms of delight rocketed through her when Kent rubbed an ice cube over her clitoris. He watched her, exulting in the ecstasy that flashed over her face. He hesitated, waiting until she relaxed before he began to brush it over the swollen nub again and again. With slow deliberation, he stroked the melting ice cubes up and down her labia.

She did her best to contain her cries and moans, but in the end, had to clamp her hand over her mouth when the sensations threatened to overwhelm her.

He leaned closer. His lips brushed hers. "How about now, my pet? Do they feel less painful?" He growled against her mouth before he covered it with his own, effectively cutting of her cry when he slipped the cold ice cube deep inside her pussy.

"Oh, fuck," Sharon wailed the moment his lips left hers.

The cold ice melted almost instantaneously in her hot pussy and she could feel the trickle of water oozing out of her slit. Kent's finger returned to draw circles around the still sensitive nub. An orgasm winked with mutinous intent, but remained aloof, teasing her with its pleasure, but staying just out of reach. Every touch and swirl of his ruthless hands brought her closer to orgasm.

Just as the sweet heat of a climax was about to fill her veins, he took his hands away, eliciting a mournful cry to escape from her lips.

"Please," she begged.

"Ah, our dessert. Doesn't this chocolate cheesecake look divine, love? Come on, eat up. I'm tired after the flight and wish to get to bed."

The implication was clear. She wasn't going to find any relief for her aroused body any time soon.

CHAPTER THIRTEEN

"*Finalmente!*" Luca exclaimed when Damiano walked into his office. "I have my son back. I am surprised, though. I didn't expect it to take this long."

"Get out of my chair, Luca." Damiano snapped. His tone was acrimonious. His eyes glittered with emptiness—a cold malevolence, that seemed encased in a black void.

He, of course, exulted at what he saw. *The Devil's Spawn is back.* Luca gloried, as he caught the pitch-black darkness swirling in the depths of his son's eyes; a sign that the beast had been unleashed inside Damiano.

His frosty reception and less than cordial demeanor wasn't uncalled for either, but that just made Luca smirk. This was the man he'd been waiting to unleash. And now, he stood in front of him.

Boldly demanding and without a speck of fear in his body. Luca's eyes narrowed speculatively. Damiano was clever, cunning and had pulled wool over his eyes before.

"And what did the little wife say about your decision to come back here? You *are* back for good this time, right?"

"Yes, I am, and Ceejay?" He scoffed. "She's a woman. She'll adapt."

"Will she? From what I've seen of her—"

"*Basta di questo!*" Damiano sat down in the chair Luca had vacated. "My wife or how I chose to treat her is none of your concern. Besides," he leered at Luca, "What she doesn't know won't hurt her. Should I feel the need, I might avail myself of the abundance of eager pussies in New York." He shrugged belligerently. His tone of voice warned him to drop the subject.

"And you would let her go?" Luca queried. The disbelief was shallow in his gaze.

Damiano laughed. "I wouldn't have to. Ceejay knows I'll take my son with me if she decides to leave."

"That must have been an unpleasant discussion," he remarked.

Another negligent shrug. "It matters not. It's done. If I want to make a success of my position as the Don, I have to be here all the time. I can't cart back and forth every two weeks. You and your cronies have proven your incompetence more than enough."

"Now, wait a minute, you insolent pup!"

"No, Luca, *you* shut the fuck up. You're not gonna fuck with me. *Nessuno è!* You wanted me here and you'll take me the way I am. *Your* Don. Now, get me up to speed with the fuckups I have to fix."

Luca simmered in anger. He'd forgotten how compelling Damiano was in full command. On one hand, he was delighted; on the other, it grated on his ego that Damiano had no fear of him.

"And what about Mason? The bracelet of death he carries?"

Damiano pinned Luca down with a searing glare. An air of eeriness and unsettling coldness emanated from his gaze.

"You said it, Luca, he's my successor and I will personally mentor him as he grows older. Beware, my dear father. I don't need you around to rule. I already have all the support *and* fear I need from the other bosses. A dead man can't detonate that needle." Damiano basked in the sudden gray pallor of the man across the desk. Luca knew it wasn't an idle threat. "He is my son and if you wish to see him grow to a man, you know what to do."

It disconcerted Luca that he didn't elaborate or demand him to deactivate the device. He just barked to be brought up to date. That settled Luca's mind. In front of him sat the real thing. It was the Devil's Spawn. He relaxed in his chair and reached for a file folder.

Damiano stood in front of the window, gazing over

the city below once he'd dismissed Luca. His decision to come back here was two-fold. First—to make sure Mason's life wasn't in jeopardy and second—to see if his presence back as the head of the Occhipintis would flush out Jay Vick.

He would get rid of two flies with one swat. Jay wanted the power. When he hears that Damiano was back, he would know that Luca had double crossed him again. He felt it in his gut; those two were in cohort with each other.

"And they're at odd ends. I'm sure of that. Luca might know what Jay's after, but he sure as hell doesn't know what our father's agenda is."
It bothered Damiano that he didn't either.

His dark hair reached the collar of his tailored blazer, which was left stylishly open, over a crisp white shirt. Upon closer inspection, his hair was speckled with gray and more prominent on the sides. He stood tall but leaned on the cane in his right hand. His face was obscured by a dark, bushy beard and a full moustache, with his full lips peeking through and effectively hiding his prominent cheekbones and well-defined chin.

He looked around and captured the gazes of the trio of men who were having lunch in the far corner of the small restaurant. His cerulean blue eyes glittered behind the heavyset glasses when they continued their meal without taking any notice of him. His lips twitched upward camouflaged by the black beard.

The server led him to a table and people took note of his gait when he began to walk. He concentrated to keep his steps faltering and uneven like something was weighing him down on one side and his muscles were struggling to compensate for his lack of balance as he leaned on the cane.

"What can I get for you, Sir?" The young waitress asked with a friendly, compassionate smile once he'd settled, with pretend difficulty, into the booth.

"Let's start with some strong brew, missy,

while I peruse the menu." His voice had a husky drawl with a heavy Australian accent.

He settled back in the chair and hid his smile when the young woman's eyes followed the cords of muscle knotting in his neck and straining the shoulder seams of his jacket, his shirt tenuously buttoned across his bulging chest.

No one recognized him. Sally Cooper, the server, had joked and flirted with him numerous times over the past number of years.

He tested the theory by looking directly at some of the people who had known him very well in the past. Apart from friendly smiles and nods, no one showed any flash of recognition. Jay smirked; the feeling of self-righteousness added a sparkle to his eyes.

Over the years, he'd become a master of disguise. It had been a risk to walk openly into a restaurant he used to frequent with the three men sitting in the corner. He glanced their way. They were in an animated discussion and had no interest in him.

Hah! The biggest test. My one-time best friends don't even recognize me.

He deliberately met Seth Harris' eyes, who gave him a brief how-do-you-do nod before he returned his attention to Nolan across the table from him.

Jay had grown gray over the past couple of months which added to his disguise. He always used to be clean shaven and the bushy beard gave him an entirely different appearance. The blue contacts were irritating, but a necessity. One look into his usual black irises, and they would know who he was.

Sally returned with his coffee and took his order for a medium-raw steak with a baked potato, corn, and vegetables. It was the only thing he missed about this town—the good food.

"There you go, Sir. I can vouch for the steak. We have the best meat in entire Texas," Sally said and broke into a broad smile when he winked at her.

"It looks very appealing. Thank you, miss."

He was halfway through his meal when his

phone vibrated in his pocket. With an irritating snort, he pulled it out and smirked at the name that flashed on the little screen.

"I'm busy having lunch. Can this wait?"

"No, it can't. You better get your ass back here."

"Jesus. You just sent me here. Do you think I'm a puppet who'll jump to your every demand? I'm not moving. I have a job to do and I'm going to see it through."

"And how the fuck do you propose to do that if your target is back at the Occhipinti head-office?"

"What do you mean he's back?"

"For good, asshole, and exactly where Luca wanted him to be."

"You said he denounced the seat as the Don at the annual meeting and gave the bonds back to Luca. Or were you lying to me?"

"I have no reason to lie to you."

"Then what brought him back? What the fuck aren't you telling me?"

"Luca is prancing about like a peacock, so I

can only assume he had something to do with it. The only thing I could get out of him was a cryptic, '*you always have to be one step ahead and do the unexpected. No one is immune to certain triggers. I just knew which one to use.*'"

Jay struggled to keep his voice low so his conversation couldn't be overheard.

"Well, his trend has been to be in the office one day every two weeks, so he'll be back tomorrow. I'm not budging."

Silently, Jay was fuming. This was exactly what he'd been trying to avoid. But, no. Luca Vitale had been clever. His assumption that Damiano would mentor Jay, was ludicrous to say the least.

"Aren't you fucking listening to me? He's back for good. He's not planning on commuting to Jacksonville."

Jay's fingers tightened around the fork until his knuckles turned white. He has been double crossed. *Yet again! Fucking bastard. This is the final straw.* If Damiano was back, his only aim, according to Luca, would be power. There was no chance he would give it up; least of all, to his long-lost brother.

The vertical line that slashed in the center of his forehead turned his expression cruel.

What the fuck was Luca up to and why hasn't he said anything to me about his plans? Jesus! I've been such a goddamned fool. Was that why he'd sent me here? To get me out from under his feet so he could concentrate on bringing Damiano back?

"Luca fucking knew Damiano would be back. That's why he sent me here."

The silence that followed his gruff statement made Jay curse. He'd been careful to keep Luca's instructions secret from this man. Now, *he* knew that he was playing on both sides of the fence.

"Luca also sent you to Jacksonville? What the fuck for?"

"It doesn't matter now, does it? He got what he wanted after all these fucking years. His blue-eyed boy back in charge."

"Just get the fuck back here. We need to come up with a strategy. I don't trust Damiano. We need to make him slip up. Luca has to see he's playing him for the fool."

"Is he? Or are you the fool? If he's gone dark, he wants the power as much as we do and guess what? He's got it now—with Luca's blessings. Just how do you propose to remedy that?"

A string of Italian curses followed. "Debating this over the phone isn't going to achieve anything. Get back here and let's find a way to rid ourselves of Damiano Vitale for good."

"You're a fool if you believe Damiano is the problem. Haven't you got it yet? As long as Luca Vitale breathes, neither one of us will ever become the Don."

The silence was brief and the voice that floated back to him was cold, doused with intent. "I'm well aware of that but we have Damiano now. He can do us a favor by getting rid of Luca. All it will take is a few slip-ups from Luca that could be potentially threatening to Damiano's reign. As dark as he is now, he won't stand for it."

"That would be brilliant; setting them up, to get rid of each other. This needs proper planning. I just have one or two things to take care of, but I'll be back in two days."

Jay paid his bill and walked out. He was halfway to the door when he remembered to limp. A glance over his shoulder set his mind at ease that no one noticed.

Luca recalled the brusque order from Damiano as he made the call.

"I believe it's time my brother and I get to know each other better. Get him here, Luca."

"Me? I don't know where he is. I told you I haven't been in—"

"Cazzate! I'm not a fool, Luca. I know you've been in contact with Jay ... or as you've christened him, Jayanni. Get him here."

He was uneasy about the order, but the black look from his son warned him not to deny him. Sometimes, Damiano scared him. This was one of those times. When he got that glacial look in his eyes and his irises glowed with a red flash, he was at his most dangerous.

"Exactly what I wanted him to become; a force no one would dare oppose. Jayanni, least of all." Luca mused aloud.

"Father?"

"Ah, I was beginning to believe you weren't going to answer."

Luca's mouth slashed into a straight line when he didn't respond.

"There's been new developments, Jayanni. Damiano is back for good. Now is the time to harvest his knowledge."

"Back for good?"

"Yes. He's decided it's time to take up the reign full time. He wants you here."

"He *what?*"

The shocked surprise was a sharp reminder of how little Jay trusted Luca's vision—that Damiano and he could become friends.

Luca smirked. He loved keeping Jayanni unsettled. But at the same time, he had a suspicion that the only reason Damiano wanted him closer was to keep him away from his family. He still didn't trust him one-hundred percent.

"He asked to see you. He said it was time the two of you became better acquainted as brothers."

"And you believe him? The only reason he would want me there, is to kill me. You forget I'm the one who kidnapped both his wife and son."

"I haven't forgotten but ... well, I guess I forgot to mention it's the devil that's back. He doesn't have one ounce of feeling running through him. All he sees in front of him now, is power. Just think, Jayanni, how strong the two of you could be together."

Jay didn't respond. Luca sighed. It would take a lot of cajoling to entice his eldest son to trust his twin. They've been on the opposite sides of the fence for too long.

"Get over here, Jayanni. With Damiano running the family business, you've got nothing to play for in Jacksonville. Here, you at least have a chance of becoming the next Don."

"I'll be back in two days."

"Two days? No. I want you back here tonight."

But Jayanni had already cut their connection. Luca frowned, concerned at what the hotheaded man planned to do.

CHAPTER FOURTEEN

His large, muscular frame slouched negligently in the posh leather chair. He stretched his legs out with a grunt. Looking around, he noticed many people he recognized from the days this used to be the hotspot.

Damiano cringed at the memory of debauchery that had gone down in this place all those years ago. His eyes were half-lidded as he watched Vito walking toward him, carrying two tumblers of what could only be his favorite single malt whiskey.

"See anything you like?" Vito smirked as soon as he sat down across from Damiano.

He was aware that his half-brother was watching him like a hawk. Not totally unexpected. He had a pretty good idea why he'd invited him to his BDSM club—Masters, in New York. It was a test. One, he assumed, was ordered by Luca.

If he was truly his dark, old self, he would fuck the night away.

Jesus. Is that really how shallow these people are? To believe that's what defines a man? Sex, drugs, and booze?

Damiano shrugged. "A couple." His response was curt.

Vito was visibly uncomfortable with the glance he received from him. He'd always been wary of the darkness in his brother. Now, it seemed like his glare sucked something out of him. Vito could feel his self-confidence wilt before those black orbs that looked through him; like he knew why he'd invited him to the club.

He'd seen the reaction from the patrons when they'd walked in. Damiano was a powerful man in his own right—in dimension and stature, and his compelling aura brought the temperature down the moment they entered the club.

Vito swallowed and squirmed again.

Damiano's gaze felt like an act of malevolence—a glare to stop intent before a thought was formed. It was then that Vito realized that the Colt his family and friends loved, was nothing more than a role—an act. *This* was the real Damiano and for some reason he was no longer afraid to show it.

"I haven't received notification that the bonds have been returned to the vault, Vito. Care to explain the delay?"

Vito felt a warm blush spread over his cheeks. He prided himself on his competence and hated it when questioned.

"I stayed behind in LA for relaxation. I only returned a few hours ago. It'll be done in the morning."

"See that it does. I have big plans for the family business. It's time we sow the benefit of those bonds."

"Plans? Anything you're willing to share?"

"Not yet. Soon though, and I'm going to need both you and Jayanni involved."

Vito's eyes widened. He didn't even attempt to

hide his shock. "Jayanni? Your twin brother? Since when have you become buddies with him?"

"I haven't, but now that I'm back, I am more than determined to turn this family into the biggest and most feared one in the US. It's time to bury the hatchet and besides, I don't blame him for acting the way he did. If the tables had been turned, who knows, I might have been the one acting up like that."

"I find it hard to believe that you would want him by your side. He kidnapped your son, for god's sake, and your wife too, a couple of years ago!"

"So, he did, but I've decided to let bygones be bygones. Besides, the bonds are back where they belong and that's what all of you were after, isn't it?"

Vito stuttered and his complexion turned beetroot red.

Damiano smirked. "Yeah, you too, little brother but fear not, I don't hold it against you. Jayanni? Well, he will have to decide who he's going to side with. Because if it's not with me, I'm afraid … *lui nuota con i pesci.*"

The warning rang crystal clear in his voice. Vito would follow the same path as Jay Vick if he opposed him in any way.

"You know I've always stood by your side, Damiano. Nothing has changed."

Damiano's attention was drawn by a small commotion at the entrance. His gaze turned hard as he observed the man jovially greeting his friends.

"Since when does Luca hang out in a place like this?" He grunted irritably.

Vito followed his gaze and was visibly startled to notice his father walking toward them.

"He's been popping in now and then. Although, he didn't mention he'd be here tonight."

Damiano was livid. Luca wanted to be a first-hand witness to his darkness.

Fuck! I won't get out of here without giving him something to ease his doubts.

He had no intention of cheating on Ceejay. Not even for ... but then he sobered. He might not have a choice and she'd known it. She'd prepared herself for it. He'd been the naive one. Until he had the means to get that fucking bracelet off Mason's arm, he'd have to jump through every loop for this fucked-up bastard.

"Well now, this is what I love to see—my sons having fun together." Luca laughed engagingly. He sat down next to Vito on the sofa. He leaned back with his arms spread on either side on the backrest. He looked around with interest.

"Quite a crowd here tonight, Vito, my boy. Ah, thanks, little lady," he said, taking his drink from one of the servers.

The *little lady* grated on Damiano's nerves, especially since Ceejay had identified him as the mastermind behind the fuckup their lives had become.

Luca took a large sip and then savored the taste in his mouth before he swallowed. He glanced toward Damiano.

"So, planning on having some fun tonight? I'm sure with all the *stress* at home, you've not been ... satisfied properly."

Damiano refrained from snorting in his face.

He settled for his trademark shrug.

"I might. There are a couple of subs that give the best head. I haven't had one of those in a long time."

He apologized to his wife in his mind for the lie but chose this intimacy as the lesser of two evils. There was no way he'd be able to force himself to put his cock inside another woman's pussy.

Luca beamed. The glimmer in his eyes was a dead giveaway to his purpose for being here. He'd come to verify firsthand if Damiano was acting like a douche bag; proof that he had no heart or soul.

"Did you get hold of my brother?" Damiano asked. His voice was cold and bitter but no different to what they were used to.

"Yes. He should be here in two days."

"Why two days?" Damiano didn't like the implication. It might mean that he was up to no good.

"Come now, son. Surely you don't expect him to jump with joy at the prospect of meeting you? He suspects that you hate him and your only purpose is to kill him. Surely you can understand his hesitation?"

Another shrug. "I don't give a fuck about his feelings. I want him here, Luca. Tomorrow. Not in two days. Make it happen."

His stare was so lethal and piercing; it felt painful to Luca. He blinked and sharpened his gaze on Damiano again. His anger wasn't aimed at Jayanni. It was centered on him.

Luca drew a staggering breath. *He knew.* Another glance at his furious eyes confirmed it and Luca worried about the possible repercussions—for himself.

Somehow, Damiano knew that he'd been the one responsible for every single action that had molded his live over the past three years—ever since Ceejay had come along.

"I will call him. Relax, son. Tomorrow is another day. *Divertirsi un po.*" Luca tried to pacify him and draw his attention away from himself.

"Yeah, I might as well." Damiano got up and walked toward a tall, dark-haired sub who had been flirting openly with him since his arrival. He didn't want to approach anyone with whom he'd scened in the past, for obvious reasons.

His stomach churned at the prospect of what lay ahead, but he forced his feet to continue until he stood in front of her.

She smiled seductively while she ran her hands over his chest.

"Did I give you permission to touch me?" His voice was harsh and raw. Her hands immediately fell away. She clasped them behind her back and lowered her eyes in a submissive pose.

"That's better."

"My apologies, Sir, but I was overwhelmed when you picked me. All the subs have been eagerly waiting for your attention. I've heard many stories about you."

"Then you would also know that I don't appreciate a forward sub. You do what I tell you. You accept what I offer and don't demand anything else. Do you believe you're up for it, sub?"

Damiano had to ensure he played the old

Damiano to the T. He was irritated that she'd already heard all the tales and by the glint in her eyes, she had expectations of the full six-course meal usually on offer by the powerful Damiano Vitale.

Well, was she in for a surprise?

"Yes, Sir."

"Master Devil. That's what you'll call me."

Her eyes lifted to gaze longingly at him. Her eagerness to please was there for everyone to see.

"Master Devil, how may I serve you?" She almost begged in a whiny voice.

"I'm in the mood for a deep, hard throat fuck, sub and after that, if you appease my lust, I want you on the St. Andrew's cross for an erotic flogging."

"Oh, Master Devil, it sounds exactly like what I need. Shall we?" She asked and turned toward the dungeon entrance.

"Where do you think you're going, sub?" His voice cracked icily.

She turned wearily to face him. He sat down on the barstool and pointed at the spot between his feet. He could sense Luca and Vito's curious looks but didn't glance their way. This was a show for their benefit. He had to keep his mind focused only on this moment because if he allowed it to wander, he wouldn't be able to see this through.

He had to do this. For Mason.

"Right here. And make it hard and quick. I don't have the patience for a rookie blowing me off."

Damiano clenched his teeth when the sub unzipped his pants and caressed his cock. She had the touch of a seductress and he felt his blood rushing south to fill his shaft.

"I told you what I want. Now get to it," he rasped, watching as she eagerly licked his length before she curled her tongue around the blunt tip and locked her lips around it.

He clamped his fist around a tuft of her hair to guide his cock deeper into her mouth, intending to get this over with quickly. She gagged and looked at him, tears were filling her eyes and spittle began to run down her chin.

"Do I need to do all the work myself, sub?" he

asked snidely, drawing laughter from others standing around to watch the devil at work. He tilted his cock at the right angle that would ensure a quick release. Her hot, wet mouth slid down his length sensually. He felt his balls tightening.

"That's much better." Damiano blanked his mind and allowed the primal urges to take over. He forced his cock all the way down her throat, gripped her hair in both hands and set to fuck her in a fast, steady rhythm.

He could feel his climax rushing to the edge and he pounded harder, faster. With a low grunt, he thrust as deep as he could, once, and his load jetted down her throat.

His eyes were half-lidded as he glanced toward Luca, who looked like a cat that'd just had his fill of cream.

Fucking asshole!

"Did I please you, Master Devil?" The sub asked with eager anticipation for what was still coming. She obviously assumed the flogging would end with her ass up in the air and fucked all the way to kingdom come.

"We shall see, sub, once we're in the dungeon. Shall we take care of that flogging?"

"Yes, Master Devil."

He zipped up his pants and rose. Luca ambled closer, still smiling like the fucking asshat he was.

"I'll be on my way, son. I just popped in for a shot. I'll see you in the morning."

"With Jayanni, or don't bother coming in."

Luca's face became splotched with red dots at being cut down in public, but then he smirked. This was the successor he'd been dreaming about. Nothing and no one would be able to stop him now.

Luca Vitale stood on the verge of becoming the most revered man in the US and his son, Damiano, was going to help him achieve it.

Damiano watched him leave after he had a brief chat with Vito. He sighed when his half-brother glanced his way and got up to follow him to the dungeon.

Fuck. Can't they be satisfied with what they got? Now I'll have to see this flogging through.

Unfortunately for the sub, it isn't going to end with sex she'd been hoping for.

Damiano was resigned to his plot. He ordered the Dungeon Master to tie the sub spread-eagled. Seeing as he had no intention of fucking her as part of the scene, he might as well do a good job with the flogging.

"What's your name, sub?" He asked while checking that the cuffs on her ankles and wrists were not too tight.

"Roxy, Sir." The excitement was apparent in her voice which drew a sigh from him.

"Do you think you did a good enough job bringing me off, Roxy?"

She looked at him wearily, shaken by his cold voice and dark glare. "I thought I did well, Sir."

"But not without me guiding you. That, to me, was a failure. You do know what that means?" His brow lifted in sardonic amusement. He hated using the sub like this and as a Dom it grated on him but he had no choice.

Her face fell and she whispered with

disappointment in her voice, "No fucking, Sir."

"Exactly. However, I might be moved to bring you off with my hands ... if my floggers don't do it for me."

Her eyes widened as she watched him select two long, black floggers. He swung them in his hand, snapping the strips together. She jerked at the sharp sound echoing in her ears.

"Don't worry, sub. I don't intend to hurt you ... much ... but I do promise pleasure. This will be an erotic flogging."

He'd decided on a double flogging to ease himself out of having sex with the sub. He might as well turn the debacle into a demonstration of his skill. His fluid arm movements weaved a form of the number eight in the air. Watching the sub, he followed with slow circles using only a slight twist of his wrists. Her trepidation morphed into excitement when he flung the floggers over his shoulders and approached her.

"Ooh," she moaned as he sensually ran his hands over her buttocks and then her stomach to fondle her breasts. His movements were calculated to arouse and entice without the usual excitement it offered him when he was with his wife. She'd ruined him for other women. Not that he minded. He was fully committed to his marriage and their love.

Damiano stepped back to stand with spread legs behind her. "Ready, sub?"

"Oh yes, Master Devil."

He swung the strands against her skin with light caresses, aimed at heating her skin. He circled her while swinging the floggers in beautiful seamless motion. It was continuous and smooth as it connected with her back, her buttocks, then her stomach, her abs, and her thighs. Her gasps grew louder as the strikes began to sting.

He threw the floggers over his shoulders and pressed lightly against her back. He squeezed her breasts while rubbing her clit. She thrashed against his hand. He chuckled and with a final pinch of her nipple and clit, he warned, "Now, Roxy, are you ready to scream?"

This time every hit was harder, aimed at

achieving the maximum impact as he circled her faster. She moaned and whimpered as the force of the hits intensified. Her body jerked with every strike. With the next round, the sting became a flashing burn.

"Oooowww!" Her cry rang through his ears.

"That's more like it, sub."

He circled her to stand behind her. He swung the floggers in a full circle, which lashed against her in a rotation of nonstop hits. As soon as the one flogger connected, the next one lashed at her skin.

"Ooowww! Fuck!" She screamed, writhing against the chains holding her in place.

"Now, sub, that is much better."

He repeated the same process on her buttocks. Her screams and sobs tore from her throat as she jerked against the chains.

"Owowoowey. Aargh."

"That was a good scream, Roxy. Deserving of a little reward, I think."

He flicked the floggers over his shoulders again and stepped closer to grab her burning, stinging cheeks in his hands and squeezed. *Hard.* She cried out and he laughed, which caused the spectators to join in and spur him on to continue.

"Behave, sub," he warned when she yanked on the chains.

Tracing a slow path toward her breasts, he pinched, alternating with rubbing his palms over them. She let out an elated sob when his finger circled her clit and rubbed it. He could smell her arousal and drove one finger inside her pussy. She was hot and soaked his finger instantly. She was helpless against his expertise and the way he played her. No one watching would guess that he was completely unmoved and his actions were purely technical, aimed to arouse.

"Shall we go for the finale, sub?"

"Oh fuck, Master Devil, I can't take much more. I need to come."

"And so you shall, Roxy," he promised with a devilish chuckle.

He started again and found his rhythm within the first two strikes. He circled to her front, smiling when she whimpered at the glint in his eyes.

"Yeah, sub, now the fun starts."

Damiano began with her thighs, working up to her stomach, and abs. The first strikes were soft, then stinging, then hard and ruthless. Her screams delighted the audience. They watched in awe when he flicked the floggers in tight circles—a movement that mesmerized them—all with precise flicks of his wrists. He spread his legs to brace himself.

"Here we go, Roxy," he warned, lowering his wrists and then flicked the floggers in a continuous circle against her nipples.

"Oooow! Fuck."

He aimed directly on her nipples. Her screams and cries incited the group to frenzy of lust. He moved the strikes to her stomach then back to her breasts, alternating in revolving circles. The strips landed with precision on the nerve spots of her belly, and finally, her pussy. His rhythm was smooth and constant, connecting with her pussy over and over at top speed.

She screamed as he alternated the strikes

between her nipples and her pussy until she shuddered uncontrollably.

"Please! I need to come!" She sobbed.

Pain had morphed into need—pure scorching need—long ago already. Her cries were of desperation. The heat of the burning lashes had warmed her blood and she'd been on the verge of a climax since he began hitting her breasts.

"Now, Roxy, you may come."

His voice was gruff as he aimed the floggers at her pussy, the hits were continuous—clit, labia, repeat. When her sobs turned to screams, he pulled his hits upward right at the end, ensuring the tips of the strips, stung just inside her pussy.

She exploded. Streams of clear liquid gushed from her as she squirted. He continued until she climaxed again and begged him to stop. The crowd erupted in applause, praising him for his skill. He handed the floggers to the coordinator and assisted the Dungeon Master in untying her.

He looked around until he found Vito watching him. The awe on his face would've been funny had Damiano not been so irritated and angry at their manipulation.

"Vito." His voice was sharp among the noise around them. "Take care of her. I need a drink."

"With pleasure." Vito didn't question Damiano's gruff order. They used to scene together often and he wouldn't mind giving the sub what she craved once she has recovered from the flogging.

Damiano didn't stop at the bar. He walked out of the club and didn't relax until he stood under a hot shower in the penthouse apartment he used when in the city. He kept his thoughts blank, stealthily locking the memory of the throat fuck away in the back of his mind. One never to be revisited.

Linzi Basset

CHAPTER FIFTEEN

"Since when do you smoke?"

Damiano looked up. It was obvious that his mind was elsewhere as he glanced at Kent, who was hovering in the doorway of his office at the Occhipinti head-office.

Kent was somewhat shaken when he looked into his eyes; a well of jet black ink. For the first time, he could see what made him such a good leader. That gaze was as fearsome as a tiger attacking.

A thin cigar hung from Damiano's bottom lip. Kent's gaze followed the small trail of smoke that escaped from the corner of his mouth, to dance its way to the ceiling.

Damiano's eyebrow raised in amusement at his reaction; but other than that—nothing, not a flinch, not a single damn emotion flashed in his eyes.

He waited until Kent came next to him where he stood by his usual spot, gazing out of the window.

"Part of the disguise, my friend. I hate these fucking things, but to make my *morphing* more believable, I had to become the same blackguard I was before." His voice was gruff and low. He rolled his eyes to the one corner. "Hidden camera," he muttered softly.

Kent nodded his understanding and kept his voice low. "Do you think this is gonna work?"

"It has to. Anything—to make Luca trust the change in me. I expected him to hand me the means to get that bracelet off Mason's arm after last night, but I've seen him twice this morning and nothing."

"Why after last night?"

Damiano's jaw became more rigid—if that was even possible. He shook his head. "Not something I intend to remember or talk about. I'm just glad you were still in New York and could come here today. Your presence might prevent me from choking Jay

Vick when he walks in here."

"Yeah, if I don't get to him first."

Damiano wanted to unsettle Jay and pacify Luca. Two flies with one swat. Jay was already weary of him and finding Kent here would put him on a back foot.

His cell vibrated in his pocket. He read the text from one of his newly appointed bodyguards from Bracus' team.

"Showtime. They just entered the building. It should take them less than five minutes to get here."

"Well, let's hope we pull this off. I hate that man, more than I thought possible and might just lose it when I see him."

"Keep your cool, Kent. You have it in you. Think of Mason. It's all that matters now."

He detected the sound of approaching footsteps and went to sit behind his desk. It was Kent's cue.

"You're a fucking asshat, do you know that, Colt?"

"Damiano, Kent. Colt is no more. I've fooled

myself too long. This is who I am. Who I was meant to be? Playing a Good Samaritan to the entire community—*Gesù*! If only you knew how I hated being Mr. Nice Guy all the time."

"Bullshit. I don't believe you. What fucking drugs has that shitfaced father of yours got you on?"

"Watch your mouth, young man!" Luca sneered from the door. "And leave my son be. He made his choices and it's time you—bunch of backwater people, accept it."

Damiano looked up. His first impulse was to tear into Jay Vick and beat him to a pulp for the trauma he'd put his wife and son through. It was sheer self-preservation and the picture of his son in his mind that kept him rooted in the chair.

"Well, well. Look who's here. Come in, Jayanni. You remember Kent Gibson, your *friend*, I imagine?"

Kent ran his hand through his hair a couple of times in quick succession—a gesture to calm himself. The stare he fixed on Jay could have frozen the Pacific.

"I'm no fucking friend of this shithead," Kent snarled in his former partner's direction before he turned to Damiano. "What the fuck is this? Are you now brushing shoulders with the same man who kidnapped your son? Get a grip, Colt! For fuck sake, what are you doing?"

"I told you, Kent, my name is Damiano. Remember it or you can get the fuck out of here, right now."

"You're a goddamned traitor and believe me, if this is who you associate with; then I'm done with you. *For good.*"

Luca and Jay barked with laughter. Their enjoyment at the scene they were witnessing was obvious in their expressions.

Kent turned to Jay. Damiano noticed the cold fury that burned with dangerous intensity in his friend's eyes.

Jay's laughter dried up when he too recognized the look in his former partner's eyes. He'd seen Kent explode just twice in the years they'd worked together, but he knew, just how dangerous the otherwise complacent man could be when angered.

Kent took a step toward Jay, a vein pulsing in his temple with his fists tightly clenched.

"You better wake up, Jay Vick and do it soon. See this as your one and only fair warning. Because believe me, *friend*, when I find you outside of this building, you won't live to see the next light." The promise was made with glacial intent and Damiano knew he meant every word he said. This was no play acting.

"Come now, Kent. Damiano forgave me, otherwise I won't be here. Why is your dander up?" Jay mocked him.

"You're nothing but a virus, Jay. You survive by killing—not just other people, but yourself too. You think you're soaring high now because you have these two men to hide behind? Beware, because it will drag you down. I know you, better than they—"

"Fuck you, Kent. You don't know me. Not the real me. You know who you believed I was. The role I was playing." Jay was annoyed when he found himself trembling at Kent's words, which further triggered his insecurities.

"No man can hide his true emotions under certain circumstances, Jay, and I was by your side to experience all of yours. You're about to come to a fall—"

"Shut the fuck up!" Jay shouted. His control was on the verge of snapping.

Kent continued unperturbed. "Do you know why? Because, sooner or later, your anxiety will get the better of you. You will begin to question everything. *Every* action and *every* intention. You had friends before; people who loved and respected you; who would've killed for you. Can you say the same for this man standing by your side?" Kent smirked at the expression on Jay's face. "Hah! I didn't think so."

"That's enough, Kent. If you can't accept my brother and the man I am *now*, you're not welcome here. And let me give you a warning too. Stay away from Jay. You know me well enough to know—I protect family at all cost," Damiano growled.

Luca gaped. He couldn't hide the surprise at Damiano's reaction. Maybe his doubts had been unfounded. For the first time since his son had walked back into the building, he relaxed his guard. Now he was content.

Kent seared the three men with a condescending look. He walked to the door, where he said, "There's a saying that the wheel turns. Well, Vitales, brace yourself, because I am going to be at the helm of turning that fucking wheel!"

Damiano didn't watch him leave; he kept his gaze on Luca and Jay. The smiles on their faces said it all. Their little act had been a success. Now he had to cement their confidence and trust in him.

"Fucking moron. It's time those Jacksonville losers realize I'm done with them." He appeared pensive for a moment. "Yeah, I think that's it. It's time to move on from there. My little wife and son have to join me here. It's time to live the good life."

"Now, that is the best thing I've heard in a long while." Luca beamed as he approached Damiano and thumped him on his back. "I think we should celebrate, don't you? Do you still have that one-hundred-and-fifty-year old Macallan whiskey in your bar?"

"Indeed, I do. Come, Jay, don't look so reserved. It's time to let bygones be bygones. We're twins and it's about time we get to know each other as brothers."

He got up and walked toward him with his hand held out. Jay searched his expression, but like always, it was blank and emotionless. He shook his hand.

"I find it hard to believe that you are ready to just forgive everything I did, Damiano. What game are you playing?"

"No game, Jayanni, but make no mistake, I will be watching you. *Very* closely. Step out of line just once, and you're done. I don't threaten, as Luca knows very well—I act. Don't fuck with me, brother, and we'll get along fine."

Jay nodded and took the tumbler Luca held out to him.

"Let's raise a toast. For the most feared Vitales

this country has ever seen." Luca couldn't contain his excitement. Everything was falling into place, much easier and quicker than he'd anticipated.

"Oh, Damiano. I believe I can hand this over to you now. All you need to do, to deactivate the trip switch in the bracelet, is to code in your birth date."

Damiano had difficulty keeping his expression unchanged but his heart threatened to jump out of his chest with joy. Now, his son would be safe.

He juggled the device a few times with his eyes searing Luca. "Just like that?"

Luca shrugged. "As you said, you're Damiano and back for good. Little Mason is the future of this family, so ... go ahead. Once it's done, you can let the little lady know to remove it."

"I'll get to it later. Let's celebrate first. Tomorrow, the three of us begin our strategy to fold the rest of the bosses in the mob. It's time for only one ruling family in the mafia. The Occhipintis."

Luca's eyes glimmered with greed. He'd never had such a vision. He'd been aiming at the Government, but combining that with what

Damiano was suggesting, would make him an even bigger force to be reckoned with.

Jay, on the other hand, watched his father with narrowed eyes. The glee in his expression was evident. There was a hint of the victory in his smile. And he didn't bother to hide the pride he felt for Damiano. Jay didn't like that he saw Mason as the future of their family. So far, neither one had made any commitment to what his position was going to be.

Damiano might intend to watch him closely, but he would be watching the two of them as well. This time, no one would fuck him over. He had made it into the hallowed walls of the crime family. He had no intention of failing to reach his goal ... or to leave again.

On the way to the hotel Kent struggled to let go of the fury inside him. His lips curled and his nostrils flared in memory of the self-righteous smile that Jay

Vick had sported. He was cognizant of the fact that hate colored one's soul with negative energy.

He had come to hate Jay Vick.

Would I feel anything if I killed him?

Nothing. Not one damn thing.

"It is time to end his reign of terror," he gritted out through clenched teeth.

"What's that, Sir?" The cabbie asked.

"Just thinking out loud."

He forced his anger and resentment down all the way to the hotel room. His beautiful sub was reading on the patio. Her face lit up when she saw him.

"You look stressed. Is everything okay?"

"Looking at your beauty makes everything perfect. Come here, my pet and kiss me."

The kiss they shared was one of companionship, mutual respect and finally of the warmth they shared for each other in their hearts.

He ran his finger over her cheek. A vision of a knife cutting into such perfection darkened his mind. He had to keep her safe. Jay Vick knew how to cut someone to leave a permanent scar. One that not even plastic surgery couldn't fix.

He didn't share Colt's belief that Luca and Jay would back down and stay out of their lives. Luca might, now that he had his son back at the helm, where he wanted him, but Jay? His soul had become black. He didn't need motivation for anything, except his own demented drive for power.

"This past week alone with you has been wonderful, Sharon and made me realize how much I've changed since I was married to my slave wife. Maybe it's been too long, or the fact that I had only been around submissives all these years, but it cemented the fact that I don't want or need that anymore."

"What are you saying? That it's over between us?" Sharon felt the world begin to dissolve under her feet.

"No, love. I'm mucking this up. That's not what I mean at all. I have noticed that you keep expecting me to fall back into a Master/slave role. Yes, love, I've seen those looks. You can relax,

Sharon. I am happy with my choice to have a normal Dom/sub relationship. Sexual domination only. I've outgrown the Master/slave dynamic. I want to see more of the cheeky and sassy woman that's coming back to life. I want you to challenge me—physically and emotionally and not wait for an order from me to do so. And, yes, I love the times you did just that—even in that subtle way of yours. I want us to have a normal life outside of the bedroom."

Her eyebrow lifted in a sensual sweep to her hairline. "Only the bedroom? Sooo ... if I were to seduce you here on the patio, you wouldn't ... oooh!" she shrieked when he ripped her dress off with one hard yank, then giggled when he pushed her down onto the chaise lounge after divesting himself of his clothes. "Whatever are you doing, Kent?" she asked breathlessly.

"Yes. My name, that's what I've been craving to hear from your sweet lips. Not only my Master or Master Kent. *Just* Kent."

She cupped his cheeks and looked at him with smiling eyes. "Are you sure about this? You're not just doing this to help me become a stronger person?"

"I'm doing this for selfish reasons, my love. I want to have freedom in our relationship. Not just for me, but you as well. You have too much passion and energy to be suppressed under another's will. I find that I want to be the recipient of that."

Sharon searched his eyes. "Kent?"

He smiled gently and leaned in to kiss her in a meshing of passion and need; a need that was borne from the emotions he couldn't deny any longer. Not to her, and not to himself.

"You're an amazing woman, Sharon. You've made me feel things I've never felt before," he said in a raw voice.

His arms folded around her and pulled her into a protective cocoon. He buried his face in her fragrant hair, to breathe in her familiar scent. Jasmine—the perfume she favored—mixed with her own spicy bouquet, was an accelerant that set alight the flames of lust in his mind. He smiled at her tenderly as he untangled her arms from around his neck to look into her eyes.

"You're so beautiful. A gift that keeps on giving. And I've barely unveiled you. I can't wait to unwrap the balance of your heart and soul; just like you have done with mine. I love you, Sharon. More than I thought possible."

"I can't begin to tell you how happy that makes me. You are my future, my love, and knowing that you love me ... god, that makes me the happiest woman on earth."

"Hm, now about that seduction you mentioned . . ."

"Well, if you would move off me, I might—"

"No, I'm quite comfortable where I am. Maybe we can leave your seduction for when we're back home. For now . . ."

Her carnal moan sounded in his ears when he pushed his cock, slowly, but firmly forward, until he was fully embedded within her wondrous satin folds, encasing every inch of him, pulling him deeper, as if she would draw him all the way inside her.

"That's the best feeling ever, honey; your hot, tight sheath hugging me tighter than a handmade glove."

He dragged her hands over her head to weave their fingers together as he pinned her gently to the chase lounge. He pulled back and began to slowly submerge his thick erection deep into her with steady rhythmic thrusts.

"Aahh, Kent, you feel so good. You know just how and where to ... mmm."

Kent's breathing turned choppy as he became consumed by passion. The hunger in him compelled a fervent moan from her lips as he plunged into her, thrusting harder, to the hilt against her wet pelvis, macerating any doubts that she might have had of the effect she had over him.

He had an urgent desire to free her from her past and alleviate the pain that still haunted her in her sleep. He longed for the day he would not be awakened by her thrashing and crying out to some unforgotten, painful memory.

Sharon wrapped her legs high around his

waist, tilting her hips in a trusting gesture of subjugation. He grunted as that small act nearly robbed him of his control.

Kent slumped on top of her, breathing harshly as he fought to bring his rampaging lust under control. This was a special moment in their lives. Not one to be anointed with a rough, hard fuck. She deserved more.

"Honey?" Sharon asked hesitatingly.

He lifted his head. "I love that, baby; when you call me 'honey' from your luscious lips." Her loving smile tiptoed through the chambers of his heart. "I meant what I said, Sharon. I love you and I want to marry you. *Soon.*"

Sharon was overcome with emotion and couldn't keep the tears from slipping from her eyes. Kent smiled.

"That's not the most romantic proposal I've ever heard," she smiled through her tears.

"No more tears, love."

"These are happy tears, honey. *You.* You make me so happy."

He felt her tremble against his body and he tightened his fingers around her hands. Watching her, he began to stroke his cock into her in a slow, steady rhythm. The moment her breathing accelerated and her pupils dilated, he felt the involuntary spasms around his hard shaft. Knowing she was on the edge of a climax, he powered into her, slamming his hips hard against her pelvis. Her cries sounded throughout the room, which he tampered with his mouth, as they both gave in and erupted with a ferocity that shook them to the core. They were lost, swirling in a wave of bliss so acute, both of them could do no more than just bask in the radiance that left them exhausted.

It was like the universe had adjusted the colors of the world overnight. Everything was brighter than it should be. The trees in the hotel garden were not just green, but radiant virescent hues that delighted Sharon.

That was what happiness and love did to a person. Kent smiled at the vivaciousness of the woman walking by his side as they left the hotel. It was time to go home and she was more excited than him.

She glanced at him before she got into the cab waiting for them at the curb.

"Are you sure, honey? I mean, your house is beautiful as it is."

"Yes, love. I want you to change everything to what you like. Most of the decor in my house dates back to my marriage. I meant it when I said it's time to move on. We need to put *our* stamp on the house. Yours and mine."

Sharon beamed with an ebullient smile that made her eyes shimmer like diamonds and brought out her porcelain beauty. Her fingers itched to start redecorating. It was her vocation. Interior designing. Converting Kent's home into *their* home was going to bring her for a lot of joy.

"Come on, daydreamer. I have a flight plan to keep."

Kent's voice yanked her from her reminiscence and with a quick kiss on his lips, she got into the cab.

"What now? I thought you were in a hurry?" She queried when he didn't follow her.

Kent looked around. He'd had an eerie feeling of being watched since they'd stepped outside. His gaze fell on a man leaning negligently against the lamp post across the street. The smirk on his face was discernible even over the distance that separated them.

He saluted him and made a point of looking at Sharon in the back of the cab before he swaggered off.

"Don't move, love. I'll be right back." Kent ordered before he sprinted across the street.

Kent's mind was filled with rage, like a ticking bomb waiting to explode. He careened into Jay from behind, slamming him against the wall of the building. He ignored the gasp of the woman passing by, witnessing the violent act. He yanked his arm back and pushed it upward, ignoring his enraged cry.

His silence, while he waited for Jay to catch his breath, was a sign of his rage. He didn't raise his voice but his muscles tensed and he got right into Jay's face for maximum impact.

"Now listen to me, you fucking useless piece of shit. Coming here to taunt me? Hah! You don't scare me. But you better take note of the warning I gave you yesterday."

"Come now, Kent. Like Damiano said, forget about how I managed to fool you for years."

Kent battled to control his temper. This time the smirk was on his face.

"You know what, that doesn't matter anymore. You were a brilliant surgeon and I respected you. You had a good name and future most men only dream about and you threw it away. And for what? To become a fucking thug? A gofer for every Tom, Dick and Harry in the mob?"

Kent had hit a sore spot and he could see the fury flare up in Jay's eyes. He retaliated with a sneer, "You think you're holier than thou?" He yanked his head toward the cab. "But that's the best you could do? Taking on Vitale's scraps? Can't say I blame you. She is a good fuck. Cunt and ass—I had them both," he jeered with a snide laugh. "Yeah, I've always been one step ahead of all of you. I was on Roberto's team when he came after Nolan. It was the best opportunity to get near Seth and I got to fuck your woman as a bonus."

Kent forced back his revulsion, remembering the state Sharon had been after Roberto had given her to his men.

"Boasting about raping a chained woman? How pathetic can you get? And Seth? Well you fucked that up really well, didn't you? You couldn't kill him even though you shot him in the back." Kent slammed the motherfucker's head into the wall when he tried to bear back.

"Let me go, you fuck! I'm bleeding," Jay wailed.

"You know what, making you weep like a little boy is just gonna be so pleasurable. And, I am going to, fucktard. It's become a necessity. You've proven to be is a coward who goes for women and innocent children. Jesus, look at you! I haven't even swung a punch yet and you are already quivering. You are nothing without the strength of Luca or Gianni behind you? Removing you from this earth isn't cruelty; it will be an act of mercy and justice, combined."

Kent stepped back and flung Jay's arm against the wall. Being in the public stayed his desire to end him there and then. Jay groaned but didn't move. With a disgusted snort, Kent turned away with a final warning, "Stay away from Jacksonville, Jay, and stay away from me and Sharon. Because as God my witness, the next time I run into you, I *will* make good on my promise."

He walked across the street, half expecting to feel the searing pain of a knife in his back at any moment. He got into the cab and took off without looking back.

CHAPTER SIXTEEN

"How sure are you about this, honey? I don't trust that man. What if he lied to you?"

Colt could see the panic in Ceejay's eyes and for once he struggled to set her mind at ease. He never trusted Luca, but he had to believe that he wouldn't lie to him in this. The repercussions for him were too high.

"I don't trust him either, baby, but he knows all too well what would happen if he lied. No, don't worry."

"I don't believe I'm hearing this! What about everything else he's done to you *and* to me? Don't tell me you're going to let him get away with this, Colt!"

Colt sighed and ran his hands over his face. He'd only been back at the mob a week and he could already feel the tension in his body. Because of the threat to Mason, he'd not been sleeping. He felt drained and stressed—tired beyond imagination. Not just physically, but emotionally as well. He was on the brink of exhaustion, hoping for a respite from the storms raging inside him, but he knew until he closed this chapter of his life, there would be no rest for him.

"Ceejay, please understand. There are a lot at stake. No," He placed his fingers over her lips. "Listen to me, baby. I need to know what demented plans Luca has in place and put an end to them before he destroys everything. All I ask is that you remain patient and give me the time to do this in the right way. I do promise you this; Luca Vitale will pay for what he has done to us and our family"

She came willingly into his embrace and clamped her arms around his back. He could feel her trembling. His eyes closed. It didn't take a genius to know what was in the back of her mind.

He tilted her chin and kissed her deeply.

"I love you, my beautiful, sweet wife. Always

remember that."

"I know, honey and I . . ." she fiddled with her hair. "I know I said that you ... but I can't help ... I hate the thought . . ."

"Ceejay, stop. No matter what happens in the coming weeks, my heart belongs to you. As do my body. I have no intention of fucking another woman—even with your permission."

Her eyes filled with tears. He cuddled her against his chest and buried his face in her hair. The memory of the scene in the club threatened to escape from the depths of his mind, but he punched it right back. Soon, he'll be able to forget it all together.

"Come, let's get that fucking bracelet off our son's arm."

They found Quade and Maxine in the kitchen where their little girl, Chelsea and Mason were playing together.

"Dada!" Mason screamed and ran on his short legs to catapult himself into his father's arms. Colt hugged him so tight that he began to squirm.

"Mason miss Dada," he complained with a toothy smile.

"I missed you too, tiger. Have you been a good boy and looked after Mommy while I was at work?"

His head bobbed up and down while he peered at Ceejay, like he was expecting her to deny his claim. She laughed and then nearly burst into tears again when he leaned over to wipe the tears still visible from her cheeks.

"Mommy huwt?" He wanted to know, with his head tilted to the side. The small frown between his brows was a mirror of his father's, who looked at her too.

She shook her head. "No, my love. It's tears of joy."

"Joy?" What's joy?"

"Happy, little one. Mommy is very happy."

"Goody!" He chirped and clapped his hands.

The movement drew Colt's gaze to the bracelet and he went to sit at the kitchen table. He stabbed the code into the small square amulet he took out of his pocket. He hesitated and looked at Quade.

"You're the only one who knows Luca and if it's safe to trust him, Colt. I can't tell you what to do," he answered the unasked question.

Mason complained loudly when Colt reached for the bracelet.

"Daddy needs to fix it, son. The clasp is broken."

"Oookay," he conceded with an unsure look.

Colt took a deep calming breath before he reached for the clasp and with a quick yank removed it from his arm. He inspected it immediately but the needle was still secure in its slot. The moment was too much for Ceejay, who burst into tears and took Mason in her arms to hug him tight.

"I want you to have this tested, Quade. I want to know if there is really anything in that needle and if so, what it is."

"I'll get it to the lab in the city. The head scientist, Rob Cole, is a good friend of mine." He looked at his cousin with searching eyes. "What are you planning to do if there is a virus in here?"

"Then Luca's final moments wouldn't be as

painless and quick as I had originally intended. He would feel the pain and suffering he put all of us through."

Colt had made up his mind long ago about the man whose seed gave him life. Not his father. He'd never thought of him as his father, and he never would. This act had been the last straw.

Ceejay was still struggling to control her emotions. Colt rubbed her hands where they were clenched together around their little boy's body.

"Baby, let go. You're upsetting him and he doesn't understand why. He's safe now. Let go," he cajoled her.

With a final hug and a kiss on Mason's brow, she lowered him to the floor. He immediately rushed back to Chelsea, to join her in playing with the blocks on the floor.

"Come. Let's go for a walk."

Colt led her to a beautiful, tranquil spot under a large oak tree on the banks of the river. He sat down and pulled her onto his lap. They stared out over the water in peaceful harmony. Relaxed and relieved for their child's safety at long last. He stroked her arms.

"I'm not blind to the emotional pain that still seeps through your words when you remember Dean. It hurts to hear them. I see the suffering in your eyes. I am in awe of your bravery, tenacity, and ability to face each day with such passion. You hold on like a fighter; every morning rising with renewed fervor. It's nearly over, my love. I wish I could go back and change things for you, but I can't. All I can offer you is a brighter horizon, a hope that one day we'll be free of all the ugliness that surrounds *me*."

His voice cracked and he swallowed back the regret that *he* was at the core of how her life had been molded—however unaware.

Ceejay turned in his arms and pressed her lips against his. It wasn't a kiss. It was a gesture of warmth.

"No, honey. You're not to blame. Don't ever think that you are. And yes, I still think about Dean and how he and Stephen died. It was ... ugly, cruel, and so unnecessary to kill an innocent child. That's the only regret I have. I stopped remembering Stephen as the man I used to love the day I found out how he'd deceived me. *He*, ultimately, was to blame for Dean's death. And my love, however sad it was, if it didn't happen, we would never have met. I wouldn't be married to the most wonderful man, with a gorgeous son."

Colt looked out over the field of daffodils on the other side of the river, a sunny yellow blanket. They were many, but so delicate, and he imagined their gentle swaying in the breeze was a wave like tomorrow was guaranteed. They stood rooted, soaking in the sunshine, and taking in yesterday's rain through their fine roots. If only life was that simple. His arms tightened around Ceejay. He needed to protect them and he wouldn't stop until they were safe.

Yeah. And the only way to make that happen is to get rid of the festering puss in my life. Luca Vitale.

Damiano sat behind his desk, his eyes were hooded. His expression, as usual, was dead-pan. It irritated Luca that he couldn't read him. He never could. Not even when he was a teenager.

"How was it, visiting your son?" He asked colloquially, trying to draw some kind of reaction from him. He grunted when it bore no fruit. Luca was aware that he'd gone to remove the bracelet because Damiano had given him a brusque warning when he'd left.

Damiano allowed his gaze to slide over the man so feared and revered by all in the mob. He might have the ability to awaken the fear of God in men lesser than him, but Damiano didn't see it. Without his muscle surrounding him, he was less than powerless. He was so sick and tired of their propaganda. The fear and misdirection of the gangsters. They tell you who to hate, who should live and die. Luca was the master at it. To make those around him believe how the enemy was barbarous and the powers that controlled their lives were heroes.

And he, Damiano, had become like him all those years ago. More so because he didn't need bodyguards to do his bidding. He took action himself. Which was why he was now feared more than Luca in the realm that was the mafia.

"My visit with my family is of no concern to you." Damiano replied, lighting a thin cigar. He puffed on it while watching Luca.

Vito arrived with a brief knock on the door. His expression was surly and angry. When Jay followed close on his heels, Damiano knew why. The two men had met the day Jay had arrived and taken instant dislike to each other.

Damiano suppressed a pleased grin. His plan was coming to fruition. Vito would be the only one walking out of this meeting feeling empowered. The play-off between Luca and Jay was about to commence. He was aware that there was animosity between the two half-brothers because of supposed promises made by Luca. Damiano intended to use that to kickstart their demise.

"Let's begin. We have a lot to discuss and I

need your full attention."

He looked between the men who silently offered their agreement. Luca remained mute. He'd expected to share power with Damiano, but he'd made it clear it was either him in charge or Luca. He refused to share his position.

"The *Cosa Nostra* as we know, protect racketeering and secondary activities such as gambling, loan sharking, drug-trafficking and fraud. The Occhipintis have become known as the *mafiusu* in the business. We stand for what the original Sicilian mafia families strived to achieve. It's time to kick our position up a notch."

"A notch? In case you missed it, son, we're at the top already," Luca smirked.

That earned him a demeaning look.

"And that's good enough for you? Hm, seems you're losing your touch, Luca."

"Now, listen here—"

"In here, *I* am the boss, Luca, so *tenere la cazzo bocca chiusa!*"

Luca's face turned crimson, his eyes popped

and the anger was visible in the swelling veins in his neck.

Damiano didn't miss the enjoyment on Jay's face, bearing witness to the mighty Luca being cut down to size. The eagerness to gain power made men predictable and easy to manipulate. He was glad his estimation of the silent battle between the two was accurate. Jay could already smell victory.

Bah! Your turn is coming, bastard!

"What are your plans, Damiano?" Vito asked with eager curiosity.

"Full control—over every branch of mafia family in the US. There should be one voice in control, who makes the decisions and rules over the mob in this country."

"And that voice would be yours, I imagine?" Jay's voice was gruff.

Damiano shrugged. His voice was coldly indifferent. "The Occhipinti family and by default, of course, mine."

"Very commendable prospect, my son, but completely unachievable," Luca rasped, although his gaze sharpened at the possibility.

"Is it?" Damiano said. The smirk on his face made Luca sat upright.

"Just how do you propose to get twenty-five bosses of *Cosa Nostra* families to give up such power? Not to mention the other four main mafia families in New York. Those devils will never bow to you, Damiano." Luca said with an expression of ridicule on his face.

"That has always been your problem, Luca. You think too small. I've never backed away from a challenge and this is something I *will* achieve. Either you stand by my side, or you *vaffanculo.*"

Luca sat back in his chair.

"I already have the buy-in with the Russo family." Damiano laughed at Luca's expression. "And the Marino's are discussing it already."

"I don't know what you did or how you got Joey Russo to agree to bow down to your rule, but if he's in, the others will follow," Vito exclaimed. He could barely contain his excitement.

Luca stared at him with narrowed eyes. Jay

followed the discussion quietly, but it was clear that he stored every piece of information in his mind.

"What did you do, Damiano? What promises did you make?"

"Not promises, but intent of change. The mafia is going to become more than a crime organization. We're going to turn it into such a lucrative enterprise that everyone will want to jump on board. I am offering the top five a seat on the board of directors with equal share in profits."

"What! Are you crazy?" Luca exploded. "We are at the top because we have the highest profit. Why the fuck would we want to share with them?"

"Because, my dear Luca, with them at the helm, together we will be able to achieve so much more. You wanted to play at politics? Well, just how much more powerful do you think we will be in unity? We will have the entire country eating out of our hands without becoming involved in the propaganda of the Government."

That left the three men pensive as they thought it over.

"Now, I need the strongest team around me to get this in place as soon as possible. With immediate effect, Vito will take over from Luigi Campo as consigliore."

"Now just wait a minute, here. I promised Luigi that he'd not be ousted—"

"Well, I guess you shouldn't have made promises that you can't keep. *Silenzioso*, Luca. It's not up for debate. I've made my decision. I will leave it to you to explain his position to him. You can find some other menial position for him. As a consigliore, Luigi failed miserably."

Vito smiled broadly. The announcement was a victory in his opinion.

"You, Luca, may decide whether or not you're going to support this endeavor and I will gladly involve you in the discussions with the top families. If not ... stay the fuck out of my way."

"Relax, son. I happen to think it's a brilliant idea. You just caught me by surprise."

"Very well. For now, that's it. We will discuss more details tomorrow. Any questions?"

"Where do I fit into this plan of yours, Damiano?" Jay snapped. He simmered with anger at being ignored so blatantly.

"You? Well, Vito's region would require a new caporegime, so I suggest you get up to speed quickly. I need him by my side pronto."

"You're fucking crazy," Jay managed to sneer. He was livid at the insult.

"Why, my dear brother, you have to start somewhere and what best way to learn than to become a caporegime and learn from the best one in the family?"

"Me a capo? Are you fucking crazy?" he spattered with anger. "Luca, tell him," he demanded.

"Tell him what, son? I told you, he has the power and will take us to grander heights and that's exactly what he's doing."

"I'm not going to become a useless capo! You had intimated that I would be leading side by side with him!"

Damiano barked out a laugh. "You? By my side? What a fucking joke. Not until you have what it takes, Jayanni. Your actions over the past two years have proven that you're a hothead. You need to learn how to lead. Killing? Yeah, I guess you're good at that, but let's be honest, any lackey can off anyone. Leading an empire such as this? It takes a real man to do that."

"You bastard. Who the fuck do you think you are?"

"Why, I thought you knew when you came here, Jayanni? I'm Damiano Vitale, also known as the Devil's Spawn. The Don of the Occhipinti family." He leaned forward and said with narrowed eyes. "And, my dear brother, this time, I'm here to stay. So, I'm afraid if you had any delusions about being the one in charge ... hahaha ... you'll need to unseat me. And, believe me, Jayanni, you don't have what it takes." Damiano mocked him.

Jay stormed out of the office with the laughter of his nemesis ringing in his ears—finally coming to the realization that Luca had played him. Damiano had treated him like the court jester. Perhaps it was his way of taking revenge on Jay for what he'd done over the past two years. But none of that mattered in his mind, except the shattering of his only dream.

"They all will pay for this humiliation. *All of them.* No one treats Jayanni Vitale like a fool!"

CHAPTER SEVENTEEN

At moments like these, Damiano's rage turned chillingly cold. This change was ephemeral. Vito had seen that godless look before. His knuckles were white from gripping the phone too tight; a sign that his fury was going to boil over.

'*This is a first*', Vito thought. He'd never seen Damiano struggle so hard to keep a lid on his anger. He was on the verge of losing it.

"Yeah, he's the villain in his own story." Damiano's voice was clipped with frozen disdain. "Leave it with me. Thank you for reporting back to me so quickly."

"Anything I can help you with?" Vito asked when the cell phone clattered on the desk. He frowned at the vacuous look in Damiano's eyes. He blinked and it was gone.

"No," he said curtly. "Where is Jayanni?"

"I have no idea. Since he stormed out of here yesterday, no one has seen him."

"Get hold of him. I want someone keeping an eye on him all the times, Vito. I don't trust him. He's volatile and likely to be a danger to all of us."

"Yeah." Vito grimaced. "Especially since the meeting yesterday didn't go as he expected. I still find it hard to believe that you've just forgiven him. After all he's done to you and Ceejay?"

The dark, foreboding eyes returned—pitch black, fathomless—like looking into an abyss. It was this unknowable part of Damiano, the small piece welded unmovable into a crease of his consciousness that beat slowly in a dormant malevolence. It took possession of Vito's mind and sent chills up his spine.

"Fuck it. It's irrelevant now, Vito. I have only one goal and that's to turn this family into a force of nature. He, unfortunately, doesn't have what it takes and after yesterday, he knows it."

"That's how you intend to take revenge on him. *Cazzo*, that's brilliant! You'll break him down slowly, chip away at his self-confidence. That'll serve him right."

"He's a weakling. I don't have time for slackers. He'll realize soon enough he's no patch against me. His whole life he's been ruled and controlled by others. He's a follower. He'll never be a leader."

"Then why make him a capo?"

Damiano didn't respond.

"Of course! You want him to fail."

"Do as I said, Vito. Find Jayanni and make sure we know every move he makes."

"On it. I'm outta here."

Damiano replayed his conversation with Quade in his mind. It had been interrupted when Vito had walked into his office.

"You, know, until I spoke with Rob, I didn't believe that Luca Vitale could be that heinous."

"Are you saying it was the pox virus in that needle?"

"Yes, but not exactly."

"Whaddaya you mean?"

"It seems the formula that Carmen Oliver handed over to Julio Cortez wasn't the real thing. According to Rob, who was on the team that worked on its development with her, it was deliberate. No one was allowed to leave the lab with any of their notes. It was a decoy. The only complete formula of the pox virus is still kept in a locked and controlled environment in the lab."

"So, she fucking died for nothing?"

"Yeah, so it seems."

"Then what was in that needle?"

"Nothing more than the common flu, but Luca didn't know that."

"Yeah. He believed it was the pox virus and he had no qualms about using it on my child!"

The ringing of his phone yanked him back to reality. His eyes narrowed when he answered the call.

"Seth, I trust you have good news?" He listened intently, a smirk forming around his lips as he listened.

"And you're at the location now? Good. Get hold of Quade. We need to get Rob Cole involved before you take over that lab. I want everything they've worked on, confiscated and then ... blow up the fucking building."

A deep, volcanic rage began to ooze like molten lava through him, consuming all rationale in its unstoppable path.

"You should never have targeted my son, Luca. You knowingly used, what you believed to be the actual pox virus ... well, you fucking monster that was the last straw." The words tore open a seam of seething vengeance laced with such a toxic hatred that it filled Damiano with fear that it would loosen his tenuous grip on self-preservation which had guided him through the labyrinth of the mob. "Now that I'm in control of all your devious plans, I don't need to postpone your demise."

Damiano fed off his anger as he made another phone call.

"Bruce? Where is he? Good. This is what I want you to do . . ." He quickly gave detailed instructions. He shut down all emotions to prepare for the confrontation ahead. It was the first time he would kill a man with deliberate intent.

It was no use trying to contain his anger. He didn't want to anymore. The veneer of *La vera famiglia* had finally worn thin.

He was determined when Bruce's text came through an hour later.

It was time.

"What is the meaning of this, Damiano? And why the fuck are we meeting in a back alley?" Luca spat when Damiano arrived.

He smirked at Luca. "You're asking me? *You?* The most feared Don of all times? Haven't you ended countless men's—or no, what do you call them again—ah yes, *douche bags*, lives in alleys such as these?"

"What the fuck are you talking about?" He snapped ferociously. An uneasy feeling was creeping up his spine, Fear; it set his heart hammering against his ribs. Damiano's face was closed off. His demeanor was rigid, cold and it scared the hell out of Luca.

He glanced sideways at the bulky shape of Damiano's bodyguard, who had picked him up from his house under the guise of an invitation from his son to join him for dinner. The reason why he'd told Tony to stay behind. Damiano was negligently leaning against the car, watching them.

The yellow lights above a doorway, a little further down the street, flickered, casting an ominous glow through the darkened alley.

The wind howled around the corners, whipping up any unmoored detritus and thrashing it against the narrow width of cracked and spoiled concrete that lay underfoot.

"Are you threatening me, Damiano? Me? Luca Vitale?"

Damiano smirked as he looked around. "See anyone else here?"

Luca's fuse began to spark like fireworks in a chilled autumn breeze before he exploded with unrestrained fury.

"*Figlio di puttana!* You've lost your mind. What's this about, Son?"

"You know, I could never figure out why you continued to call me Son, especially now, after what you did to *my* son. You, Luca Vitale, have never been a father to me."

"So, this is what it's all about? The bracelet? I gave you the means to remove it!" Luca threw back.

"Too little, too late. Ceejay could've removed that fucking thing before I could warn her, but you didn't care."

"Well, that's not true. I do care about you, which is why I want you by my side," he attempted to cajole Damiano.

"Funny thing is ... hahaha ... he would've ended with nothing more than a flu."

Luca went cold. He could already see all his plans to control the country crumble to pieces. "What are you saying?"

"I had the contents of that needle analyzed, Luca. It seems Carmen Oliver was clever enough to fool you. Something you should've realized. The bio-chemical faculty is very careful with their research. The original formula, the only one that exists, is safely locked away in the research lab."

"You're lying." He said with a smile, scrambling to find a way to appease Damiano. "Come now, let's just forget about all the unpleasantness and go to dinner."

Damiano snorted. "The Occhipintis are experts at extraction, aren't they? You take hold of the beast by the jaw and remove its tongue. After that it's easy to subdue and defeat the others." He laughed. "Who said defeating evil isn't going to be fun? Yeah, I have every intention of ridding the universe of *you*."

Luca exploded in a froth of Italian expletives. Damiano just watched him, as stoic as a monolith, unblinking against his onslaught.

"You won't get away with this, Damiano. No one will believe my death was an accident!" He raged, looking around wildly for an escape. Bruce straightened and tensed, preparing for him to run.

"No? Isn't this how it's usually done? You, know, dismembering the body and dumping it, like bloody buckets of chum, off a boat, fifty miles out to sea? I could have your hands and head stored in a freezer somewhere between here and New Hampshire. But I won't. Your death will look like an assassination. I want your body found. You, Luca Vitale, are going to be my message to the rest of the wise guys."

Luca had gone pallid. His hands clenched and unclenched as he shuffled around. He knelt, pretending to tie his shoelaces, growling when Damiano chuckled.

"Come now, Luca. Do you really think I'm that stupid? Yeah, I know you're carrying a knife, but I came prepared."

Luca straightened with a knife gleaming in the dim light. It was a Sabatier, a single piece of finely honed, razor-sharp, carbon stainless steel, a neat six- inches long. Damiano had felt the cutting edge of that blade during his training. The one thing Luca excelled at, was a knife fight.

Luca approached him carefully, watching his every move. He ground to a halt when Damiano pulled out his own knife. Luca's eyes widened as he watched him weigh it in his hand. It was a killer's knife, serrated to rip through flesh and bone like shark's teeth.

"*Che non va*? Forgot that you taught me how to fight with a knife?"

Luca's lips flattened into a straight line. The memory of how expertly Damiano could handle a knife at a precocious age of eighteen, sent a hot shard of fear through his bowels.

"Yeah, I daresay I was an equal match for you ... then. Now? Well, let's see, shall we?"

The knives gleamed in the moonlight. Luca knew that only one would walk away from this. Damiano didn't move, just waited patiently. With a primal growl, Luca charged and swung the knife. He was fighting for survival. Damiano dodged to the side in one fluid move, taunting him as Luca swiveled back in his direction. His eyes were menacing, blazing red and his features were indistinguishable in the darkened alley. Luca charged again, grunting when a sharp searing pain sliced through his side.

"*Cazzo!*" He exclaimed when his hand came away bloodied from the deep cut in his side.

"Did you think I would make this easy on you? Oh, no. You're gonna feel pain and I'm not going to stop until you're cut to ribbons and bleeding like a butchered pig."

Luca charged with a mighty cry, thrusting blindly. Both knives met in the air with a resounding 'clang'. He could feel himself tiring. With renewed vigor, he slashed his blade back and forth but without any success—Damiano had mastered the knife warfare.

He screamed when Damiano laughed. "Playtime is over, Luca." Then he began slicing at Luca's body with every swipe of his arm. Blood seeped through Luca's white shirt and soon it turned into a crimson soaked canvas.

"Any last words, Luca?"

He looked at Damiano and knew he was facing his final moments on earth. His expression was pure hatred—the first time he allowed his emotions to show. The knife glittered ominously in Damiano's hand, dripping with his blood.

"I'm your f-father, Damiano," he stuttered—a note of desperation and pleading filtered through the syllables.

"My father? Don't make me laugh, Luca. You're a snake—an evil. Do you know why?" He asked colloquially, walking in a circle around him. "They don't require love to raise their offspring. They don't have the ability to feel love, only to survive.

Like you—fucking psychopath that you are. You've never experienced any emotion. Not for your wife and sure as hell not for Vito or me, for that matter."

Luca lunged and sliced horizontally in a wide arc ... and missed. He screamed when Damiano stepped in and slashed the knife deep into his side to sever the muscle that held his viscera in place. He stumbled back, trying to push the protruding intestines back into the gaping wound. The calculating way Damiano circled him brought the realization home that *this was it*. He was looking death in the eye.

Damiano continued unperturbed. He wasn't even breathing hard. "Now, here's the thing, Luca. If we don't take the threat of psychopaths like you seriously, they will continue to dominate our world, driving us into a hellish dystopia. Just like you did to me and Ceejay. You can deny it all you want but you've exulted in the pain and emotional distress you've caused us over the years. Playing us like puppets. *Cazzo!* You have no morals and because of that, no restraints."

"Stop, please. I'm sorry. All I wanted was to have my sons by my side." Luca was now begging for his life.

"Don't bother with an apology, Luca, because it doesn't mean shit coming from you. Do you want to know how you're gonna die? Hmm? I'm going to leave you here to bleed out. *Alone.* Like you deserve. No one is going to cry and mourn your death. Instead they will be filled with jubilation."

In a final attempt to save himself he lunged toward Damiano. This time Damiano blocked his arm and stepped into him. Luca's eyes widened when he felt the knife meet his flesh, as the tip of the blade sliced through skin, muscle, and sinew. He puffed out a scream. He felt the knife twist as Damiano pushed it deeper and deeper.

Damiano watched the fear in Luca's eyes, his mouth wide open in reflex to the pain. Damiano felt nothing. No anger, no guilt, and no regret. He twisted the knife and tore away at muscle and sinew.

"*Brucia all'inferno*, Luca," he growled. With brute strength, he thrust the knife all the way into his body, ripping, slicing, and tearing away at his flesh.

Luca's cry was no more than guttural chokes, mixed with an agonized moan. Damiano pulled the blade out and watched the once mighty Don of the Occhipintis, sinking to his knees, his face contorted in a painful grimace. He convulsed and shuddered like a rabid animal. His dark blood flowed freely from the gaping hole in his stomach onto the alleyway. The cascade of his life source trickled out of his wounds.

Damiano turned away when his pleading became quieter, the coppery tang of blood tingled his nostrils. He nodded to Bruce as he got in his car. His voice was the last thing Luca would ever hear.

"Leave him to bleed out. It shouldn't take too long."

Luca crumbled to the ground, struggling to breathe. The light dimmed and the sounds became muffled, like he was swimming underwater. Aside from the beat of his heart, no muscle moved. It pounded to a rhythm of the words of his execution, of the cold steel and, Damiano—the judge and jury.

Luca felt himself grow weaker and weaker. His breathing turned haggard and shallow. He looked up to the sky. The moon looked pale and wan. It hung above him like a specter. Silhouetted against it, stood the walls of the dark and dank alleyway. His dying place.

"No one should ... die ... alone," he groaned and gurgled on his own blood; the light in his eyes shimmered one final time, before it went out.

For good.

Linzi Basset

CHAPTER EIGHTEEN

Jacksonville ... 3 weeks later

Jay stood hidden amidst the dense shrubs on one side of the garden. It was quiet in the early afternoon. Nothing moved, other than the slight breeze. He cast his eyes upward. The blue sky peeked from above his green camouflage. His heart thumped against his chest. He tried to calm himself in an order to ease his breathing.

The anger, at yet another betrayal, was numbing. The only person he'd considered a true friend, who had patiently mentored him over the past couple of years, turned out to be no better than Gianni and Luca Vitale; his greed for power was all encompassing.

Jay should've seen it coming. They were all

the same. Even Damiano.

"The fucking fraud!"

He had been pretending for years! His desire to turn the mob into an almighty unit was nothing but a fluke to fool Luca.

"Yeah, Colt Fargo never fucking existed. He's fooled everyone. He wants it for himself. All the power and for that he had to destroy Luca."

And now that Luca was dead, his real ambitions had been exposed. The mob had been turned over to the Devil's Spawn. He had become it—he embodied it, in the true sense of the word; cold and calculating, dismembering the mafia with the precision of a surgeon, piece by piece.

"And they're all too fucking stupid to stop him. No, they'll bow and scrape their knees to stay on his good side. Bah!" He spat into the ground in front of him.

He scowled at the thought as he perused his surroundings. Everything was quiet. The farmhands were out in the field, busy with harvesting. *She* would be alone inside.

Luca's death still haunted Jay. It was shocking and all too sudden—too blatant. No one said it out loud, but everyone speculated that Damiano himself had taken out Luca Vitale. But again, when he mentioned it to *him*, he had scoffed at the absurdity of the idea.

"You're grasping at straws, Jay. Luca had many enemies, especially after the LA meeting. Everyone suspected he was the one who wanted to wage a biochemical war."

"And you truly believe it was one of the other families that offed him?"

"Who else? Drop it—"

"Jesus! Not you too! It's him. I'm telling you, Damiano killed Luca."

"C'mon, Jay. Why would he do that? He had Luca's full support and backing. No, it was someone who'd had enough of his conniving and underhanded dealings; cutting the rest of the mob out."

Jay decided to keep his thoughts to himself.

"When are you pulling me back in? I'm not going to be left out in the open to swing in the wind."

The brief silence should've warned him, but he trusted this man. He'd believed they had formed a bond.

"I don't know yet. Things have changed, as you very well know and I have to tread very lightly myself. With Luca gone ... my position is precarious too, to say the least," he hedged.

"You bastard! You're backstabbing me, too!"

"I'm what? Get a fucking grip, Jayanni. Being a capo isn't so—"

"Fuck you! Fuck the whole lot of you. You better start looking over your shoulder because you're fucking gonna be next. I will be the Don of the Occhipintis and nobody is going to stand in my way. NOBODY!"

Jay was out to prove that Damiano's loyalty didn't lie with the family. He was adamant in his quest to unseat him. His first impulse had been to use the virus in the same way that Luca had intended, but Damiano had turned over all the prototypes that Luca had been developing, over to the Government. That move had a bigger impact than anyone could have ever have foreseen. He had the ear of the President himself—a revered hero in all their eyes—at least that's what the rumors were.

Now, it was time to unmask Damiano's true nature to those who mattered. The moment his friends started dropping dead, he'd be back in Jacksonville in a flash where he was vulnerable.

"Yeah, you bastard. Then, it will only be you and me. And this time, you won't see me coming."

He looked at his watch. The corner of his mouth twitched into an unconscious smirk to combine with the cold, pathological detachment in his eyes. He drew in a deep breath of the fresh air, savoring the moment.

It is time.

Something set Kent on guard the moment he opened the front door. It could have been a smell or the temperature being too cold—like a window had been left open.

Instinct warned him not to call out to Sharon. He closed the door silently behind him. He stood quietly with his eyes closed, like Seth had taught him to, allowing the nuances of the surroundings to filter into his mind. He disconnected from everything but the ever-present sound of his drumming heart. Then he heard it—a smothered sound, no more than a soft sigh, caught his attention.

The kitchen. It came from there.

He took out his cell and sent a message to Parnell.

He's here.

They'd all been on tenterhooks since Luca's death. Colt had warned them that Jay had once again vanished.

He'd been expecting him. His gut instinct had warned him that Jay would target him first. Jay was, if nothing else, predictable. His only goal now would be to discredit Colt as the leader of the Occhipinti crime family. And if he came running when his friends were in danger, that would prove his point.

But Kent knew—this was personal. Jay hated

being ridiculed. The way he'd bested him outside of the hotel in New York had been enough to trigger his hatred.

Apart from that, it was almost like he had something to prove to Kent; like he was better than him at *something*. He used to resent Kent's popularity amongst the patients.

He began making his way toward the kitchen, wondering where the bodyguard was. They had agreed to keep their loved ones safe and Bracus had sent his best teams to protect them. Chances were that Jay had already killed the guard.

He tried to ignore the tight feeling in his chest. It was the first time that someone he loved deeply was in danger. Kent had never before felt such dread. He suppressed the thought that Sharon might already be dead.

No. He would keep her alive to taunt me; to weaken me. Remember Seth's lessons, Gibson. Remain calm. Detached. Don't let him force your hand!

Not knowing where she was tore at his

insides. He held his breath and listened. His emotions didn't reflect on his facial muscles. His complexion remained normal; his eyes steady. With a deep breath, he stepped into the kitchen.

His gait was casual without hesitation as he walked in a couple of steps, taking in the scene without turning his head. His heart hammered when he noticed the bodyguard on the other side of the large table, his chest covered in blood. Sharon was tied up in one of the kitchen chairs with a cloth gag tied over her mouth. She looked disheveled but he couldn't detect any bruises or blood in the brief glance. Tears ran down her cheeks. She shook her head wildly when she saw him.

Kent recognized the horror in her eyes. He smiled gently. "It's okay, love. Be calm. I'm here."

"Well, well, it's about time. I was just about to start having fun with this whore of yours." Jay snorted when he noticed Kent glance toward the guard. "Forget about that loser. He's as dead as the past."

"Yeah, I can see that. Shot in the back by a

coward like you."

Kent took a chance taunting him, especially as he stood behind Sharon but he had to keep him occupied until Parnell arrived with help. They'd agreed beforehand if anyone raised the warning, one would arrive with a chopper and medical assistance while the other arrived with help on foot. With Jay, they knew it was better to be prepared.

"I'm no fucking coward. You don't scare me, Gibson. You and your *buddies*—with all your ops and military experience—are no match for me. Yeah, my friend, I've got you right where I want you now."

"First of all, you piece of shit, I am not your *friend*. You're a degenerate; a fucking no good, useless snail crawling along, leaving a trail of slime."

Jay's only reaction was to laugh, although the glimmer in his eyes was proof that Kent's taunt had hit home. His laugh morphed into a smirk as he ran his hands over Sharon's body and squeezed her breasts so hard that her garbled scream echoed in the room.

Kent surged forward. He didn't see the gun

but felt the sharp pain before the explosive sound of the shot mingled with Sharon's suppressed screams. The bullet had penetrated his left thigh. From the tingling burn, he knew it was no more than a flesh wound.

"You think you can best me? Fuck you and fuck all the motherfuckers you call friends. This whore of yours?" Jay taunted, yanking her head back with his hand fisted around a clump of hair. "I'm gonna cut her face to shreds and then see how you live with that regret for the rest of your life."

With those words, he pressed a knife against her cheek, keeping the gun trained on Kent.

Sharon tried to stay calm. She could feel the blade against her throat as she stared helplessly at the man she loved, more than life itself.

Kent saw the fear in Sharon's eyes and could detect the trembling of her body from where he stood. Jay tipped her chin up into the sharpened edge and chuckled in glee at the small stream of blood that trickled from the cut. Kent felt the fury rising inside him. He focused his eyes on Jay and didn't flinch at the cruel smile that stretched out across his gaunt features. He was about to cut her. Kent growled a warning but was helpless as he watched Jay's steadfast grip on the polished weapon shift. He began to drag it down her cheek toward her chin, causing more crimson liquid to flow from the raw wound he had inflicted.

Sharon screamed in pain and Kent saw red. Without thought of consequence, he charged; dodging the first bullet that Jay shot, but the second round impacted into his shoulder. He was high on a cocktail of adrenaline and rage carrying him closer to his nemesis. The third shot tore through and exited his right side at the same time he tackled Jay, slamming him to the ground. The knife and gun clattered to the floor under the power of his assault.

Fury drove Kent. He didn't feel pain of the gunshots. All he saw was the vision of red blood seeping over ivory smooth skin from the deep wound as he ruthlessly dragged the sharp edge of the knife into skin, muscle, and sinew.

No sooner had they hit the floor than Kent's

fist connected with Jay's chin. He grunted from the pain and saw the second blow aimed at his abdomen. He was caught beneath Kent's weight and could do nothing to prevent it.

He felt the rush of pain jolt throughout his body while he struggled to find his breath. His stomach ached, his arms lost strength but he shoved with all his might and bore upright.

He won't get the better of me. Not him!

He wiped his mouth with the back of his hand. His tongue was soaked in blood. Bruised and winded, with his leg in agony, he glared at Kent.

"What the fuck happened to you, Jay? You were like a brother to me! Now you're nothing more than a killer. I trusted you! I cared for you—"

"Oh, please! Cut the sentimental bullshit!" Jay sneered and charged at Kent. His head was pounding. He brought a fist to his face, aiming for his nose, but Kent pulled back and his knuckles grazed his temple.

He might have landed a punch, but while his fist slammed into Kent's face, he reciprocated with vicious force, a punch into his stomach, followed by an uppercut. Jay's head snapped backward. Blood pooled in his mouth and he choked for breath.

There was sudden stillness on both sides. Then suddenly, they were moving again, brutal force in every blow. Kent rained blows onto Jay like he wanted to smash him into the very earth.

Kent's eyes narrowed in reaction to a powerful punch to his cheek, before he tilted his head back and slammed it into Jay's. Stars burst in Jay's vision, but he shook it off, blindly throwing a sloppy kick in Kent's direction.

Kent stepped back with a grimace, as he easily evaded the kick and taunted him. "Is that all you got? I've got three bullet wounds and I still can best you," he gloated, smirking infuriatingly at Jay.

With an enraged growl, Jay threw himself at Kent, who jostled to one side, easily avoiding him.

"You bastard! I'll fucking kill you!" Jay screamed and with blood surging through his veins, determination and anger took over.

He threw his body weight behind the fist that

edged closer to Kent's face. It connected with his jaw with such force, blood splattered from his mouth. Pain erupted from the point of impact.

"Enough of this shit," Kent sneered and grasping Jay's head in his hands, he brought his kneecap to his nose with force. He grunted in satisfaction at the blunt crack. Kent shoved him back, blood spattered over his shirt from Jay's crushed nose.

Jay drew his fist back again and slammed it into Kent's stomach.

This was brutally repaid with the pointy end of Kent's right elbow was brought down in hard repeated thrusts meeting Jay's open mouth, splintering teeth and jawbone. He continued battering with relentless accuracy until Jay collapsed like a rumpled doll.

"You're a fucking coward and that will never change," he rasped gruffly.

"I knew you are too weak to kill me," Jay stuttered, bearing upright. His face and mouth were torn with chunks of flesh ripped away by the force of Kent's fists.

Kent stumbled a few steps. He bent to pick up Jay's knife.

"Oh, you fucking useless piece of shit. I promised you death and it's exactly what you're gonna get."

Kent turned in time to see the gun explode. The concussive sound blasted in his ears as he hurled the knife toward Jay.

The bullet slammed into Kent's chest with such force that he was thrown backward. Sharon's gargled screams echoed in his ears as he slid down to the floor, sucked in by the black void of unconsciousness.

Sharon was hysterical and screamed at Parnell who she noticed standing in the door with his smoking gun trained on Jay. He rushed over to remove the gag.

"Untie me! I have to help him. Parnell, please! He can't die!" She sobbed hysterically.

"Easy there, Sharon. You're bleeding quite badly." He cut the ropes with one slash of his knife and rushed over to Kent, glancing back at her. "Are you okay?"

"Forget about me," she cried, kneeling by Kent's side.

"Oh my god! Look at all the blood. He's taken so many hits. We have to get him to the hospital. Parnell! Do something!" She screamed, clasping Kent's head in her arms.

"Seth is already on his way with his chopper, Sharon. We'll airlift him to the hospital." Parnell tried to calm her down while he checked Kent's open wound for any signs of bubbles. He didn't see any but he detected a faint sound of air passing through his chest cavity. He found a plastic bag in the drawer next to him and covered the wound.

"Find me some tape. Sharon! Tape!"

She jumped up and came back with a roll of insulation tape. He used it to tape the plastic down on three sides to prevent air from building up in Kent's chest.

"He won't make it. It's too far!"

Parnell shook her. "Calm down, Sharon.

Being hysterical isn't going to help Kent. I've done what I could. Seth's bringing the local doctor with him. Relax, Sharon. He's breathing," Parnell said while pressing a cloth hard against the wound in his chest.

Seth came rushing through the door with a man who immediately went over to Kent.

"There's no time to do anything more than what you've already done, Good job, Parnell. Let's get him in the chopper. I'll try and stabilize him on the way," Doc Martin ordered brusquely and turned to Sharon.

She snapped at him when he tried to tend to her wound. "Forget about me. It's nothing worse than I've ... just attend to him. Please!"

"Very well, but you will come with us. We need to stop your bleeding."

Seth stood looking down at Jay. The knife stood up straight in the center of his chest. A round bullet wound in the center his forehead. He looked at Parnell.

"Good fucking job, Parnell."

"I think Kent's knife killed him seconds before my bullet did. I just wish I could've gotten here earlier. Then Kent wouldn't have been shot."

"No more regrets, Parnell. It's fucking over. At long last, Colt can come back home and we all can go back to living a normal and safe life."

They avoided talking about Kent's condition. They had both been around death often enough to know his chances of survival, with that bullet in his chest, were slim.

CHAPTER NINETEEN

"Tell me he's going to make it. *Please*, Sasha. I beg you! I need to know he's going to pull through," Sharon pleaded. She clung to her like a lifeline.

Sharon had refused to leave Kent's side until he went into surgery. Doc Martins had managed to stop the bleeding from the cut on her face, but she wouldn't let anyone treat her until she knew that Kent was going to survive the operation.

"Sharon, he's in very good hands. The surgeon is the best there is for trauma wounds." Sasha tried to cajole her to the bed. She'd been allocated a private ward but had been pacing the room like a caged tiger.

"I need to be there, Sasha! I have to be close to him," she said and with that, stormed out the room and ran toward the operating room.

Parnell jumped up from where he, Nolan and Seth had been holding vigil in the hallway outside the OT.

"Easy there, Sharon. You can't go charging in there. It's a very delicate operation."

Tears were running down her cheeks but she allowed him to pull her down next to him.

"Please tell me he's going to be okay. That bullet ... his heart . . ." She began to sob.

"I'm not going to lie to you, Sharon. His condition is critical," Parnell said with a look at Seth and Nolan, who nodded. She needed to know the risks.

"With bullet wounds, the chest is vulnerable, because it causes destruction to organs with its trajectory into the body, crushing vital nerves along the way. Extensive hemorrhaging is also a danger. It is impossible to say."

"Do you think ... his heart?"

"No, he would've died immediately if it had caught his heart, but the bullet didn't go right through, so it must be lodged somewhere. It was a high velocity bullet; they fragment when they strike. That's the danger. All we can do is wait and pray, Sharon."

"They've been in there for hours already." She smiled tremulously at Sasha who had followed her and wrapped a blanket around her shoulders.

"He's healthy and strong, Sharon. And now he has something in his life to fight for. You have to be strong. He's going to need to know that you are holding together when he comes to. That's the most important stage of his recovery. The first twenty-four hours." Sasha seemed to be the only one who could manage to calm her down. She pressed a cup of coffee in her hands. "Drink this. You need to warm up and it will help the shock."

Sharon followed her instruction blindly. She felt numb with concern for Kent. Fearful thoughts looped around in her mind, until there was no room for anything else. These next few hours would either pass as a blip in the course of her life, or it would be the final trauma that'll break her.

"He can't die. God please. I can't live without

him." Sharon didn't realize that she'd muttered the words out loud, but the others glanced at her.

They never realized how much Sharon had come to love Kent. Watching her slumped in fear, with despair running through her mind, was a revelation. She was gentle and caring; with strength of character they'd never expected to see from her. Kent had much to do with the change in her, it was evident.

Seth and Parnell got up when the surgeon stepped out of the operating room. Sharon couldn't get her legs to obey and remained seated. She clenched her hands, watching his face. He looked tired and sedate. Her heart felt like it was about to stop beating.

"We managed to get the bullet out, but the hemopneumothorax damage was extensive. We inserted a chest drain. There is still danger of bleeding, which we need to look out for."

"What happens if he starts bleeding?" Nolan questioned.

"If it doesn't drain and gets worse, we'll have

to perform a thoracotomy. For now, he's stable and in the recovery room. The next seventy-two hours, however, will be crucial."

His eyes turned to Sharon. "Don't worry, miss. Everyone here loves Kent and he'll receive the best of care. Now, come with me. It's time to take care of that wound."

"No. I need to be with him. Please. May I see him?"

"Not until we've dressed you wound. He's very susceptible to infection now. And an open wound like that? Come, Sharon, is it? Kent will never forgive me if I don't take care of you and get someone to fix this beautiful face."

The thought of causing him more harm was enough for her to follow him. She missed the wink he gave the others, who sighed in relief that she finally conceded to have her wound looked at. Parnell had seen how deep and vicious the cut had been. Even with plastic surgery, she might still end up with a scar on her cheek.

Sharon opened her eyes and looked around the room. It was a private hospital room. She glanced around. It was luxurious. There were flowers on the desk, beautiful paintings adorning the walls, leather chairs and soft music. Her eyes fell on the large plasma television screen and she sighed. The bed was bigger than the usual hospital beds and very comfortable but she missed their home.

She turned her head and froze. It had been two weeks. Two weeks, during which Kent had been riding on the edge of life and death. He'd had heart failure twice and had contracted fever. At least he didn't start bleeding again and that had been the biggest relief. She didn't think his body would've been able to withstand the trauma of another operation.

Sharon became lost in the warmth reflecting in his eyes, like she was falling into a pool of dark chocolate. They shone in the early morning light; his gaze was unwavering. She couldn't seem to look away.

He was awake! At long last.

Colt had demanded that they put her in the same room as Kent because she refused to leave his side, even after her cheek surgery. She would sit in the chair next to his bed until she fell asleep. Eventually, their beds had been pushed up against each other.

Her hand lifted of its own accord and she caressed his cheek, touching the corner of his eye. She detected a slight glimmer in their depths. They filled with the warmth and love she'd become used to when he looked at her. Her smile was tampered by the shadows that danced across his face.

Her hand moved involuntarily to the bandage covering her cheek. The plastic surgeon had told her she would carry a scar for the rest of her life. The damage had been too deep for complete recovery.

"No, my love, don't," he rasped. His voice was gruff from not being used for so long. "Your beauty comes from within, Sharon. Haven't you realized it yet?"

"There's a scar, Kent ... I'll always—"

"Be the most beautiful and courageous woman I have ever met; whom I love with body, heart and soul."

Kent had known the cut would leave a permanent scar. If the surgeon had done a good job, it would be a neat thin line on the side of her cheek.

"I'm sorry, my love. You have to be the one to bear the memory of yet another man's demented obsessions."

"All I care about is that you're here with me. I was so scared. I don't know how I would've been able to survive—"

"It's over, Sharon. It is past. Let's bury all those bad memories forever and concentrate on our future. Together, as man and wife."

Sharon sat upright and looked at him. He looked so pale and had lost weight over the past two weeks, but he was still the most handsome man ever. The keeper of her heart.

"Kent?" She whispered wonderingly, a

whimsical smile brimming on her lips.

He reached up to caress her good cheek. His smile was tender and filled with the love in his heart.

"I love you, Sharon and I can't think of anything I want more, than to spend the rest of my life with you. Will you be my wife, my love? To have and to hold until death do us part?"

She leaned closer and whispered against his lips, "Yes, my one and only true love, I will. You have been my heart for so long now."

Their lips met and the world fell away. It was a slow and soft kiss, comforting in ways that words would never be.

"And here we thought he was lying in ash and dirt, on the edge of death."

Nolan's voice drew them apart but Kent pulled her against his side, cuddling her into his embrace.

"Me? In ash? Pfft, from that little bullet? Not a chance, my friend."

Suddenly the room became smaller as all his friends and their wives followed behind Nolan to stand around the bed.

He looked at them. His eyes met Colt's. For the first time in all the years since he'd come back to Jacksonville, Kent saw him smile with relaxed ease.

"What happened with the mob, Colt?" Kent asked with a frown.

"I've given enough information to the FBI to curb their organization for a long time. They effectively will have to build their forces up from the ground. It's going to take a long time, which might be enough for those still in the running, to give up. No, I didn't divulge their names and if they're clever, they'll go clean. Or face the consequences at some time."

Kent relaxed against the pillows. They were free of the Occhipintis. Finally.

"Kent sleepy?" Mason asked from where he sat in his father's arms. His little face was scrunched up as he looked at all the machines bleeping.

"Yeah, he's a lazy bugger."

"Ooh! Nol said bugil! Noty Nol!" Mason piped

up.

The laughter that filled the room was a mixture of love, happiness and friendship that would last until the end of time.

Three months later . . .

Her eyes fluttered open; once again to the sight of a hospital room. Only this time, it was with hope. She turned her head. A smile curved her lips. Her eyes shimmered with unshed tears as she looked upon her husband slumped in the chair next to the bed with his hand clasped around hers. Even in his sleep, he coveted her touch. He always did. It humbled her. How much he loved and cared for her.

Her savior. Her rock. The man she had come to love more than life itself.

"You're awake," he said in a sleepy, raspy voice.

"Kent? My face? I thought you said there was

nothing more you could do with that scar?" Sharon asked in a tremulous voice when her fingers encountered the bandage covering her cheek.

His smile turned gentle, warm, and drew her into his soul like it always did.

"I've been working on a new technique to build up damaged muscles, especially severed ones like yours. You'll still have a scar, my love, but a faint one and hardly noticeable unless someone looks for it." He leaned closer to kiss her lips. "That, my sweet wife, is the only scar left. I managed to fix all the others. You are even more beautiful than I ever imagined you could be. Not because of the scars or the lack of them, but because I can see the love and joy in your eyes when you look at me."

Sharon began to cry earnestly. Her life had come full circle. This man, her one true love, had fixed her. He'd reached deep inside her soul and healed all the ugly scars from her past life. Meticulously. One by one. And now, he'd done the same to her physical ones.

"No more tears, Sharon. Especially now. So,

my loving wife, when were you going to share the news with me?"

"What news?" She asked between sniffles.

He pushed the sheet away and lifted her gown to caress the rounded curve of her stomach.

"Of our baby. The one already growing inside your body." His voice had deepened with the emotion running through him.

Her eyes widened and her hand lowered to press over his.

"Pregnant? I'm pregnant?" Her mind swirled while she frantically made calculations. "I thought it was because I was stressed about the operation. Oh, Kent, is it true? Really true?"

"Yes, my love. We found it during the pre-op checks. We're going to become parents in seven months."

Sharon beamed. There was nothing she wanted more in life. She had the love of her life by her side. Her protector, who would always care for her.

"Now, you just have to get well soon."

"I am already. You gave me the cure to all the pain; the day you found me in Club Tiberius."

"Destiny has a strange way of molding our lives. I, for one, am filled with joy at how mine has turned out. You make me happy, Sharon. More than I've ever been."

"Well, remember that when hormones take over and turn me into Attila the Hun."

He laughed and hugged her fiercely. "I will grin and bear all your demands, my lovely wife. I love you, Sharon."

She cupped his cheek. "And I love you, Kent."

Meanwhile ... in Brooklyn, New York.

He was selfish, in ways no one else would ever have believed. To him it has always been a form of pragmatism.

For years he'd kept the true part of his nature locked in a steel cage; a necessity to achieve his end goal. It was the part of him that was selfish. That didn't think a baby was cute or kids were adorable. Fuck—it didn't even care for another's life. That part of his soul had no care for the less fortunate. They were the weaklings—the inconsequential elements in this world. All that mattered was what benefited *him*.

The rest of his cognitive functioning had built that prison long ago, something strong to keep it hidden from prying eyes and clever minds.

Until now.

The time for hiding was over and he could show his true colors now.

"Ha! I played them all. And now I reap the reward, after all the years of suppression; of being ridiculed by the 'oh so mighty' Luca Vitale."

His laughter crackled in the quietness of the room. It was the sound of pure evil. He turned from where he'd stood gazing out of the window at the glimmering lights of the city below.

His eyes circled the room as he took in the luxury. The deep leather sofas, the dark mahogany desk. His eyes came to rest on the intricately carved cigar box on top of the desk. He sat down behind the desk, reached for one of the Cuban cigars and lit it.

He puffed on it and leaned back in the chair, blowing the smoke in the air with obvious relish.

"Ah, yes, this is the life."

Yeah, he'd fooled them all. Of all the players, who'd played the game for ultimate power, he'd been the master puppeteer. The one no one bothered with. The one who jumped through hoops for everyone.

But in the end, his gamble had paid off. It had been a long, tiring road at times, but finally, he had it all. From the day he found out that Luca Vitale had secretly been mentoring Jay Vick, he'd put his plan into action and played an Oscar deserving role.

"Fuck, yes. Ten fucking years. It took ten shitty years but look at me now."

He barked another laugh. He'd played the game carefully. In the end, it had been easy to play off everyone against each other and it ended exactly how he'd planned. Everyone vying for the role of the

Don was dead, because of their incompetence.

No one had the foresight that he had. Luca might have believed Damiano was the answer, but he'd been a fool. *He* had known that Damiano had never been invested in the family and that he'd been biding his time to leave for good. Using that as his game plan, it had been easy to manipulate everyone in the direction he'd wanted; for them to kill each other.

And the end result? Now, he had a bigger empire than Luca Vitale had ever dreamt of having. Because of the steps Damiano had taken to take over as the reigning family.

"Yes, Luca Vitale. You were the blind one. You wanted your successor to be just like you and yet you never saw yourself in me. That was your biggest mistake. Your downfall. Because the irony is, I am just like you. Ha, well, I'm probably worse than you because your death meant fuckall to me. *Niente!*"

He got up to stand in front of the window once again. His lips curved in a self-satisfied smile.

"Yes, now I am the Don of the Occhipintis and

the ultimate boss of the mob—the entire mafia regime of the US." The smirk reflected in the window glass in front of him.

"Me ... Vito Vitale."

A new reign of terror has begun.

The End.

Read on for an excerpt of Book 1 of Club Devil's Cove – His Devil's Desire. The series you've all been waiting for. Rhone Greer and Keon LeLuc!

EXCERPT: HIS DEVIL'S DESIRE

Club Devil's Cove: Book 1

Prologue

Being an assassin in the Kill Squad for the CIA had its perks—a new city every week, casual hotel life, with no dishes or chores, new clothes every day. Although, she donated the old ones to charity or the homeless. She chuckled.

"Yep, there are some finely dressed homeless walking around all over."

Ace—her code name, of course—swallowed a gulp of double espresso and browsed the newspaper. She had an hour before her next job officially began, or rather, until she received the target's identity. It was how she operated. She didn't want to know anything about them. She only needed their location to set shop and take the shot. She left the planning to the operations team.

What they didn't realize was that she always double checked everything. She wasn't a fool to leave her life in other's hands.

She'd learned early on to maintain a cool detachment from her targets. Mostly, she tried not to think of them at all, but when she did, it was with indifference; like they were already dead. She thought of them as meeting their destiny and she was merely the conduit. Everyone had to die sometime, and most of her targets got off easy considering the lives they'd lived. The way they'd made others suffer—they shouldn't go from happy and oblivious one second, to dead the next. Simple. Convenient. Painless. No, most of them should be put through Hell's fire.

She'd barely raised the cup when her phone beeped.

Damn! Trust Bulldog to be early! She snorted reading the text message. Her *targets* were already on the way. She frowned. No one had informed her there would be two targets. Ace hated surprises. She punched a reply and sent it, tapping her fingers on the table waiting for a response. In true Bulldog manner, it was curt and to the point.

Be ready. Price is double. Lock and load, Ace. They'll be there in thirty minutes. I'll send the photo in twenty.

Leaving a perfectly good cup of coffee on the table offended her morals. So, she gulped down the rest and paid the bill.

"The breakfast is on me," she told the server who protested her leaving without eating her food.

Within fifteen minutes she was in position on rooftop of the Hilton Hotel. Her targets were to arrive at the apartment building across the street. She perused the street and nearby rooftops through the telescope of her XS1 TrackingPoint sniper; the best and the most accurate one in the market. It was early morning and apart from the hum of the traffic below, it was quiet so high up. Everything seemed in order. Ace sat with her back against the wall and waited for Bulldog, her handler, to send her the photo of the targets.

No one who'd met her would believe she executed people for a living. Most definitely not at twenty-six years of age. She was as agile as an Olympic gymnast, and just as fast. When she'd embarked on her career, she hadn't been in a sound frame of mind and they had used her vulnerability to recruit her. Of late, she'd come to realize it wasn't the right choice for her. Her questionable career choices didn't reflect in her personal life, which was pretty low-key.

She was efficient at her job. Instead of dispatching paperwork and emails, she dispatched people to whatever came after life; but only the ones who had it coming. Only those who posed danger to the people of this country; or that's what she kept telling herself to keep going.

The photo arrived seconds before the limo came around the corner. Ace settled behind the rifle. Her lips pursed in an annoyed pout.

"What danger could such a beautiful woman pose to the country? Or is this another one of Bulldog's own vendettas he's got me taking care of again?"

Ace had become uncomfortable with her assignments of late. The last two jobs just hadn't felt right. This one smelled foul as well.

Her mark stepped out from the black limousine, her curly brown hair falling in soft layers around bare shoulders. She had the right physique and the right hair, but Ace would have to wait for her to turn to get a positive I.D. of the face. She never assumed anything in this line of work. A loud siren drew the woman's attention and she turned around. Ace froze and then her finger relaxed on the trigger. She drew a ragged breath, staring at the child the woman held in her arms. She looked at the picture again.

"The little girl ... no, she can't be the second target." She sat frozen in shock, staring at the picture.

"Fuck you, Bulldog. I'm done doing your dirty

work," she growled. Her actions were methodical as she began disassembling her firearm. This was where she drew the line—killing innocent women and children. There was no way that innocent little girl could've done any wrong. She was barely six years of age, if that much.

Ace wasn't heartless. She didn't kill for the joy of it. She did if for protecting the innocent. The only time she had done it for revenge had been the very first time—for her family.

Bulldog's voice crackled over her earpiece. "Shoot! What are you waiting for?"

He had a direct link-up to her earpiece and was probably in the ops control room watching the scene via satellite, but she ignored him and detached the magazine from the sniper.

Then all hell broke loose. *Ping! Ping!* She heard the shots and picked up her firearm to peer through the scope. She spied another shooter on an adjacent roof, taking shots at the mother and child. She jammed the magazine back into the rifle and took aim. When she squeezed the trigger, she knew she'd killed the shooter on the other roof, even before the bullet hit him.

She looked back to the limo below and froze. The young woman was lying in a pool of blood on the black tarred road. The white frilly dress of the little girl she was slumped over was tainted red. There was no movement apart from a large man who was screaming and running toward the limo, closely followed by another. More shots were fired. Samantha aimed her rifle at the window of yet another building, where the shots were coming from this time. She released a folly of bullets in that direction.

"Ace! What the fuck are you doing? Get your target. Now!"

"Target is already dead," she snapped into the mouthpiece.

"Get the fucktards trying to get to the limo. They are not to reach that child! Ace, I gave you an order!" Bulldog snarled in her ear.

"Fuck your order. This is bullshit, Bulldog! Fucking bullshit and you know it! Who the fuck are these people?"

"It doesn't matter. Do what you get paid for! Shoot those fuckers!" he screamed into her ear.

"You know what?" she said with a calmness that belied the trembling of her hands. She'd almost done something she would never be able to live with. Kill an innocent woman and child. Had she not waited for her to turn ... "Do your own fucking dirty work. I quit!"

She took one final look down to the street. She caught the big man's gaze, who was kneeling by the body of the bloodied woman. He probably saw a dark figure in a cap and a sniper rifle in hand. He didn't know that she had tried to save them.

She saw him scream at her. It was too far to hear but in her mind she knew what he said. "I will find you, fucker! You will pay for their deaths!"

Ping! Ping!

Two more shots fired in quick succession. The force of the bullet, impacting his chest, threw him back at the same time the man running toward him went down from a hit. Ace found the third sniper and this time took careful aim. Her bullet hit him dead center.

The sirens and screeching tires of police vehicles came around the corner and spurred her into action. She picked up her duffel bag and ran, disassembling her rifle at the same time.

Ace was always prepared for the unexpected. She'd just locked the gun away in a secret compartment and jumped under the shower of the room in the Hilton Hotel she'd rented two days prior, when there was hammering on the door.

The police officer searching the rooms on the floor for a runaway assassin was disarmed when a petite, blonde woman wrapped in a small white towel, dripping wet, answered the door.

Click here and start reading this dark, suspense romance series now: www.books2read.com/CDC1-HisDevilsDesire

BOOKS BY LINZI BASSET

Castle Sin Series
Stone – Book 1
Hawk – Book 2
Kane – Book 3
Ace – Book 4
Parker – Book 5
Zeke – Book 6
Shane – Book 7
Danton – Book 8
Billy & Mongo – Book 9

Club Devil's Cove Series
His Devil's Desire – Book 1
His Devil's Heat – Book 2
His Devil's Wish – Book 3
His Devil's Mercy – Book 4
His Devil's Chains – Book 5
His Devil's Fire – Book 6
Her Devil's Kiss – Book 7
His Devil's Rage – Book 8

Club Wicked Cove Series
Desperation: Ceejay's Absolution–Book 1
Desperation: Colt's Acquittal – Book 2
Exploration: Nolan's Regret – Book 3
Merciful: Seth's Revenge – Book 4
Claimed: Parnell's Gift – Book 5

Decadent: Kent's Desire – Book 6

Club Alpha Cove Series
His FBI Sub – Book 1
His Ice Baby Sub – Book 2
His Vanilla Sub – Book 3
His Fiery Sub – Book 4
His Sassy Sub – Book 5
Their Bold Sub – Book 6
His Brazen Sub – Book 7
His Defiant Sub – Book 8
His Forever Sub – Book 9
His Cherished Sub – Book 10
For Amy – Their Beloved Sub – Book 11

The Stiletto PI Series
Fierce Paxton – Book 1
Fiery Jordan – Book 2

Billionaire Bad Boys Romance
Road Trip
Rogue Cowboy

Dark Desire Novels
Enforcer – Book 1

Their Sub Novella Series
No Option – Book 1

Decadent: Kent's Desire

Done For – Book 2
For This – Book 3
Their Sub Series Boxset

Their Command Series
Say Yes – Book 1
Say Please – Book 2
Say Now – Book 3
Their Command Series Boxset

Romance Suspense

The Bride Series
Claimed Bride – Book 1
Captured Bride – Book 2
Chosen Bride – Book 3
Charmed Bride – Book 4

Caught Series
Caught in Between
Caught in His Web

The Tycoon Series
The Tycoon and His Honey Pot
The Tycoon's Blondie
The Tycoon's Mechanic

Standalone Titles

Linzi Basset

Her Prada Cowboy
Never Leave Me, Baby
Now is Our Time
The Wildcat that Tamed the Tycoon
The Poet's Lover
Sarah: The Life of Me

Naughty Christmas Story
Her Santa Dom
Master Santa
Snowflake's Spanking

Box set
A Santa to Love – with Isabel James
Christmas Delights – with Isabel James
Unwrapped Hearts – with Isabel James

Books Co-Written as Kimila Taylor
Paranormal Romance
Slade: Blood Moon
Azriel: Rebel Angel
Zaluc's Mate

Books Co-Written as Isabel James

Zane Gordon Novels
Truth Untold

Decadent: Kent's Desire

The Crow's Nest
A journey of discovery on the White Pearl

Christmas Novellas
Santa's Kiss
Santa's Whip
Mistletoe Bride

Box sets
A Santa to Love – with Linzi Basset
Christmas Delight – with Linzi Basset
Unwrapped Hearts – with Linzi Basset

Poetry Bundle by Linzi Basset & James Calderaro

Love Unbound - Poems of the Heart

ABOUT THE AUTHOR

"Isn't it a universal truth that it's our singular experiences and passion, for whatever thing or things, which molds us all into the individuals we become? Whether it's hidden in the depths of our soul or exposed for all to see?"

Linzi Basset is a South African born animal rights supporter with a poet's heart, and she is also a bestselling fiction writer of suspense-filled romance erotica books; who as the latter, refuses to be bound to any one sub-genre. She prefers instead to stretch herself as a storyteller which has resulted in her researching and writing historical and even paranormal themed works.

Her initial offering: Club Alpha Cove, a BDSM club suspense series released back in 2015, reached a Bestseller list, and she has been on those lists ever since. Labelling her as prolific is a gross understatement as just a few short years later she has now been published over seventy times; a total which excludes the other published works of her alter ego: Isabel James who co-authors.

"I write from the inside out. My stories are both inside me and a part of me, so it can be either pleasurable to release them or painful to carve them out. I live every moment of every story I write. So, if you're looking for spicy and suspenseful, I'm your girl ... woman ... writer ... you know what I mean!"

Linzi believes that by telling stories in her own voice, she can better share with her readers the essence of her being: her passionate nature; her motivations; and her wildest fantasies. She feels every touch as she writes, every kiss, every harsh word uttered, and this to her is the key to a never-ending love of writing.

Ultimately, all books by Linzi Basset are about passion. To her, passion is the driving force of all emotion; whether it be lust, desire, hate, trust, or love. This is the underlying message contained in her books. Her advice: "Believe in the passions driving your desires; live them; enjoy them; and allow them to bring you happiness."

STALK LINZI

If you'd like to look me up, please follow any of these links.

While you're enjoying some of my articles, interviews, and poems on my website, why not subscribe to my Newsletter and be the first to know about new releases and win free books.

Linzi Basset's Website and Isabel James' Website
Linzi Basset Twitter and Isabel James Twitter:
Friend Linzi on Facebook or Friend Isabel James on Facebook
Linzi's Facebook Author Page and Isabel James' Facebook Author Page
Linzi All Author-Page and Isabel James All Author Page
LinkedIn
Instagram
Goodreads
BookBub
YouTube
Pinterest

Like my Facebook pages:
Linzi's Poetry Page

Club Wicked Cove
Club Alpha Cove
Club Devil's Cove
Castle Sin Series

AND, don't forget to join my fan group, Linzi's Reading Nook, for loads of fun!

Don't be shy, pay me a visit, anytime!

Made in the USA
Las Vegas, NV
03 October 2022

56459622R00256